GRIZZLY JUSTICE

APRIL CHRISTOFFERSON

STORY MERCHANT BOOKS

LOS ANGELES • 2019

GRIZZLY JUSTICE

ISBN-13: 978-1-970157-00-0

Story Merchant Books
400 S. Burnside Avenue, #11B
Los Angeles, CA 90036
www.storymerchantbooks.com

www.529BookDesign.com

Other Works by April Christofferson

For Dad,
builder of bridges

At what point in our evolution as a society did it become okay to run over wildlife?

—Ted Zoli, bridge engineer and MacArthur Fellow

GRIZZLY
JUSTICE

PROLOGUE

IT WAS AS IF THEY KNEW. It was as if they were welcoming their old friend home.

Will could not bear to look at Annie as she rode alongside him. The two were separated by the palomino gelding Eleanor Malone had taken days to pick out at the Yellowstone National Park stables located just a quarter mile above the stone house where she lived with her daughter, adjacent to Mammoth Hot Springs. While Will had gotten frustrated with the delay, Annie believed it had given Eleanor purpose, something to occupy her days since it had happened. But the wait had about killed Will, who was not good at grieving. Who wanted nothing more than to get back out into the backcountry, where he could begin healing.

An urn had been tied to the palomino's saddle. It contained the ashes of their dear friend, Annie's predecessor in Yellowstone, Magistrate Judge Sherburne.

At first it had just been a lone wolf, crying in the hills above the rolling, expansive meadows of the Lamar Valley, but now, by the time the trio of horses had started to climb, by the time that Eleanor Malone, seated in the car Will had parked along the road, would lose sight of them, an entire pack had joined in the chorus.

"This is it," Will said, as the voices rose and fell, pulling his gelding to a halt.

He finally looked over at Annie. Tears stained her cheeks. He didn't have to tell her what he meant in declaring they'd arrived at their destination. Annie had accompanied Will three years earlier when Judge Sherburne had watched from his parked car—just as Eleanor Malone did now—as the pair disappeared to spread the ashes of Rosemarie Sherburne, his wife of thirty-eight years. On that day, too, wolves had played a pivotal, comforting role—a limping number 22, the alpha female of the famous Druid pack, whose life Will had saved the previous summer, and two of her pups had stood watching from a nearby knoll, within sight of the car, as Will and Annie lifted the ashes to the wind.

"Could it be her?" Annie asked now.

"She's gone, Annie," Will replied, his usual indignation at such statements—actually, not at the statements, but at their reality—nowhere in evidence. Not with Annie. "The Druids are *all* gone."

Annie's jaw jutted forward as she listened to the cries. "I don't believe it. I've never believed it."

A grim smile crease Will's weathered face. He reached across the palomino's back for her hand, which met his.

"I'm glad you don't," he replied softly.

• • •

"Mom," Kylie Blessings said into the phone, "it's me. We're just leaving Yellowstone. I had the most amazing time. I know what I want to be now, Mom. A ranger. I want to live here, in Yellowstone. Will you move here with me?"

This was followed by the nervous giggle Tracy recognized well, especially when her daughter wanted approval for something about which Tracy harbored normal parental doubts.

"I love you, Mom. We're driving straight through, so I'll see you in twelve hours. I can't wait! I have so much to tell you."

A pause, and Tracy could hear exuberant laughter and voices in the background. Apparently Kylie wasn't the only teenager enthused about the "Seattle Youth Empowerment" trip Tracy had signed her bored and confused daughter up for at the beginning of the summer.

"Oh," Kylie added then, "my cell's about to die and the charger in the van isn't working, so don't worry if you don't hear from me again. Love you so, so much!"

Tracy held the phone to her ear, straining. She did it every time, but each time the idea that she might have missed something—any kind of utterance, even the sound of Kylie breathing—caused her to hold it, press it against her ear with force, until she heard the automated voice.

"To erase this message, press 7. To save it, press 9."

Switching on the lamp on her bedside table to make certain she did not accidentally press the wrong number, Tracy Blessings saved the message one more time.

She had already forwarded it to her most trusted assistant at the station—a young, techy, and ambitious UW intern—who had promised to make a copy of it so that Tracy would never have to worry. But until she had that copy in hand, Tracy wasn't taking chances.

Not with this.

Not with the last time—the last words—she would ever hear from her beloved little girl.

1

WILL MCCARROLL FIDGETED, HANDS REFLEXIVELY
balled into fists, foot tapping the floor impatiently.

No one looked his way.

God how he hated meetings. Being forced to sit in a room with
a bunch of bureaucrats was enough on its own to make him crazy,
but he'd come to this one already in a foul mood.

He'd come to this one downright furious.

He could see he wasn't alone. Even though he was better at this,
the bureaucratic crap, Trevor Nolan's coloring—red hair and a
complexion to match—always gave him away. Trevor had grown up
in Yellowstone, the son of a famous interpretive ranger, and worked
his way up from being one of two bear biologists to becoming the
park's bear management program leader. Between his father's
teachings and that climb up the ladder, he'd learned to wear a mask,
play the game. But today Trevor was pissed, and even without the
red blush of his cheeks, that fact was obvious.

"Two bears. That's how many we've got in captivity right now,"
Trevor reported. "And I've got a biologist out there who just
radioed to say she's located the Swan Lake Flats sow."

Sitting at the head of the new conference table, on the top floor of the newly renovated Albright Visitor Center, Yellowstone Superintendent Al Gonzalez looked unimpressed.

He turned his attention to Ron Max, public affairs officer and official spokesperson for the park.

"I don't want the fact that we've located the Swan Lake Flats sow to get out," Gonzalez said. "She's got a fucking following that we don't need to hear from right now. Is that clear?"

Avoiding the eyes of the others in the room, Max nodded obediently.

Then, to the rest of the room, Gonzalez proclaimed, "In keeping with our new policy, we keep looking until we find the culprit."

Zeroing in on Will McCarroll, thirty-year veteran in Yellowstone backcountry law enforcement, he added, "And until we do, I want you, Ranger McCarroll, to focus entirely on trails, no backcountry— if someone off trail gets in trouble it's a whole different ballgame than some hiker on a trail. And I want you to open up some of trails we'd closed. The press is doing a nice job of reporting on our efforts to find the grizzly that killed the hiker on Bunsen Peak, which seems to be appeasing our critics. Now we're getting complaints about too many closures."

"We should be closing *more* trails," Will replied, "not opening them."

Peter Shewmaker, Will's boss, shot him a warning glance. "We'll open as many trails as we can, Al," Peter replied, his usual deference to his boss, the park superintendent, in place. "But Will's right. The right thing to do is keep all the trails in that area closed, until we find the offending bear."

The offending bear.

The euphemisms used to make what they were doing sound justified only served to fuel Will's fury.

"What we should be doing is jailing hikers who don't carry bear spray," he said, ignoring Peter. "In both these incidents they were doing everything we advise them not to do: hiking alone, not carrying spray, and both ignored at least three signs saying there was a bear in the area. Yet who do we punish? The bear. If we're looking at policy changes, we need to implement a rule *requiring* hikers to carry bear spray, and fine them a shitload when they don't. Let me enforce that and see what kind of reduction we have in incidents like these."

Gonzalez shot Peter Shewmaker a look whose message was clear. He'd had enough of Will McCarroll's insolence.

He turned to Max.

"What's the public sentiment right now—close more trails or open them?"

Max, a stout man who took his work seriously, had been waiting for this. Standing to his full five feet six inches, he pulled half a dozen newspaper clippings out of the leather folder bearing the National Park Service logo he'd precisely aligned with the tiles on the table in front of him.

"These are all op/ed pieces and letters to the editors over the past four days, since the latest mauling. The sentiments run the gamut. *Billings Gazette* says we're not doing a good enough job of posting signs and protecting the public, but that's obviously politically motivated. Everything is, since it's an election year."

Max didn't have to explain that the current political gamesmanship was aimed at changing the whole regime at

Yellowstone, which had been put in place seven years earlier with the election of a Democratic president. He didn't need to.

He flipped through the clippings with the practiced hand of a card dealer.

"Seattle says it's a shame bears are being sacrificed for the sake of record tourism numbers."

Selecting another, he said, "Helena paper says the public needs better education...."

Trevor couldn't take this one in silence.

"Better fucking education? They're all given explicit instructions at the gate. There were signs everywhere on both trails, and at least one interp and one LE spoke to each of the guys who were mauled, told them to turn around. What more are we supposed to do?"

Sheepishly, Max pulled another article out.

"Unfortunately, they're even weighing in in the nation's capital. The *Washington D.C. Reporter* interviewed our glorious state senator, Liz Conway, who was apparently in D.C. when the first mauling took place. She says, and I quote"— adjusting his glasses, he lifted the clipping and, bringing it closer to his nose, zoned in on it—"this is another example of what's going on in Yellowstone. First it's a rogue ranger taking away guns—guns that are perfectly legal—in a campground. Now it's mismanagement that's cost an innocent tourist his life."

Will watched as Gonzalez reached for the article, practically snatching it out of Max's hands.

Trevor finally broke into a smile. Looking at Will, he said, "Well, look who's getting a little national press?"

Two years earlier, in response to a shooting that left a young man dead over a drunken game of cards at the Pebble Creek campground, and in anger about the recently enacted guns-in-parks legislation, Will had confiscated all the weapons in the campground—an act that had culminated in his being deported for a year to Yellowstone's famous sister, Glacier National Park.

After the fleeting pleasure derived from embarrassing his friend and colleague, Trevor turned serious, adding, "What's that right-wing nut job doing back in D.C.?"

Max, whose job it was to keep track of such things, replied, "There was a convention back there. The Alliance for Economic Progress. They're the ones pushing for the transfer of federal lands to states."

"We've been wanting to move up to Mammoth for a year, but we stayed in Gardiner just to vote for whoever runs against that woman," Trevor responded, eyes ablaze. "After the election, we make the move."

While most of the park, including the housing available to employees just a quarter mile south of Mammoth, was situated in the state of Wyoming, the north entry gate and town of Gardiner were located in Montana, where a slate of ultra-right politicians had taken office after the previous election.

"Hell," Max said uncharacteristically, "if Conway wins the seat in the U.S. Senate, Maggie and I may join you. Though Wyoming's bound to be next."

Amid the groans and comments ranging from "amen" to "nut jobs" this brought from the rest of the room, Will turned to Gonzalez.

"Didn't I hear you just got back from D.C.?"

Ignoring his question, Gonzalez stuffed the clipping Max had just given him into his shirt pocket, saying as he did, "What's in the *Chronicle?*"

Max rifled through the articles again, grabbed one. "An op/ed by Hadley Black," he replied.

Shewmaker and Gonzalez groaned simultaneously.

When Max stretched his arm across the table toward Gonzalez, neatly clipped article pinched between manicured forefinger and thumb, the superintendent held his hand up to stop him.

"Just read me the parts I absolutely need to know about."

Once again adjusting his glasses, which had slipped halfway down his nose, Max planted his feet hip-length apart and began reading from the newspaper with the biggest circulation in the Yellowstone Ecosystem, the *Bozeman Daily Chronicle*:

"Bear spray. That's all that it would have taken and two humans and two of Yellowstone's grizzly bears would still be walking the Earth today. A simple stop at a store in one of the gateway towns or inside the park, a simple purchase and taking a few minutes to learn how to use it properly…"

Gonzalez's snort of indignation, accompanied by a wave of the hand, signaled he'd had enough.

"Someone needs to muzzle that asshole," he said as Max dropped the hand holding the article and removed his glasses, signaling he'd reported the last of the media coverage—and, for all present, hopefully the end of the meeting.

"*He's right.*"

All heads turned Will's way.

Avoiding Gonzalez's glare, Shewmaker looked at Will, cleared his throat.

"Don't even say it," Will instructed his boss, rising so abruptly that his chair tipped momentarily onto its back two legs.

He paused, turned to face Gonzalez squarely.

Yellowstone and Yosemite were the only national parks with political appointees as superintendents, and this fact had made Will's life miserable, off and on, his entire career. He had been appalled by the selection of Gonzalez, who had rapidly moved through multiple national parks, leaving behind disgruntled employees, especially wildlife biologists, at each. Will took Gonzalez's appointment to be the then-new president's token gesture to the country's growing right-wing wildlife and wilderness-hating constituency.

For his part, Gonzalez had made it clear that his patience was wearing thin with the ranger who had become a national hero after saving the alpha female of the famous Druid wolf pack. Were it not for that fact, both men knew that Will would be long gone. Even sending Will to Glacier had backfired on Gonzalez when Will survived an attempt on his life aimed at preventing him from testifying before a congressional commission revisiting the guns-in-parks law. Will's televised testimony had created no end of trouble for the powerful gun lobbies and upped his popularity with the public.

But the truth was—and both Gonzalez and Shewmaker knew it—Will could care less about the leverage he'd accrued. Once, when Shewmaker had threatened to fire him for arresting a prominent local mayor's son for baiting elk with salt blocks set inches across the park boundary, in order to lure them outside the park's protected confines for paying customers to shoot—like cardboard figures at a carnival booth—Will had told his boss to go ahead. Fire him. He had told Shewmaker that he'd stay out there, in the wilderness, doing his job—only then he wouldn't have his hands cuffed by the bureaucrats.

Shewmaker had known Will was telling the truth. That his biggest nightmare would have been firing Will and then having him disappear into the wilds of Yellowstone, continuing his passion to stop poachers—vigilante style.

He had known that because Will always told it like it was. This morning had been no exception.

Staring Gonzalez straight in the eye, Will now declared, "Wild animals shouldn't be used as political pawns, their lives sacrificed to appease irresponsible hikers or politicians; people who come here wanting to see wild animals, but not *too* wild—not animals doing what animals in the wild are supposed to do."

He grabbed the felt ranger's hat on the table in front of him and turned toward the door, oblivious to the strain on Shewmaker's face, or the glee on Nolan's.

"Yellowstone isn't a zoo," he said over his shoulder. "Our bears *act* like bears. And that's what some of us *want* them to do."

• • •

Johnny Yellow Kidney hated cell phones. He was prone to not answering them, especially if he could use being out in the backcountry as an excuse—after all, dead cell zones predominated inside the vastness of Glacier National Park—but the area code now displayed on his phone read "206," and after he'd ignored calls from this persistent woman for over a week, she had apparently gone to the higher powers to get Johnny's attention. Johnny's supervisor,

Hannah Aldrich, had told him he'd better speak to this woman, this Tracy Blessings from Seattle. Hannah said she was important, some kind of TV personality, and that the public affairs office had been firm when they called to pass her message along.

Still, Johnny hesitated. Hannah knew he was headed up to Pitamakan Pass today, and that coverage up there was non-existent. He could probably get away with not answering. But then he was hit by the unwelcome thought that he still hadn't received a response to his request for a collection assistant for his wolverine DNA study. He needed that assistant. With the EPA soon to rule on the listing of this animal he had devoted his career to, Johnny needed all the help he could get to collect data—as much as possible, as fast as possible.

Better stay on Hannah's good side.

"What the hell," he muttered to Tucker, his paint gelding, before tapping the green symbol at the bottom of the beat-up, government-issue phone. "This is Johnny."

"Mr. Yellow Kidney, thank you for answering." The voice was strong, self-assured. Female.

"This is Tracy Blessings. I apologize for being so persistent, but I have an important matter to discuss with you, and I'm calling to request a meeting."

"About what?"

Diplomacy wasn't always Johnny's strong suit.

This seemed to take his caller aback, but only momentarily. "I'm the director of a new project that I think you'll be interested in. I'd be very grateful if you could spare me an hour or two. At your convenience, of course."

Johnny already regretted answering.

"Busy time of year for me. I'm in the middle of a study, not spending time in the office these days. Maybe after the fall…"

"Please, Mr. Yellow Kidney, I promise not to waste your time. I know it's valuable. And I also promise you'll consider what I have to propose very interesting."

Now it had become "propose," not just talk. Shit. He could almost feel Hannah Aldrich looking over his shoulder.

"Okay," he sighed as he let up on the reins, allowing Tucker to move forward, eager to get started on the familiar climb up the rocky trail lined with lodgepole pines. "It'll need to be first thing, early, by six a.m. Or at night, nine or so. I guess the day itself doesn't matter. They're all busy this time of year."

Blessings' reply came back so fast, it caught Johnny off guard. "Great. I'll be there tomorrow. Six a.m."

2

WILL WATCHED THE YOUNG WOMAN from a distance. He recognized her by the long blonde hair, tied in a ponytail that stuck through the opening in the back of the National Park Service cap she rarely took off. Looked like she was having as bad a day as Will. Two-way radio dangling from one hand, she limped slowly down the Thunderer Cutoff Trail.

"What's up, Emma?" Will called ahead.

"Am I glad to see you," she yelled back, picking up her pace despite what was obviously an injury to her right leg.

Will's sixth sense, acutely honed after years in the backcountry, told him it was going to be another interesting day.

"Radio out?" he said as the two met about three-quarters of a mile up from the trailhead that wound its way up to Chaw Pass and then on to the Thunderer, one of the Lamar's most famous mountains, in part because of its prime grizzly habitat.

"I forgot to charge it last night," Emma replied, her face flushing as she made her admission.

Had she been a law enforcement ranger, Will would have launched into a lecture, but park biologists were notorious for lax radio maintenance, and he had observed the new bear biologist enough to recognize her work ethic, passion for her chosen field, and sense of responsibility. He'd also observed the shit that, as both a new kid on the block and a female, she'd been putting up with from other biologists—and even some hard-edged law enforcement.

More importantly, he sensed that at that moment something besides her obvious injury was troubling her.

"How badly are you hurt?"

"It's my Achilles. I tweaked it scrambling off-trail. It's not that bad now, but I've had this happen enough in the past to know that by the time I get back to my transit, I'll be out of commission for days."

Off-trail. A red flag for a veteran like Will.

"What took you off-trail?"

Emma's words practically tripped over themselves in their rush to get out.

"I heard a shot. I was bushwhacking in its direction when I slipped on talus. I waited, listened, for over two hours, but never heard another thing."

"No question it was gunfire?"

"None."

"How far up were you?"

"About two-thirds of the way."

"Had you seen any bears? Or scat?"

"Both. I caught sight of a sow I've been seeing up there. Grizzly. And plenty of scat."

This wasn't the response Will had hoped for.

"I've been seeing her, too."

"I tried calling for LE, but…" Emma lifted the radio palmed in her right hand. "Wait till my colleagues, and the rest of the park, hear about this one."

The young biologist's chin began to quiver beneath her tightly pursed lips.

"I don't know how they'd hear about it," Will said nonchalantly. "At least not unless I end up issuing a citation and need your testimony."

Shaking her head, Emma replied, "I can't ask that of you."

"You didn't."

"They so want to see me fall on my face."

"I'm not sure that's what it is. I just think it's kind of a trial period, almost a fraternity hazing kind of thing. You're the new kid, and you're a woman. Anything you do, the good ole boys are watching."

He made a mental promise to himself to keep a good eye on Emma Day's situation with her co-workers. Recent ugly charges brought by women working in the maintenance department had become public, and an investigation was in place. Will knew one of the supervisors accused and had all but knocked him out when he ran into him several days earlier and heard him bragging about the sexual favors he'd coaxed out of a young worker. Will had the highest regard for the park's biologists and law enforcement, who worked closely with biologists like Emma. He couldn't imagine any of either group being guilty of what they were now learning about male supervisors in the maintenance department. But he could be wrong.

He'd been wrong plenty of times in the past.

"Listen," he said now, "I'll call for someone to come help you get home, but I need to get up there and see what I can find."

"I can get out alone," Emma replied forcefully. "Just hurry up there."

Will didn't like the idea of letting her go on alone, but his instincts about what had happened up on the Thunderer, what Emma Day had heard, tipped the scale toward letting the biologist fend for herself. He'd just walked the trail she'd be traveling and hadn't seen a trace of a bear. Plus, he'd passed hikers no more than ten minutes earlier.

"There are two groups of hikers heading up the trail," he said, as he stepped toward some dead branches downed by a recent storm. "Tell both to turn around. One's an elderly couple, very nice. Ask them to accompany you. That's an order."

Breaking the shorter of the branches in his calloused hands, he handed it to Emma.

"Your walking stick."

"Thank you, Will. Please, be careful."

They had each turned to head in their separate directions when Will heard Emma Day's voice again.

"Will…"

He turned.

"The DNA results came in this morning. The Swan Lake Flats sow matches the DNA of the bear that killed the hiker on Bunsen Peak."

Will stood there, eyes locked with Emma's. It was as if she had been holding this news in and now, seeing Will, literally could not stop herself from sharing it. Her tears started flowing.

14

Somehow, she had known Will would share her grief. Her words hit him like a brick.

Co-workers in an office in the city became close confidants and friends. People who worked out together at clubs developed an affection for one another.

Because so much of the work was solo, those types of attachments weren't as frequent in a place like Yellowstone. Working in Yellowstone, people like Will and Emma developed shared attachments to its animals.

Will spent as little time as he could along Swan Lake Flats—one of the busiest through fares of the park, packed with tourists trying to fit Mammoth Hot Springs, Old Faithful, and Yellowstone Lake in on the same day, causing bear jams and bison jams and even an occasional wolf jam. Will avoided it like the plague. But when he'd heard about the Swan Lake Flats sow's cub getting killed by a drunk driver, he had to go and pay his respects.

He'd climbed up above the maddening crowds with his spotting scope and watched the magnificent, grief-stricken animal for hours. A funny thing happened to him as he watched her, usually just the golden hump showing above the prairie grass, willows, and sagebrush that filled the landscape as she paced, moving in a zigzag pattern, covering acres and acres of terrain, walking off her grief, no doubt still hoping she would come across her cub. The usual respect and awe he felt at the privilege had turned into something more. Empathy. Perhaps even a kinship. The sow's grief he recognized, was a little different from that which he had felt, thirty years earlier.

The next day he'd returned, but the crowds, which had grown as news of the cub's death spread, and the knowledge that no amount of lingering would bring back her cub, had driven the sow to higher elevations. Just as the tragic deaths of Rachel and Carter had done to Will.

Unfortunately, it now appeared, it had driven her, in her grief, to Bunsen Peak.

"Damn," Will managed to utter.

Emma did not let his gaze go.

"She was the first grizzly I saw when I started here," Emma said. "It was just before her cub got hit. I came upon the two of them up near Sheepherder Cliffs. It was this gorgeous summer day and the two of them had gotten into a thimbleberry patch. She gave me a warning huff, so I backed off, but she let me stay there and watch her, maybe for a good twenty minutes. I was so excited—she's so magnificent.

"It was my birthday, and that was the greatest gift I've ever been given. I called her my birthday bear."

The irony that this one bear had symbolized such different emotions in these two humans who held such affection for the iconic species was not lost on Will.

"Listen, Emma," he said, momentarily putting aside his feeling of urgency to deal with the gunshot Emma had heard. "You're going to be told that you shouldn't give the bears names. That's why we number everything. You're not supposed to anthropomorphize them."

Emma's eyes declared her disappointment to hear such advice coming from someone like Will.

"But I've been here in this park now for thirty years," he continued, "and it's what keeps me going. Caring about them as individuals. *They* are what keep me going. So as far as I'm concerned, you've already got your head on straight, and I'd spend less time worrying about your co-workers and more time focusing on what you know is right."

As he spoke, Emma pulled something out of her pocket. A folded piece of paper. Now she unfolded it and extended her hand toward Will.

The sheet was filled with a pencil drawing of a bear. The minute detail filled the page, capturing not only the massive animal's physical presence, but somehow, through the finest of strokes, her spirit as well. But this was not just any bear. Under the drawing, in a perfect, feminine script, Emma had titled the drawing: Birthday Bear.

The Swan Lake Flats bear. Will stared at it.

"You felt the same way about her," Emma said quietly. "I could see it."

Was he that transparent? Will desperately hoped Emma would say no more. No one but Annie had ever brought the powerful emotions, his demons, to the surface so unexpectedly—emotions that he had fought to keep in check, keep hidden, for three decades. Paper in hand, the young biologist stretched her arm toward Will.

"It's yours."

"Mine?"

"You're the only one who seems to be looking out for me. And I can see what she means to you, too. I want it to be my thank-you. Please."

Will couldn't tell the young biologist that he did not want the drawing. That once he got back to his small ranger cabin above Trout Lake, he would carefully place it in a drawer, under layers of clothing he no longer wore. That it might take years, as it had with some of the pictures of Rachel and Carter, to finally take it back out and be able to look at it. Really look at it. That's how strong his demons were, that's how incapable of dealing with them, after all these years, he was.

Instead, he took the drawing—its intricate lines having captured the giant, fiercely gentle creature almost to perfection—gingerly refolded it, and placed it in his shirt pocket.

"Thank you."

Neither could find more words. With a final hug, they parted, Emma heading back toward the trailhead that began and ended across from the Pebble Creek campground, while Will continued up toward the Thunderer at a jog.

• • •

Will passed dozens of bear scats—some left by a black bear, some by a grizzly; some days old, some still steaming—as he trotted up the strenuous trail, heavy-hearted about the news that the Swan Lakes Flat sow would now, almost certainly, be sentenced to die. Hell, two bears that could not be conclusively proven responsible for the death of another hiker had been killed within just the last month. While DNA analysis and tracks indicated that up to a half-dozen bears had feasted on the hiker's body, which had gone undiscovered for at least twenty-four hours, the two who had also had the bad luck to be been seen three miles away, near the scene of another—non-fatal—mauling, received death sentences.

Circumstantial evidence.

That's what Will called it. And an unjustifiable ploy to appease the public, avoid a drop in visitor numbers and the estimated $800 million the park brought to the area each year. That's what he had argued to Peter Shewmaker, and then, when Peter wouldn't listen, to Superintendent Gonzalez when Will ran into him at an Arch Park fundraiser to reopen the old Mammoth school. The long-vacated building used to be the school for children of Park Service employees who lived inside the park, but when Gardiner built a state-of-the-art facility and just about everyone chose to bus or drive their kids to town, it closed. Now, due to the discovery that a big chunk of money the federal government had been paying to Gardiner School wasn't legal and the fed's decision to stop paying those funds—in fact, to try to collect ten years of payments that should never have been made—the old school was being reopened, and a fundraiser held to help finance the repairs after years of the school sitting empty.

Uncharacteristically, Will had volunteered to work at the fundraiser—coincidentally, the same afternoon Gonzalez's secretary denied him an appointment on the day the decision to euthanize the bear had been announced.

Peter Shewmaker had simply glared at him from afar that day at Arch Park, knowing Will never volunteered for anything but backcountry duty. The most dangerous, remote country and task and Will would be the first to sign on, but a fundraiser in town?

Will had to give Peter credit. He'd approved Will changing his day off to work the fundraiser, and then, knowing—as he had to—what Will had in mind, hadn't done anything to stop Will from approaching Gonzalez.

Of course, by the time of the fundraiser, the dirty deed had been done. Two fewer grizzlies now roamed Yellowstone National Park. Two grizzlies killed because neither hiker had been carrying bear spray, both had been hiking alone, and both had ignored multiple signs warning of a bear frequenting the area. One hiker had even declined when urged to join a group of four others who had just experienced a bluff charge of the sow with cub. A cub that had now been orphaned and shipped off to a zoo in the East.

The fact that it was too late to change the outcome—Will heard Emma Day had been forced to assist in euthanizing one of the bears, and the cub had already been shipped away—hadn't mattered to Will the day of the school fundraiser, hadn't caused him to reconsider his emotionally charged conversation with Gonzalez.

For Will knew that it was just a matter of time before another incident occurred.

But what he hadn't anticipated was that the next incident would involve the Swan Lake Flats sow.

Emma Day's Birthday Bear.

Another death sentence would now be issued; one that, like the others, would surely be carried out at a speed rarely observed in the Park Service—a rare swiftness, one prompted only by politics or public relations.

Will's anger and grief seemed to grow with each thought, each step up the Thunderer.

As he rounded a rocky bend in the trail, about two-thirds of the way up the mountain, he came to a dead stop.

A man in his early thirties, clad in plaid shirt and Cabela hunting pants, sat on a rock, staring down at the Lamar splayed out below like a Thomas Moran watercolor. He casually munched a sandwich thick with layers of cheese and meat.

"How many signs have you seen?" Will asked as he strode toward the man, taking in the butt of the Colt 45 sticking out of the holster at his hip.

"Huh?" the man replied, swiping at the mayonnaise clinging to his chin with the back of his sleeve.

His attitude and behavior, as much as the clothing and gun, told Will this guy wasn't your average backcountry hiker out to enjoy the nation's first national park.

"How many postings warning there's a grizzly frequenting the area?"

When the young man didn't reply, Will said, "Four. You had to have seen at least four now, unless you're blind or you've been hiking off trail."

"So what?" The man's eyes strayed to Will's badge. "What crime have I committed? None that I know of. I've been hiking in bear country my whole life."

"You're sitting there eating a fucking ham sandwich. That's the crime."

"You gonna cite me for it?" When Will didn't answer, he added, "No, cause you can't. I'm not breaking any rules."

Will knew he had him.

There were two kinds of backcountry hikers in Yellowstone. Those who respected LE, and those who didn't. It was clear what kind he was dealing with now.

"Where's your bear spray?"

The man grinned.

"Don't need it. I've got this."

He motioned to his hip.

Will's disdain of the guns-in-parks law that went into effect in 2010 and allowed visitors like this asshole picnicking in grizzly country to carry loaded weapons into Yellowstone and Glacier had not only gotten him transferred to Glacier National Park, but had also culminated with his being asked to testify before a Senate Commission revisiting the law.

Thanks to the powerful American Rifle Foundation and the politicians in its pockets, any thoughts of revoking the legislation was short-lived—which had only served to further inflame Will's sentiments about it. He knew, however, first hand and from experience, the consequences of doing anything about it. Even in a situation like this.

But Will had a job to do, and that was to protect both wildlife and visitors.

"Let me tell you something," he said, standing squarely in front of the young man, locking eyes with him. "If a bear catches wind of that sandwich, using that thing stands to put you in even greater danger. No one I know can kill a grizzly with one shot, and if you shoot and miss, what you'll have is six hundred pounds of rage and speed on top of you before you can even take that second shot. Bear spray is not only more effective, your chances of surviving a charge are about seventy percent greater."

Honed not only by decades of service, but perhaps also by some mellowing with age, Will's sense of responsibility for the hiker caused him to add, "If you have to carry a weapon, at least carry bear spray too. And use it first. Make the weapon your last resort."

"Guess I'll just take my chances," the hiker replied, taking another bite of the sandwich.

Recognizing that anything he said or did would only cause the young man to dig in deeper, Will decided to move on up the trail. He would turn back within a mile or two to check on him, and, if need be, follow him from a distance until he was out of the area they'd been seeing the grizzly.

But as Will turned to leave, the hiker had one more thing to say.

"You don't recognize me, do you?"

The words were said with measure, a twisted tone—somewhere between amusement and fury.

Will froze for two or three seconds, right hand instinctively opening, poised to reach for his gun if needed. Then, slowly, he turned. He stared at the hiker, silent.

"I'm Chad Gleeson's brother."

Dark eyes held fast to Will's.

"I testified at his trial. The trial that ended up taking my brother's livelihood away from him. You'll be happy to know that I've taken over his guide business."

Will didn't shy away from the gaze and the hatred-filled volumes it spoke.

"Your brother was bringing trophy hunters into this park and luring elk outside. No different than dealing drugs or stealing cars. He got what he deserved. He should've spent a year at Deer Lodge, too."

With the hiker still glaring at him, Will turned away again, well aware that he was turning his back on someone who hated him. And was armed.

That act of courage—or dismissal—proved too much for his enemy.

"So tell me, Lawman, what happens to the carcass if someone shoots a bear in self-defense? Do I get to take it home and mount it?"

Will pivoted around so fast that the kid actually drew back in surprise, hand reflexively going to his holster.

Years of bear encounters in the backcountry had allowed Will to develop radar that had almost perfected the art of distinguishing the real threats from the bluff charges. This kid was somewhere in the middle. A knee-jerk novice all too ready to resort to a firearm he should never have been allowed to bring into the park.

"Hand the gun over," Will said. "It'll be waiting for you at headquarters."

"You can't take it away from me," Gleeson said. Will caught a note of weakness in his protest. He hadn't yet become quite as hardened as his brother.

"You reach for your gun when a ranger's talking to you and you're gonna get it confiscated. Now give it to me."

Will's right hand went to his own holster as he extended the left and watched the kid begrudgingly pull his Colt out.

Will grabbed it.

The smell was what hit him first. The unmistakable scent of gunpowder residue.

He lifted his barrel to his nose, eyes now glued to the man's face to gauge his reaction.

Nothing.

"You fired this thing."

"You asking or telling?"

With carefully contained rage, Will lowered the gun, checking the safety as he did so, and closed the two-foot gap separating the two, bringing them literally face to face.

For the first time he saw something of a reaction in the dark eyes he looked into.

"I'm telling you. And you'd better do some explaining. Starting now, or pay the consequences."

"Like Chad paid the consequences?"

"Tell me what you fired at and why."

"Nothing. Never took it out of the holster."

"Where'd you hike? How far up?"

Gleeson shrugged his shoulders, nodded toward the rock he'd been sitting on when Will came upon him.

"This was it. Didn't have time to go any farther."

Will knew he was lying. He also knew he had few options at that moment.

"You better hope I don't find otherwise."

He unsnapped the can of bear spray hanging from his belt.

"Take this. This is what's going to protect you if you have an encounter."

When Gleeson didn't reach for it, Will placed it squarely on the dirt, between his two feet. He knew that as soon as he disappeared from sight, Gleeson would pick it up.

"You make a mistake like shooting a bear in this park," Will said before turning to continue up the Thunderer, "and you'll regret it for the rest of your life. You're young. That could be a hell of a long time. Now swallow that goddamn sandwich, pick up the spray, and get the hell off this mountain."

• • •

Will had gone no more than one-eighth of a mile when he saw the first tracks—recent and made by a grizzly. The placement and weight, size, the length of the claws left no room for doubt. But that wasn't what started Will's heart racing.

He dropped to his knees.

Drops of blood that had just coagulated—tiny, no more than the size of a grape, but dozens of them—accompanied the tracks.

Will slid his two-way radio out of his belt, lifted it to his mouth.

"Mammoth, do you read me?"

The radio crackled back at him within seconds.

"Yo, Will, it's me, Reggie B." Reggie B, an energetic, second-year ranger from Seattle, had already impressed Will with his absolute passion for all things Yellowstone. "What's up?"

"We have a wounded grizzly two-thirds of the way up the Thunderer. He's headed east. Close all trails, all sides of the Thunderer. STAT. Get signs posted in the campgrounds, both Slough Creek and Pebble."

"I read, Will. Peter's out sick. I'll give him a ring at home."

New or not, Reggie had apparently already been instructed that proper protocol called for the chief of law enforcement to make the judgment as to whether to close trails.

"Close the trails," Will ordered, "*then* call Peter if you want."

The hesitation was ever so slight. Reggie had worked with Will for two summers now, and they'd both developed a respect for the other.

"Okay," he replied crisply. "I'll get right on it. You be careful, Will."

"And, Reggie?"

"Yeah?"

"Do me a favor and make sure that Emma Day got back to headquarters okay. She sprained her ankle. She should be turning in her car any time now."

"Got it."

Will wasn't done.

"One more thing. I just left a hiker. Ten minutes ago. He should be headed down the mountain. Red plaid shirt, camouflage pants. Brown hair, six feet. I want someone waiting for him at the trailhead."

"To do what?"

"Arrest the son of a bitch."

3

"MORNIN', VILMA."

Stepping inside Brownies, East Glacier Park's popular bakery and deli, Johnny nodded toward the gray-haired woman standing behind a glass display of freshly baked cinnamon rolls, cookies, and cupcakes, as he reached for the cup on the countertop.

"Got yourself a visitor," Vilma replied, nodding toward the back of the cramped store.

From her tone, Johnny could already tell what Vilma thought of the visitor.

Grabbing the cup of steaming coffee Vilma started pouring every morning as soon as she'd see his lanky figure crossing the road—even before Johnny would stop to pet the stray dog that had claimed Brownie's wood-planked front porch this summer—Johnny turned toward the half-dozen tables situated between the deli's front and the refrigerated groceries section at the back, where visitors to Glacier National Park stocked up on their way to the Two Medicine entrance, and guests at the small motels lining the two-lane road found something to satisfy their night-time munchies.

Four tables housed people, two with multiple diners, but of the lone females sitting at two of the four-tops Johnny had no trouble picking out Tracy Blessings.

While everyone else was dressed in hiking clothes or jeans, the woman who had ruined Johnny's plans to begin his day collecting wolverine fur samples from the half-dozen stations he'd set up throughout the highest elevations of the park the previous week wore a short-sleeved blue silk shirt and conservative, slim-fitting skirt and high heels.

Johnny quickly guessed her to be in her late forties. She rose as he approached, hand extended.

"Ms. Blessings," he said, offering his hand back, along with a polite smile that transformed his features from slightly on the severe side to that of an extraordinarily handsome man, before delivering his dig. "You don't believe in wasting time, do you?"

"Please, call me Tracy," she replied, grasping his hand with a practiced ease.

Settling back in her seat, Blessings returned the smile. While hers seemed more sincere than Johnny's, he sensed immediately that she was anything but happy. An intensity to her—her upright posture, manicured nails impatiently tapping the table's weathered surface, along with the inappropriate clothing—nobody in East Glacier, not even politicians making a run through town during an election, wore business attire—may have put Vilma off; but Johnny suddenly found himself feeling curious, more than anything else, about the woman before him.

Blessings quickly took over the conversation—again with the ease of a successful businesswoman or, in her case, as he'd heard from his boss, a successful TV personality.

"I drove up from Bozeman yesterday, right after we talked. I'm hoping you'll be a key element in my reason for moving to Montana, so I wanted to take you up right away on your agreement to meet with me." It sounded like a business proposal to Johnny, formal and efficient. It must have felt that way to Blessings too, for she quickly switched gears—and stopped tapping the table top. "I stayed in the Glacier Park Lodge last night. It was lovely. What a quaint, historical landmark. And those gardens…"

Johnny's unease had increased tenfold with what he'd heard so far. In no mood for idle chatter, he cut her off.

"How could I be part of a reason you moved to Montana?"

Blessings didn't miss a beat.

"I understand you played a role in the People's Way Partnership."

Her answer caught Johnny off guard. The woman sitting across the table from him seemed to Johnny about the last person on earth who would have an awareness of—much less interest in—the one-of-a-kind highway project across ninety miles of the Flathead Reservation that had created forty-one safe crossings for wildlife.

He answered cautiously.

"I was the tribal liaison."

Tracy's eyes practically shouted "Bingo." She drew closer to him, leaning across the table, and lowered her voice.

"I moved to Montana to head up something we're calling the Safe Crossings Project. Just like the People's Way Partnership provides a corridor for wildlife to move east to west and west to east across the Flathead Reservation, the Safe Crossings Project will help create safe passage for wildlife—Yellowstone wildlife in particular—across Interstate 90 and all the way up to Glacier National Park and Canada."

Her tone changed ever so subtly when she added, "And for travelers on Montana highways."

Startled, but impressed—truly impressed—Johnny studied her.

Just how powerful and accomplished *was* this Tracy Blessings?

"That's one hell of an ambitious project. Whose support do you have?"

"The feds are ready to commit. But we need to assemble a lot more support, local support in particular. Ranchers, the State of Montana…"

"The tribes," Johnny added, finishing her sentence for her.

"Exactly."

"You won't have any problem with the tribes—other than getting them to work with agencies that do things mostly wrong, and for the wrong reasons. And with bureaucrats who've made their lives miserable."

"That's why I need you."

Johnny sat back, the old chair shifting with his weight.

"Me?"

"Yes. You have experience, valuable, successful experience, doing just what we need to do to succeed. And move things along quickly."

Johnny's chuckle finally seemed to surprise his visitor. Apparently, not many people laughed at ideas espoused by Tracy Blessings.

"Quickly?" he echoed. "Do you know how long the People's Way Partnership was in the works?"

"Six years. But that's been proven a success. It proved it can be done. They've been doing it in Canada for years with amazing success, and approval—national and worldwide. Netherlands is doing incredible things to improve wildlife and highway safety. Six years isn't necessary. It's not acceptable. What do you say—will you come on board?"

Johnny felt an instinctive sense of caution.

"Ms. Blessings," he said, trying to rein in his words. He didn't want his project to pay the price if he was rude to this pushy visitor. "I realize in your world things may happen when and as quickly as you want them to, but in my world, the world I grew up in—*this* world," he gestured toward the window, where two dozen spirited horses raced down the street accompanied by a young Indian man, clad in chaps and cowboy hat, whose job it was to herd them to and from the lodge each day, "in *this* world, things don't move on the same clock. And people get to know each other, maybe even spend an hour or so doing so, before they ask each other to turn their lives upside down."

It was Tracy Blessings' turn to draw back.

And then go on the offensive.

"You haven't spent your entire life in this world. You went to the University of Washington. I remember watching clips of you running for the Huskies...."

Johnny couldn't tell which cut her off mid-sentence—the look on his face or his reply:

"*The Indian runner.*"

Mustering all of his restraint not to get up and cut the meeting short, Johnny continued, "I am working on an important project here in the park. I'm no longer the Seattle press's token Indian who runs for the local university. I'm a wolverine biologist. We have one more shot at getting wolverines on the endangered species list. I have to collect data over the next few months, data that might make the difference. I'm already short-handed."

"I can get you more help."

Johnny couldn't stifle a half laugh.

"Just like that? You have that much pull?"

"Yes. I do. Please, please, Mr. Yellow Kidney. I know how busy you are, how devoted you are to your work. But this project has importance to wolverines too."

"Wolverines are high country animals. Highway mortality isn't a concern. It's almost non-existent."

"But connectivity *is* a concern."

She had done her homework.

"Of course it is. Wolverines won't make it if distinct populations can't connect. Nor will they if they aren't afforded the protection my research is aimed at getting for them."

"Exactly!" Tracy Blessings cried. "And that's why I've built a research component into the Safe Crossings Project. We'll be studying the crossing structure *designs*, specifically for wolverines, to *ensure* connectivity of populations. And of course, we'd like you to head up that work."

Johnny had to give her credit—she'd foreseen his reluctance and even come up with an antidote for it. But he'd already wasted too much time, valuable time that he'd planned to spend collecting samples on Pitamakan Pass. He'd had enough.

"I applaud your efforts, Ms. Blessings. It's not acceptable for us humans to run over wildlife. It's not acceptable, and it's avoidable. Working on the People's Way Partnership was one of the highlights of my career. But in terms of my wolverine work, which is not only my job, it's my passion, the data I'm gathering to help get the wolverine listed as endangered is a more immediate priority for me. I've invested years in the data I'm collecting. Maybe sometime in the future…"

Tracy reached across the table and grabbed Johnny's arm, as if in doing so, she could stop him from rejecting her proposal, stop him from getting up and leaving the table.

"Please, please, Mr. Yellow Kidney, don't say no. Please, just think about it. This project needs you. Without the endorsement of the tribes…"

It was as much the expression on her face, and grief in her voice as the desperation in her grasp that did it. Stopped Johnny cold.

"Why?" he asked. "Why is this project so important to you? How does someone like you come to care so much about highway mortality?"

In that instant, at those words, Tracy Blessings' face took on a dozen years. And something else—something no amount of makeup or plastic surgery could disguise.

"My seventeen-year-old daughter became a highway mortality statistic last year."

Johnny had spent a lifetime in a place where tragedy—death; by accident, violence, drugs, or alcohol; young and old; Indian and white—was commonplace. Where it constituted all-too-common news that started the day at a place like Brownies or ended it at a bar like the Trailhead just down the street.

Still, Blessings' disclosure caught him off guard.

He watched her gather herself—touching the rough paper napkin to the corner of her eye, where mascara had started to run;

then, almost comically—but in a way that somehow caused Johnny his own pain—to the lipstick accentuating her lips.

"You're right," she continued. "I wasn't an environmentalist. I was too busy being a lawyer, a gun control activist, appearing on local TV, gracing the world with my wisdom."

Sarcasm practically dripped from her voice, but her face had regained some of its former dignity.

"My husband and I divorced when Kylie was just two, and I went to work with a vengeance, determined to provide for her on my own. But it became more than that. My work became my passion, and my little girl suffered from that passion. While her mommy became more and more recognizable in public, she slowly wilted. And at first, I didn't even notice it. I was too busy, too absorbed in my own importance.

"Last summer she seemed lost. I signed her up for a camp in Yellowstone." Tracy paused, took a deep breath, before continuing. "She called me an hour before she died to tell me she had had the time of her life. That she wanted to become a Yellowstone ranger.

"I'd never heard her sound so happy, so sure of herself. I didn't know animals and mountains could do that for someone. She asked me if I'd move to Yellowstone with her. And then, on the way home, the van she was in hit an elk and rolled off the highway. Kylie and two other students died."

She looked Johnny square in the eye.

Tracy Blessings, TV personality, back in the saddle.

"That's my story, Mr. Yellow Kidney. Will you help me prevent this from happening to another child? Another mother?"

Almost as an afterthought, she hurried to add, "And at the same time, protect the wildlife you care so deeply about?"

Johnny drew in his breath. Damn.

It took him almost a full minute to respond. A full minute during which Tracy Blessings' gaze never let go of his.

"My involvement would have to be minimal until I finish my current work here."

"Anything. Anything you can do would help. I'll be honest. Right now, I need your name as much as I need your time. I need your connections."

"The timing just couldn't be worse," Johnny replied. "Let me sleep on it."

"I'll meet you here again tomorrow morning."

"No," Johnny responded firmly, "we can discuss this over the phone. Go home. Go back. I promise to call."

This did not please his tablemate.

"I may not seem like the world's most sensitive person," she replied, "but it's clear you don't want to become involved in the Safe Crossings Project. And I respect that. What's also clear, however, is what a good person you are and how much you care about wildlife, not just wolverines—and, I suspect, about what happened to my daughter.

"So I'm going to be honest with you. Completely, painfully honest. I'm staying put because I want you to feel my presence here. I'm hoping it will, in some—perhaps intangible—way, influence your decision."

She took another deep breath, as if the weight of the world had been temporarily hoisted—Johnny feared by him—from her slender shoulders.

Then, finally, Tracy Blessings let loose with one of the smiles that had made her so popular with Seattle television viewers.

"Plus, I want to experience Glacier. I can't be this close to such a renowned national park—the Crown of the Continent—and not go for a hike. Can I?"

• • •

Will had descended less than a mile of trail when his two-way came alive.

"Will, this is Emma. Reggie B radioed me the news about the wounded bear. That has to be the gunshot I heard."

"I agree. And I have the gun that wounded it. I ran into an outfitter up there, confiscated his pistol. It had been fired."

"Pistol? A hunter shot a grizzly with a pistol? Is he crazy? Did the bear charge?"

"If the bear charged, you can be sure he'd have told me. My guess is he was just taking target practice—from what I could tell from tracks and blood I followed, the bear was hit in the right rear. He's smart enough to know that if we find the bear and I'm right about it getting shot from behind, it'll discredit any claim he shot in self-defense."

Will didn't add what he was thinking: that Gleeson also knew a conviction for shooting a bear when it wasn't self-defense could cost him his guide license. And as cocky as he appeared, apparently the kid was smart enough not to want to risk losing to Will in court, as his brother had.

"I've got someone waiting at the trailhead to arrest him. Meanwhile we're closing all trails."

"I've already started assembling a group to look for the bear," Emma replied.

"Include me. But I can't go up again for a few hours. Right now, I have to clear the mountain."

"I'll keep you posted," Emily said before signing off.

Will had picked up the pace. When he rounded a curve in the trail and came upon the same group of hikers he'd passed on his way up—two men and two women—he was startled.

"Didn't you run into a Park Service biologist on this trail?"

"We did," one of the men replied.

"And didn't she tell you to turn around?"

The women in the group looked sheepish. One actually half-turned, as if she were starting to head back down the trail. But the men stood their ground.

"We asked her if the trail was closed and she said no, but that it would be advisable to turn around."

"And you didn't."

"No," the other man answered. "We're here to hike. There are four of us and we're making noise as we go."

"I didn't hear you until I practically ran into you."

No one replied.

"Where's your bear spray?"

"What?"

"Your bear spray. Where is it?"

"We don't have bear spray," one of the women said. "We have these."

She pointed toward bells hanging from the other woman's pack, twisting as she did so to show Will the bright red bells that also dangled from her pack.

"I'm *carrying*," the taller of the two men added, patting the lump on his right hip under the hem of his fleece vest.

Will had already pulled the pad out from his back pocket. Now he began scribbling on it.

"Names?"

"What do you mean?" the bolder of the two women asked.

"Names. I want all of your names."

"What for?" the armed hiker asked. "What are you doing?"

"Issuing citations. One to each of you."

"For what?"

Will didn't skip a beat before answering.

"For not carrying bear spray."

• • •

The ache in the small of Johnny's back told him he'd spent too much time in the saddle and not enough taking precautions that day as he'd scaled half a dozen trees, strategically mounting gun wire brushes below sections of road-killed deer and other animal carcasses he found almost daily, which—always with a prayer of thanks for allowing their deaths to be used to help other wildlife continue to roam his beloved mountains—Johnny had bolted ten to fifteen feet up a lodgepole pine.

Still, as his seasoned trail horse, Tucker, ambled carefully down the darkening trail toward Middle Two Medicine Lake, Johnny felt a sense of satisfaction at having retrieved four fur samples— samples that, upon being analyzed, would provide valuable information about the population of wolverines in Glacier National Park.

He knew the data he'd collected so far, what he could continue to collect on his own without the assistant he'd applied for funding to hire, was not likely to change the course of the USFWS's decision about whether to list *Gulo gulo* as a species entitled to special protections under the Endangered Species Act, but if there was a chance—any chance at all—that his research could help, he would gladly wear himself out, day in and day out.

But the fur he'd meticulously picked from gun wire today had even more importance to Johnny than the federal agency's upcoming decision. One of the samples he'd collected came from the last location his cameras had captured a specific wolverine, one that had become dear to his heart—and once the story got out, dear to the hearts of many. It wasn't a collared wolverine, nor was it chip-fitted—the preferred method of identifying and following a wolverine's movements, due to the fact that their small heads allowed them to slip out of a traditional collar.

But a chip wasn't necessary to identify this animal, who, two years prior, had had the misfortune of stepping into not just one, but two illegal traps set inside the park, where trapping and hunting were strictly prohibited. The only thing that gave Johnny more satisfaction than the long-hoped-for arrest and sentencing of the man responsible—local dentist Bridger Brogan, who Johnny had been trying to tie to illegal trapping for years—was the day Johnny's camera captured the little guy feeding on a muskrat carcass Johnny had found along Midvale Creek and nailed to a tree up on Pitamakan Pass.

Two years earlier, heart aching, Johnny had left that same wolverine for dead on a backcountry trail near what was now called Whispering Mountain, in tribute to Whisper Little Wolf, a young Blackfeet woman who had joined in the search for Will McCarroll. Johnny had actually raised his gun to put the animal out of its misery, when something stopped him—he took it to be a message from the Creator to let eh wolverine, who seemed already midway on his journey into the spirit world, pass on his own. As part of the desperate search and rescue operation underway, Johnny had had to hurry away that day, but with the wounded wolverine never leaving his mind and heart, he had returned the next day. Miraculously, the badly injured animal was nowhere to be seen—until the night camera picked him up two months later, a dozen feet up a tree, feasting on the muskrat Johnny had placed there that very morning.

Johnny had rushed back to that lure to get a fur sample, the analysis of which would enable him to identify the injured wolverine via his DNA. But after that one sighting—that one photo—Johnny had neither seen the animal again nor gotten a match back from the lab. He feared the worst, but in light of the extraordinary heart the feisty little animal had already shown, ohnny still fostered hope that he continued to roam the glacier-carved mountains that now served as one of his species' last viable habitats.

Pulling Tucker to a stop, Johnny raised his eyes to the sky.

Creator, I pray that it be your will that my brave and big-hearted little friend's DNA be amongst these samples that you, in your wisdom and grace, allowed me to collect today.

The prayer ended abruptly when Johnny began to sense—just seconds before actually seeing or hearing—commotion up ahead on the trail, around the bend.

He urged Tucker into a trot.

As they rounded the curve that brought Middle Two Medicine Lake into sight—the evening's last light and array of colors reflecting off its waters, broken only by the wake of the *Sinopah* on its last run, ferrying hikers across the lake to the campground— Johnny saw half a dozen men and women dressed in Park Service law enforcement uniforms.

Several looked up and nodded or waved upon seeing the biologist.

Johnny reined the gelding to a stop.

"What's up?"

He directed the question to a sturdy, bald-headed man on the periphery of the group. Rob Deardorff, Glacier's chief LE officer.

Rob's presence alone indicated an elevated level of concern about whatever situation had brought the forces out on the trail at that hour.

"Lost hiker," Rob replied, his expression unusually grave. "We're trying to decide whether to send an S&R out tonight or wait till morning. Details are sketchy. She went out alone."

"Damn," Johnny replied. "She a local?"

There were only two explanations for someone, especially if that someone was female, going out hiking alone in Glacier. The first was ignorance—a lack of experience in the backcountry that led to a lack of awareness of its dangers. The second was confidence (often overconfidence) that stemmed from living in or near the park and knowing just where it was safe to hike alone. And when.

Problem with that was that more than one local had lost his or her life due to that kind of confidence.

"No," was all Rob could get out before his assistant, who had also been off to the side, speaking on a two-way radio, beckoned him over.

Johnny dismounted, following Rob, and was just within earshot range when he heard the assistant say, "Someone's reported a body off trail."

"Female?" Deardorff shot back. His voice lacked the cool Johnny, and everyone else who worked alongside Deardorff, was used to hearing.

"Yes. Right age. She has a backpack. They're checking it now for ID."

"Damn!" Deardorff cried. "It's likely her. The Seattle stations have been calling me all afternoon."

A sense of horror instantly gripped Johnny.

"Is it Tracy Blessings?" he said, approaching the two men, who stood a few yards from the rest of the group, all of whom were gearing up for a night out searching for the lost hiker.

Deardorff spun to face Johnny. "You know her?"

"I met with her this morning."

Johnny's stomach felt as though a giant vise had gripped it and would continue clamping down on his guts until he passed out—or got an answer.

"Is Tracy Blessings the missing hiker?" he repeated, his voice rising enough to draw the attention of the other rangers.

Deardorff remained silent.

He did not need to reply. The look he exchanged with his assistant gave Johnny his answer.

4

ANNIE PEACOCK WAS ALMOST THROUGH her final review of the opinion she was about to walk into court at the Yellowstone Justice Center and hand down when she felt a presence.

She looked up.

Justine Pearce, Annie's court clerk, stood in the doorway, a single piece of paper in hand. She wore an uncharacteristically sheepish expression.

"What?" Annie asked too sharply. Her mood was sour. She had not heard from Will in over a week, and while silences of a day or two usually meant he was in the backcountry, five days without communication signaled something else was going on.

"You're not going to like this…" Justine started.

She stepped forward with the court calendar for the upcoming week, which she'd printed out just minutes earlier.

Annie knew Justine would not interrupt her minutes before court unless it was important. Brow creased, she picked up the document and scanned the charges she would hear later that week.

The first half of the page represented a typical week in Annie's courtroom. Speeding that resulted in the death of a black bear cub. Fighting in a campground. Deliberate destruction of one of Mammoth's fragile geothermal features by riding a mountain bike off the boardwalk. Drug deal at Canyon Campground.

But halfway down, a charge made Annie take a deep breath.

Citation for not carrying bear spray.

Her fingers tightened their hold on the paper as her eyes went to the next case.

Citation for not carrying bear spray.

And two more: *Citation for not carrying bear spray.*

She did not have to look at the final entry in a series of rows, one for each case, which included date, time, location, charge, and last, the law enforcement officer who issued the citation or made the arrest.

She looked up at Justine.

"I haven't missed anything, have I? Was there a reg issued last week requiring hikers to carry bear spray?"

Eyes never leaving Annie's, Justine just shook her head.

"I can see if Judge Morano is available to come down from Livingston," she said quietly.

Annie looked down again. Allowed her gaze to move to the last column, knowing damn well what she would see.

Will McCarroll. Will McCarroll. Will McCarroll. Will McCarroll. Expressionless, she looked back up at her loyal clerk.

"No," she replied, her voice lacking any hint of life. "I would only recuse myself if there was a chance my relationship with Will would influence me to charge these people. But that's not going to happen. I'll have no choice. I'll have to dismiss."

Justine's face displayed the grief and pain that Annie would not allow herself. At least not now, before she walked into the courtroom. Not in the presence of Justine—or anyone else for that matter.

"But that would…" the court clerk replied, unable to finish.

Annie waved her hand in the air, as if she could also dismiss the heartbreak of the situation.

"That's how it has to be, Justine. That's just how it has to be."

• • •

"Wait!" the young ranger cried, slicing the air above his head with a karate chop to make his point. "Quiet!"

Rob Deardorff, who had called everyone together and stood in the middle of a roughly formed circle barking orders, mimicked the gesture and shouted, "Silence."

To a person, the group froze.

Stunned by what he'd heard moments earlier—that the body found just off trail was Tracy Blessings—Johnny stood holding the reins to his horse. He, too, felt immobilized. He'd offered Deardorff a hurried explanation of how he knew Blessings, of her last words to him—that she was going into the park—just minutes before Deardorff called the law enforcement personnel together to formulate a plan.

What began as a search and rescue operation had become a recovery operation—and investigation.

Deardorff's young assistant held the radio to his ear. The wind had picked up, carrying the voice on the other end off and away from the group, and he was having difficulty hearing.

A sudden dog-like yelp from him turned all heads his way again. "A nurse just came on the scene and administered CPR," he yelled. Then, seconds later, ear still pressed to the radio, he followed with: "She's breathing!"

A cheer went up from the group. The air left Johnny's lungs so abruptly that he felt like he'd been sucker punched.

Deardorff spun into action.

"Call for a Medivac," he yelled to the assistant. "And ground EMTs." Then, turning back to the group, he began cherry-picking individuals.

"You, you and you," he said, pointing to two men and one woman, "head out on foot. Better yet, two of you get on the horse." In a jerky movement, he nodded toward Johnny's gelding. "Help the nurse in any way you can. Get her stabilized, while we get a board and medical team mobilized, in case this wind, or the terrain, makes it impossible for a chopper to land. I want constant radio contact. Got that?"

"Yes, sir," all three responded simultaneously.

"The rest of you, head back to the camp store and get that demobilization board old Arnie keeps on hand, plus medical supplies, and start back up this way STAT in case ground medical personnel are tied up and slow to respond."

With a sense of purpose and professionalism that comes with years of experience, the group disbanded without further instruction or questions. After Johnny transferred the reins to his gelding to the woman and one of the two men Deardorff had directed to head up trail, he approached Deardorff, who was now talking on a cell phone.

As soon as he ended the call, Johnny grabbed his arm.

"I'd like to accompany your people. It might help if she sees a familiar face."

"That wouldn't be protocol, you know that."

Deardorff didn't have to remind Johnny that his reputation had been built on his strict adherence to park protocol.

"Just this once, Rob," Johnny replied. "And if you don't give your okay, I guess there's nothing to stop me from heading back out to check traps...."

His words were cut off by the approach of the assistant, who had continued to try to communicate over the two-way, despite worsening winds and static.

"Sir," he said. "I have more information."

"What is it?" Deardorff replied, clearly rattled. An old and experienced hand, Deardorff was known for his calm demeanor during park emergencies.

The assistant glanced at Johnny sheepishly.

Johnny's heroics during the Guns-4-All attempt to kill Will McCarroll had earned him something akin to legendary status within the park. A low-on-the-totem-pole assistant hesitated to insult him.

But as with all Park Service work, there was a balance to be achieved, and this kid recognized that.

"You may want to step aside, sir, to hear it." Deardorff eyed Johnny.

"It's okay."

Eyes downcast, showing his uncertainty about having the park's wolverine biologist within earshot, the assistant delivered his news.

"The interp who found the body—er the woman—before the nurse arrived just radioed again to tell me it wasn't bear-related, or an accident after all."

He glanced Johnny's way one more time before finishing.

"Ms. Blessings…has a bullet wound. She was shot in the head, sir."

5

"WHERE THE HELL YOU BEEN?" Vilma called over her shoulder as Johnny stepped inside Brownies and out of the premature cold and wind that had hit the Northern Rockies two days earlier.

"Working," was all he replied as he reached for the coffee on the countertop and headed for a table at the back.

He already regretted leaving his house, but truth was he couldn't stand being there either right now.

Johnny had worked feverishly in the three days since he'd helped LE rangers and emergency responders carry the limp form down the trail to the helicopter that sat waiting in the parking lot at Two Medicine. Worked feverishly and avoided any human contact, including the dozen or more people who had left voicemails for him, which this morning he'd decided to begin returning—at Brownies. He'd seen the crowds dwindle enough, both in the park and at the local restaurants, including Vilma's establishment, that he finally felt confident he could find a quiet table at the back.

But the one thing—the one person—he hadn't factored into the decision was Vilma.

Now, despite the eggs she'd been grilling for a breakfast sandwich when he walked in, she beelined toward him, a woman on a mission.

"Working never stopped you from coming in for coffee."

Johnny did not make eye contact.

"Been up near Iceberg, checking traps."

"Yeah, and I been cooking my ass off for hungry hikers, but I'm still gonna come back here and check on you."

He raised his dark eyes, smiled the kind smile he reserved for true friends.

"Thanks, Vilma."

She dropped into the chair opposite him, wiping her hands on the apron that promoted the shop next door's "World's Biggest Spoon."

"You can't think you're responsible for what happened to that woman. Cause you're not. You hear me?"

Johnny shook his head, half in disbelief, half in despair.

"You're something," was all he said.

"Talk to me, Johnny," Vilma replied. When he didn't say anything, she played dirty. "I think I deserve that much at least. Don't I?"

Johnny could see through her, but Vilma had done nothing wrong.

"She told me she was going into the park. I shouldn't have let her go alone."

The caustic tone in Vilma's laugh threw him.

"What are you? Some kind of shaman? How the hell did you know she was going alone? You're a good Indian, Johnny, but you're no sage."

"She'd never been here, came alone. That's how I should have known. At the very least, I should have asked her. I should have told her not to hike alone."

"From what I hear, it probably would've happened to her no matter if she was alone or with someone. In fact, if she was with someone, maybe there'd be two people in a coma right now."

One of the calls Johnny planned to return this morning had come from Rob Deardorff the day before. He'd been dreading that call the most. Rob's voicemail yesterday had said that Tracy Blessings was stable. In a coma, but stable, and that he'd bring Johnny up to date on the investigation when Johnny returned his call. Johnny had dialed Deardorff as soon as he got back within range but hadn't been able to reach him.

Now Johnny felt he had to know. And he knew he could trust Vilma's sources.

"What's the latest?"

"They think it was someone from Guns-4-All. I guess your visitor the other morning was a well-known gun control advocate, always on TV saying we need to clamp down on the American Rifle Foundation, ARF. They think it was a message from those idiots, to let people know they're still around."

"That's what I heard, too. I thought with the guy who got killed and the two still in prison, it would be the end of those misfits."

"That's what *everyone* thought," Vilma replied. "But that's not what they're thinking now. Looks like those gun nuts managed to actually build a following over the past couple years."

Vilma looked back over her shoulder, where the only other worker frantically flipped overcooked bacon on the grill and the line had doubled during the time since Vilma had stepped away. Standing, she lifted a finger, pointing it authoritatively at Johnny.

"So you stop this nonsense about you being able to prevent what happened. You hear?"

She didn't wait for Johnny to answer, probably because she knew he never would—plus, smoke from the bacon grease had wafted their way.

Johnny watched as she marched back to the grill. His phone had vibrated in the pocket of his jacket as Vilma lectured him. He reached for it, saw that a voicemail had come in, and punched in his passcode as he lifted the phone to his ear.

He recognized the voice immediately. His boss.

"Johnny, it's Hannah. Hey, good news. Your request for an assistant to help you with the DNA collecting was just approved." Her tone sounded unusual, strained. "Anyway, give me a call and I'll fill you in...." Johnny knew Hannah well enough to know the hesitation had significance. "Uhh, I should also tell you...there are a couple strings attached."

Instead of the elation he would normally have felt, Johnny dialed Hannah's number with a cloying sense that something was wrong. So much so that when he got her voicemail, he did not leave a message.

He hadn't been to park headquarters for a long time. He avoided it—and the bureaucracy it represented—like the plague; but despite the field and paperwork he had waiting for him, and calls to return, he decided right then and there to change plans for the day and drive the fifty-two miles to West Glacier.

Intuition told him it was important to visit his boss; to hear what she had to say in person.

He couldn't shake a sense of dread as he pulled his notepad from his pocket. He could at least make a call or two while he drank his morning coffee.

Flipping the pad open, he read the list of phone numbers he'd been jotting down, then ignoring, the past two evenings.

The fourth one from the bottom had come in the previous afternoon. A 206 area code.

Jaw clenched, Johnny dialed it first and, when it was answered mid-first ring, was surprised not to hear someone spouting—in person or via recording—the name of an organization or business.

"Bob Heyka," the voice declared. "This is Johnny Yellow Kidney."

The silence on the other end lasted long enough for Johnny to pull the phone away from his ear and look to see if the notoriously bad reception in East Glacier had cut the call short.

The digital timer ticking away on the face of the screen indicated he still had a connection.

"Thank you for returning my call," Heyka said.

This was followed by the words Johnny intuitively knew would follow—the words he'd been dreading.

"I'm a friend and colleague of Tracy Blessings."

It was Johnny's turn to momentarily go silent. "How is she?"

"She's in a coma. It's medically induced. She's got a shunt in her skull, to reduce swelling and the chance of permanent damage." The man on the other end was choosing his words with extreme care. "Luckily, the bullet transected the best possible section of her brain to transect—if there is such a thing. They hope to take her out of the coma within the next couple days. We're worried, of course, but if anyone can make a full recovery, it's Tracy."

Images of Tracy sitting across from him at the same table at which he now sat flashed back to Johnny.

"I'm sorry," he replied quietly.

"Yes, I'm sure you are. I know you only just met Tracy, but I'm sure you could see how special she is."

These words approximately doubled Johnny's guilt. As if that wasn't enough, Heyka followed with, "She called me after meeting you. She was extremely excited about you getting involved with the Safe Crossings Project."

"That's what she said?"

"Yes. She couldn't say enough good thinga about you, and about what you can do for us. I'm not as involved in the day-to-day details as Tracy, but I'm the president of the board of directors. We have an impressive and dedicated group of people fully invested in this project. I'm a wildlife biology professor at UW, but the board runs the gamut—wildlife advocates, business people, another mother who lost her daughter, in a collision with a deer. Anyway, Tracy sent a text out to the entire board that morning, as she left her meeting with you, saying you're essential to the Safe Crossings' success."

Johnny's instinct—perhaps more his *need*—was to confess to and apologize for how brusque he'd been with Tracy Blessings; to correct the mistaken impression Tracy had apparently given Heyka about Johnny's willingness to be involved. But for once in his life, telling it like it was—disputing the veracity of the friend this man was clearly grieving—seemed the wrong thing to do.

"I'm sorry, too, about the project," he said instead. "It was a great concept. Important work."

"*Was?*" Heyka's voice registered something between disbelief and indignation. "We have no intention of abandoning the project, Mr. Yellow Kidney. That would double this tragedy. We are proceeding, with absolute confidence that Tracy will return to head it up."

Johnny's silence apparently did not deflate that confidence.

"That's why I've called, Mr. Yellow Kidney. This project can and *will* succeed. We have built up crucial momentum and support—namely federal funding. Tracy has exhausted her very extensive network of friends, politicians, and colleagues, called in every favor. She's very well-connected and highly thought of.

"I'm sure she shared her story with you. She sees this project as a way to make sense of the loss of her daughter, to memorialize her. Tracy went into a deep depression when Kylie died. This project, the idea of making sure another family never suffers the same loss, is what saved her, literally, from dying of a broken heart. And of course, for those of you, those of *us*, who have always championed wildlife, it's a no-brainer to climb on board."

Heyka was on a roll.

"However, it's the way of the nonprofit world, and projects like this, that if you let them linger, you lose enthusiasm and soon after that, financial support. We can't allow that to happen. That's why the board of the Safe Crossings Project needs you. This project can't lose the momentum Tracy's achieved. We must move forward, with the same sense of urgency. We are asking you to fill in for her until Tracy returns. And she *will* return."

So startled was he by this announcement that Johnny let his free hand drop to the table, almost knocking over a still-full cup of coffee.

"Me?" he replied, voice so loud and lacking his usual calm that it drew both Vilma and her worker's attention. "You're asking me to run the highway wilding project while Ms. Blessings is in a coma?"

If he detected the note of disbelief in Johnny's voice, Heyka decided to ignore it.

"Yes. Tracy felt you were key to our success. And you've been intimately involved with a project that's nearly identical to what we plan to do. No one fits our criteria—no one but Tracy—better, Mr. Yellow Kidney. We have a framework in place already, people hired. A brilliant young engineer from Montana State. Tracy kept voluminous notes on every meeting, with him and with potential funding sources. The outline is all there. What we need is someone credible and with experience to implement it. Someone to be the face of the project until Tracy returns. That's you, Mr. Yellow Kidney. That's you. This is what Tracy would want. When I sit at her bedside, I practically feel her willing the board to do this.

"What do you say?"

Johnny stifled a laugh.

"Mr. Heyka…"

"Please, call me Bob."

"Bob. I'm deeply saddened and sorry about what happened to Ms. Blessings. My spirit is heavy with guilt for allowing her to go hiking alone that day. I never even asked her who she was going with. I would undo that if I could. I would give anything to undo that, but this, this idea, this request…"

"You can't undo it, Johnny," Heyka interjected. "We can't go back. But we can go forward. We can give Tracy something to live for when she opens her eyes again. We can give her hope. *You* can give her hope. You may just be the only one who can."

Johnny couldn't believe that the madness—the sense of responsibility he'd already assumed for what had happened—was not only continuing, despite his protests, but amplifying.

"I don't have the luxury of quitting my job," he said. "Nor would I ever do so. It's work I love. I've dedicated my career to it, and this is a critical time...."

"You can take a short leave of absence." Johnny heard it in Heyka's voice.

It wasn't a suggestion. It was a statement of fact.

At those words, it all became clear. The call from Hannah. His request approved—never before had he seen the Park Service move so swiftly on a personnel request. The sound in her voice.

It all suddenly made sense.

"You've already arranged that." He paused, still letting it sink in. "Haven't you? When you arranged for approval for me to hire an assistant for my DNA project."

The last was neither a statement nor a question. It was an accusation, and it was followed by a brief silence.

"You're half right," Heyka said, "half wrong. Tracy arranged it. She said you'd mentioned needing an assistant. Right after she left the meeting with you that day, she made some calls, pulled some strings. That's Tracy.

"But yes, I did call and speak to your supervisor. I told her what we wanted to do and asked her if there was a chance you could take a leave of absence. I apologize. She told me she was certain you wouldn't agree to do it, but she said she thought she could arrange for you to take over the project for a month or two."

Even if he could not see the look in Johnny's eyes, he could apparently hear it in the silence.

"Believe me, Mr. Yellow Kidney, I don't ordinarily operate this way. But I happen to care deeply about Tracy Blessings. She is a wonderful, well-intentioned woman. And just as importantly, I care about this project. And I have learned enough about you to know that you recognize, no doubt more than any of us, how important these wildlife crossings are.

"Of course, the decision is yours. My intention was to make certain, by asking, that your position in the park would not be impacted in any way. But my top priority is this project and the lives—both animal and human, young people like Kylie Blessings— it stands to save. The populations, including your beloved wolverines, it stands to connect and allow to remain viable.

"I've been in this business a long time and I'm sure you recognize, as do I, that in an imperfect world, we sometimes do things we may not like doing, or how we must do them, but that we justify because we believe they are necessary for the greater good. We need you, Mr. Yellow Kidney. Please. Give us a month or two of your time...."

Johnny respected the honesty being shown him but remained unswayed.

"I don't mean to sound insensitive, Mr. Heyka, but it sounds unrealistic to believe that Ms. Blessings will be able to return to head up this project in a matter of a month or two."

"You could be right. So commit to us for three months. No more, and if Tracy is up and can take over before then—and if I know Tracy, she will be—we'll need you less than three months. If she's not, and you want out, we'll find someone else at the end of three months. But in the meantime, we'll have continued our momentum."

A moment ago, it was a month or two. Now it had become three. But Johnny knew it was fruitless to point this out. He also knew they had him.

He had not only been callous and brusque to this woman, a woman motivated to make her daughter's death count for something—something Johnny, above anyone, appreciated the value of—he had allowed her to go hiking alone in Two Medicine.

And now he was being asked to pay the price—for that's how he viewed this proposal, as the Creator's—and perhaps even his own—bargain for redemption.

And as if that weren't enough, there was the call from Hannah. The note he distinguished in her voice.

No trip to West Glacier, park headquarters, was necessary now for Johnny to understand it.

Johnny sensed that the silence on the line did not make Bob Heyka uncomfortable. In fact, Johnny suspected it made him just the opposite. Hopeful.

"I'll need two weeks here," Johnny finally replied. "To finish up my data collection."

He could do the rest of the paperwork he would submit for ESA listing from anywhere, as long as he had an assistant to facilitate.

"We can live with that," Heyka replied.

"And then I'll give you two months. Not three."

"Is that negotiable?"

"No. Take it or leave it."

For the slightest time—no more than two or three seconds—
Johnny dared to hope that this might save him.

"We'll take it."

6

WILL'S TWO-WAY RADIO CRACKLED to life just as he came around the bend before Pebble Creek Campground.

"Five-tango-one-five, this is five-hotel-one-four. We have a Code 3. 10-20?"

Slowing for a horse trailer turning into the trailhead parking lot opposite Pebble Creek, Will reached for his radio.

"Five-tango-one-five. Cliff, that you? What's the Code 3?"

Abandoning protocol, Cliff Utzinger responded with a quick "Where are you, Will?"

"Just came off the Thunderer. Still looking for that wounded griz. I'm westbound at Pebble Creek Campground, mile-post 22, returning to headquarters."

"10-4. I need your assistance on the highway about a mile west of the Buffalo Ranch, STAT."

Will pressed down harder on the gas pedal. "ETA ten minutes."

"Great."

The radio went dead without Cliff providing an explanation.

Eight minutes later, Will discovered the reason for the code that signified a crime had been committed. Three law enforcement vehicles, lights on, had pulled over on the shoulder of the narrow two-lane road, and what seemed to be an army of onlookers had already gathered as an interpretive ranger Will recognized from Tower worked the jam, ordering vehicles that had slowed or stopped to gawk at the commotion to move on.

It wasn't until the ranger managed to wave an obscenely large RV out of the way that Will saw the first body.

A bison. Motionless, its huge bulk lying not more than a dozen yards off the road.

Will pulled over, put his hat on, stepped out of his Jeep.

Cliff Utzinger had seen the Jeep approach and was the first to meet him. A slender, soft-spoken man, he managed to remain contained as he delivered his report, but Will could see rare emotion as Cliff pointed toward the rolling grassland on the south side of the road.

"There are three of them, Will. Two cows, one still nursing a calf—poor little son of a bitch is right over there," he said, hand visibly shaking as his finger moved to a distant, lone figure, brilliant orange in color, "and a bull. All shot."

The two-lane road had become a parking lot. Will was in the midst of yelling orders to onlookers to get back into their vehicles when his radio crackled to life again.

One of the few things Will appreciated about his long-time boss was Shewmaker's disregard for radio formalities. No "10-4"s or "10-20"s with Peter.

"Will, this is Peter. Where the hell are you?"

"Where do you think I am, Peter? I'm in the Lamar, working the bison killings."

"We had a meeting set for ten a.m. It's now eleven-thirty."

Striding toward a tourist he'd just watched jump out of the back door of a tour bus and bypass the ranger working the jam— and who was now pointing a camera at one of the dead bison—Will replied, "Do you really mean to tell me some goddamn meeting takes precedence over what happened out here last night?"

They had worked together long enough for Will to be able to picture Shewmaker's eyes hardening, pursed lips beginning to twitch, as the radio went briefly silent—a silence that allowed Will to snatch the tourist's camera with an expression that told the park visitor this ranger was not one to mess with.

"Get your ass to headquarters, Will. Now."

• • •

When Will pulled up behind the Albright Visitor Center, he saw Peter Shewmaker's outline centered in the window of his third-floor office. He had been standing watch, waiting for Will's arrival.

This did not bode well, but—incensed at being called off the horrific scene in the Lamar—Will refused to glance up as he exited his car and strode toward the building's back door.

Hurrying through the visitor-packed lobby, he ignored the calls and waves from young rangers working the counter—who considered Will the rock star of badass backcountry rangers—and took two stairs at a time.

Without knocking first, Will opened the door.

Superintendent Gonzalez sat in one of two chairs on the opposite side of Peter's desk. His presence did nothing to temper Will's words.

"There are three dead bison out there, with the people who did it still on the loose. Maybe still in the park. And you're telling me a meeting with me is so goddamn important it can't wait?"

Gonzalez spoke first.

"We realize you are upset, Ranger McCarroll," he said calmly. "So are we. We've just issued a press release announcing a five-thousand-dollar reward for information that leads to apprehension of the person or persons responsible."

Will's laugh was so sudden and caustic that even his long-time boss, Shewmaker, looked startled.

"How ironic," Will replied. "The park that sent nine hundred bison to slaughter this past winter now wants to position itself as upset about three being shot."

"You know damn well this kind of thing upsets me," Peter interjected.

It wasn't like Peter, who consistently towed the company/Park Service line, to express any disapproval of its actions. But in the next sentence, any satisfaction Peter's statement afforded Will evaporated.

"But the superintendent has had his hands tied with that goddamn IBMP."

Will shook his head in disbelief.

"Aw, come on Peter. Don't give me that IBMP bullshit. The Interagency Bison Management Plan is archaic and simply wrong, dead wrong. You've known it, I've known it, *everyone* has known it for years. It's based on a myth—that park bison who carry brucellosis will transmit it to cattle if they leave the park. We all know that's not true. Never happened, never will. *Science* has told us it's not true. The IBMP was never honest or science-based. It was done to appease the livestock industry. And it hasn't even succeeded at that." Will looked directly into Gonzalez's hooded gaze. "All it would take is for someone in authority, someone in your position, Superintendent Gonzalez, to get serious about calling it obsolete, like it is, and refuse to send more bison to their deaths, over grass and a political myth."

Gonzalez sat silent, but his eyes darted to Shewmaker, who rose from his chair.

"That's enough, Will. We can debate the IBMP forever, but that's not what this meeting is about."

That was enough for Will to turn his fury on his boss.

"I know what it's about. The citations I issued. Punish me however you want, Peter, but not during this investigation. That can wait. I want you to pull me off backcountry and let me be the lead on the bison killings."

With what seemed to take monumental effort not to allow any commiseration he was feeling to show, Shewmaker's gaze held steady as he cleared his throat.

"We're pulling you off backcountry, Will." Involuntarily letting his eyes drop to the floor, just as quickly, he lifted them again. "But not to work the bison killings."

"Peter, I'm the man to head that investigation. You know it. I can still be looking for the wounded grizzly while I find the bastards who killed those bison."

When Gonzalez spoke up again, the gleam in his eyes made a lie of his somber expression.

"Ranger McCarroll, what Pete's trying to say is that you won't be working *any* investigations. You are hereby notified that

Yellowstone National Park and the National Park Service are firing you. For just cause."

Will had imagined this day would come for years, perhaps even decades. But actually hearing the words seemed somewhat surreal.

"Just cause? How many other LEs have you fired for issuing citations that didn't hold up in court?"

"You think this is just about the most recent issue—your citing hikers for not carrying bear spray," Gonzalez replied, his voice rising an octave, "even though no such regulation exists within this park? How about kidnapping Judge Sherburne from his nursing home—how many times? And confiscating all the legally held weapons in Pebble Creek Campground..."

Will interrupted him.

"Yeah. And look what just happened. Those three bison shot dead. A calf that might not make it. You better believe that the assholes who did it might have thought twice about bringing guns into the park if it weren't for the guns-in-parks law. We've given them a free pass. And that grizzly on the Thunderer wouldn't be walking around with a bullet in its hindquarters—sentenced to die, either from the bullet wound itself or another park decision to avoid bad publicity—if it weren't for the ARF holding everyone in this country hostage, including the Park Service. Including *you*, Superintendent Gonzalez."

Standing next to his desk, Peter Shewmaker slammed a fist against its surface.

"Will, for once, just shut up, will you?"

Will was in no mood to be silenced.

"And what does my taking the judge who presided over this park for over thirty years for a midnight ride a couple times to get him out of that depressing nursing home and back to the place he loves have to do with anything? How the hell is that a Park Service issue?"

"It became a Park Service issue when the nursing home reported it to the police and the Park County sheriff wanted to arrest you. We promised him you weren't going to do it again," Peter answered.

The room fell silent. Will felt all eyes upon him, but he would not look up. He could not.

It had finally come to this. He took a deep breath and directed his gaze to Peter.

"Okay, fire me if you have to. Just wait until I finish the bison investigation."

Gonzalez slid a sheet of paper across the desk to Will.

"It's too late for that, Mr. McCarroll."

Mister. Will could not remember ever being addressed as mister. Gonzalez was clearly enjoying himself now.

"You'll have to be at the initial appearance for the four hikers you issued your invalid citations to, then you're done. That document spells out the reasons for your dismissal, the benefits you are entitled to, and what legal recourse you have."

Silent, Will stood, grabbed the paper, and then, without so much as glancing at it, crumpled and threw it into Shewmaker's wastebasket as he walked out of the office where he had visited, reported, asked for and given advice, been alternately chastised and praised, for thirty years.

Before shutting the door behind him, he heard Peter call to him one last time.

"Will?"

In the rush of emotion and disbelief, Will almost, for a second, looked back. Later he was glad he hadn't. For the words he heard as he walked away would echo in his head for long enough— without adding the visual of them coming from his long-time friend and advocate's mouth.

"Since you're no longer with the Park Service, please attend the hearing in street clothes."

• • •

Bill Stucky, still dressed in his Wildlife Services uniform, dried coyote drool tainted with blood adorning his pant leg, grinned a mile wide as he walked backward, waving the cattle truck down the long drive to the gate next to his house, which sat on the banks of the Yellowstone River.

"Left, left," he yelled to the truck's bearded driver, who hung his head outside the driver's side window.

Dogs barked as they ran alongside the livestock trailer, their voices blending with the bleating coming from inside of it. Stucky's grandchildren, aged four and six, ran alongside as the transport vehicle backed its way, adeptly following Stucky's signals.

Stucky held his hand up, flat palm facing the side mirror on the truck's cab, and with a screech of the eighteen-wheeler's un-oiled brakes, the truck came to a stop.

Stucky had already opened the gate to his eleven acres. Now he strode purposefully to the back of the trailer and, with a practiced hand, lifted the metal bar that latched the door in place.

"Zach, Emily," he yelled before pulling the door open. "Come see."

Zach and Emily arrived just in time to giggle and shout in delight as the door opened and out jumped thirty-six woolly, terrified sheep. Between Stucky and his well-trained cattle dogs, within less than a minute all thirty-six had dashed through the gate, which Stucky walked shut behind them, and headed toward the pasture.

Pulling a wad of money several inches thick from his pocket, Stucky strolled back to the truck, where the driver stood admiring the scenery.

"Nice land," he said, eyeing the ridge to the west that towered directly over them, which was disrupted dramatically by a deep red slash that ran from its top to the river's edge. "What the hell…"

"Devil's Slide," Stucky announced without looking up as he counted hundred-dollar bills.

The driver's eyes lit with a spark of wonder.

"How close am I to Yellowstone? I was thinking of driving down there. Never been in the park before."

"Nine miles," Stucky answered.

"You work there?" he said, eying Stucky's uniform.

"No. I'm with Wildlife Services."

"What the hell is Wildlife Services?"

Stucky was getting irritated.

"When there are problems with wildlife, we're the ones who're called in to solve them."

The driver looked confused for a moment. Then, like a threatening storm cloud suddenly parted by the sun, a light of comprehension crossed his face.

"Oh, you're the guys who get to kill 'em. Like poisoning them. Or aerial gunning. I bet it was you guys I seen in a helicopter last summer, down the Madison, just laying a whole pack of wolves down. And all those prairie dogs, and coyotes. And beaver," he added with delight. "You poison them, dontcha?"

Stucky pushed three bills into the man's hand, turned, and began walking back to the gate, which the kids had managed to open, letting the dogs inside. Thrilled to now have a job, the blue heeler and his pal, an Aussie, circled and barked, but the sheep, clearly accustomed to herd dogs, had already come upon the good grazing to be found along the Yellowstone River and ignored them, though several lambs moved closer to their mothers.

"Hey, aren't you worried about wolves getting the sheep?" the driver called to Stucky. "I mean, this close to Yellowstone."

Stucky just kept walking toward the gate, without turning back to reply.

Not to be deterred, one hand on the door, before jumping on to the cab's running board, the driver yelled after him.

"So whaddaya do with the wolf and beaver pelts? Sell 'em?"

7

"ALL RISE."

Annie stood, frozen, just behind the door leading to the courtroom. Never had she felt so nervous, so shaken, before walking into the airy, high-ceilinged room at the heart of the four-year-old, state-of-art Yellowstone Justice Center.

While she had heard stories about the lack of security at the old courtroom, which for decades had been housed in the Pagoda Building, just two doors down and across from Mammoth's Visitor Center, it wasn't lack of security that had her rattled now. The new facility with all the latest and most high-tech screening equipment, plus the presence of multiple guards at all times, seemed, if anything, like overkill to Annie.

No, what had her rattled now had nothing to do with safety. And everything to do with Will.

She took a deep breath before pulling open the right side of the tall double oak doors leading from her chamber. A gentle hand—Justine's—brushed her forearm as she passed the court clerk on her way to the bench.

"Please, be seated," Annie said, her gaze intensely focused only upon the bailiff—a stout, stern-looking man now, but one whom Annie knew to be extraordinarily jovial and kind when stationed at the screening area just inside the center's front door. "You may call the first case."

As the bailiff read the case number, Annie allowed her eyes to scan the courtroom.

No sign of Will. A rush of relief steadied her hands.

The first case involved a twenty-four-year-old from Billings who had struck and killed a young black bear on the bridge between Mammoth and Tower. He had refused the breathalyzer test requested by Cliff Utzinger, who had arrested him and was now seated in the front row of the courtroom. Witnesses called 911 immediately after the cub was hit to report the newer-model Audi had been speeding and failed to slow down when the young cub-of-the-year, who had been separated from its mother by tourists with cameras, had been running across the narrow, two-lane bridge. After reading aloud the charges he faced—driving under the influence, reckless driving, speeding—Annie placed the docket on her bench and lifted her gaze to study the young man.

She saw so many different types in her courtroom. Visitors from all over the world and, like this defendant, an occasional local. Some appeared visibly irritated to have had their vacations disrupted—or often, ruined—by ending up in court. Some appeared embarrassed or contrite. Almost all seemed nervous. But this well-groomed and -dressed young man appeared downright nonchalant.

"Are you represented by counsel, Mr. Raymond?"

"My dad's a lawyer. He's going to represent me. He told me what to do today."

"Then are you ready to enter a plea to the charges against you now, at this initial appearance?"

"I am."

"Do you understand the charges against you?"

The defendant nodded his head.

"I need a verbal answer."

"Yes, Your Honor, I do."

"And you realize the severity of the charges?"

"I do now," he replied sullenly.

"And how do you plead?"

"Not guilty."

"To which charge?"

"To all charges, Your Honor."

"Very well. A trial date will be set within thirty days. Until then, Mr. Raymond, you are not to leave the state of Montana without first filing notice with my office. Is that clear?"

"Yes, Your Honor."

As Annie turned to the bailiff to ask him to call the next case, the back door to the courtroom opened.

In stepped Will McCarroll.

He paused, and for a moment Annie felt he would avoid looking at her, but then he directed his gaze her way, nodding slightly, before slipping into the back row. Annie was as startled by his overall appearance as she was by the sight of him in a jacket and jeans.

She issued her next instructions to the bailiff.

"The next two cases may be called together."

She had already explained the situation, so the bailiff didn't skip a beat as he read two case manes and numbers in rapid succession and asked the defendants in each to rise.

Two persons stood: a man and woman in their mid-thirties.

"Please identify yourselves," Annie said.

The man spoke for both when he replied, "Sharon and Manny Cernack."

"Mr. and Mrs. Cernack. Thank you for attending. And again, the court apologizes for the fact that we were unable to locate you to notify you there was no need to attend today's initial appearance."

"We were camping along the Bechler," Manny Cernack offered. "It would have been nice not to cut that short."

"Again, my apologies. We did make every attempt to find you, including sending a ranger out to the Black Canyon, where you had reserved a campsite." She couldn't help but add, "Not the Bechler."

In light of the situation, Annie decided not to press the fact that the couple had not registered their change of plans with the backcountry office. She had been advised by Pete Shewmaker that the decision had been made not to pursue that matter and by Ron Max, of the Office of Public Affairs, to keep today's appearance short and sweet. Yet word had apparently gotten out. As a local reporter scribbled frantically in the front row, Annie saw a TV van from the NBC affiliate in Billings roll by the courtroom window.

She kept her voice steady and did not look at Will.

"And as you can see, we succeeded in notifying the defendants in the other two cases."

A hush had fallen over the courtroom.

"Mr. and Mrs. Cernack, I have been instructed by the superintendent of Yellowstone National Park, Superintendent Gonzalez, to inform you, as we have already informed the other two defendants, that any and all charges brought against you as a result of the citation issued to you by Ranger Will McCarroll, for not carrying bear spray as you hiked in the backcountry, have been dismissed...."

Annie's voice faltered.

She had been asked—a "request" from Public Affairs—to say more, to apologize for the citations ever having been issued, but that's where Annie Peacock decided to draw the line.

"Yellowstone National Park has no regulation requiring hikers to carry bear spray. Charges are hereby dismissed, and this court is adjourned."

While his wife turned to walk away, Manny Cernack stood his ground.

"That's it? No apology? I'd been told you were going to apologize...."

"Court is adjourned," Annie repeated, meeting the man's gaze.

Sharon Cernack had returned to her husband's side. She whispered to him nervously, but he ignored her, angry eyes glued to Annie.

"Where's my apology for the citations?"

Annie met his gaze.

"You are flirting with contempt of court charges now, Mr. Cernack. It is not the job of this court to apologize. Court is adjourned. Bailiff, please escort the defendant out."

Annie stood, turned to leave.

As Justine called out, "All rise," Annie could not bring herself to look Will's way. She did not see the expression on his face at her dismissal of the charges without even calling him to the stand, or when the defendant passed by where Will sat.

She did not see the young, high-heeled reporter stick a microphone in Will's face when he finally stepped outside the courtroom.

Nor did she hear her question.

"Ranger McCarroll," the reporter started, her posture erect, hair falling perfectly into long golden spirals, one of which she tossed over her shoulder with a practiced shake of the head.

"The entire state of Montana, the entire nation, wants to know," she called out after him as Will pivoted and walked away.

"Is it true you've been fired?"

• • •

Justine stood in the middle of Annie's office, holding her boss's fleece jacket in the air.

Ordinarily, immediately following a hearing, the two women would sit together over coffee at Annie's desk, making notes regarding how the hearing went and what they hoped to accomplish the rest of the day or week.

Not today.

"Go," Justine said. "His car is still behind the Visitor Center. Those damn reporters were all over him, so he ducked into the clinic, but about ten or fifteen minutes ago I saw him sneak out the back and head on foot up the Old Road."

Annie threw off her robe and dropped it on her desk instead of neatly hanging it up in the closet, as was her norm.

She slid her slender arms into the jacket Justine held open.

"I thought you didn't like Will," she said as she flopped down in her chair and reached under her desk for the pair of hiking boots she kept handy for those afternoons her mom brought Archie, her golden retriever, over for a mid-day walk.

"When did I say that?"

"Do you think I never notice the way you look at him when he stops in here?"

Annie glanced up at Justine as she finished lacing up the boots. In an attempt to combat the drooping of her eyelid, Justine had recently begun wearing black eyeliner that she extended beyond her eye by an eighth of an inch, drawing the final section up, like a smile.

Now her wounded expression caused her droopy lids to swallow the smile.

"I just don't like all the grief he causes you."

Rising, Annie took the light backpack she kept in her closet, which she had watched Justine retrieve as she tied her boots.

"I like what he stands for, what he fights for," her court clerk and confidante said as she helped Annie slide into the backpack before literally pushing Annie through the door that led to the back stairwell of the Justice Center.

Annie's steps echoed in the stairwell as she hurried down the flight of stairs toward the metal reinforced door one floor below, which faced west, away from the chaos of the park headquarters and toward the town of Gardiner—toward what locals referred to as the "Old Road."

Stepping outside into the afternoon sunlight, she instantly regretted leaving her sunglasses in her desk drawer, but she would not waste time backtracking for them. She knew how quickly Will moved along the trail. They had walked Archie together along the Old Road on several occasions.

Maybe, it suddenly occurred to her, his taking off in that direction meant he *wanted* to see her—though it was more likely he had headed there solely to avoid the media.

As she started up the unmarked trailhead behind the Chittenden House, Annie glanced toward the row of parking spots outside the courthouse, directly opposite the west side of the newly remodeled Albright Visitor Center. The TV truck no longer sat idling, but several youthful, ambitious-looking reporters lingered, talking amongst themselves. One had cornered Cliff Utzinger. Will would not have risked the same fate by heading back to his old Jeep, which she could see still parked behind the VC.

Hopefully she would find him somewhere along the trail, but Annie knew Will had any number of hidden places along the road that were special to him.

While the backcountry held Will's heart and was home to him, early on he had managed to find escapes from the craziness of Mammoth—places he went during staff trainings, or on the rare occasion he was called to duty at park headquarters. Annie hadn't been surprised by Will's confession that during day-long trainings, he often snuck out the back of the small auditorium in the Albright Visitor Center and headed up the Old Road, returning just before the end of the session to sign out.

Finding him in one of the places that provided Will sanctity would be nearly impossible—with one exception. On one occasion, Will had actually shared one such spot with Annie.

The heat radiating in waves off the desert terrain, along with the sun's glare, made seeing any distance difficult, but Annie paused at each rise to scan in every direction for Will.

Now, trusting her instincts, and seeing the stand of scrub pine in the distance about to be swallowed by the growing shadow cast by Electric Peak, Annie veered off the trail.

• • •

"I was hoping I'd find you here."

His back to her, Will McCarroll squatted, one knee on the ground as he reached for something in front of him.

At the sound of Annie's voice, he glanced over his shoulder, then slowly rose. It wasn't until he stood that Annie saw it.

"Oh my god," she cried.

Will had taken her to this spot once before. They had walked the Old Road—now mostly grown over and little more than a wider-than-usual trail that climbed and rose across a mostly wide-open expanse between Mammoth and the north entry gate—for over a mile before Will had stopped to look around. Seeing no one, he had reached for her hand, diverting their hike off trail and toward Electric Peak.

Another quarter mile, then some switch-backing that had them climbing over boulders and rocks, and Annie could see they were approaching a small clearing. That day, just before they entered it, Will had hesitated, and Annie suspected he was considering turning around. But later, after thinking about it, she came to believe that what she saw in him was something else, something akin to a priest pausing before stepping into a chapel.

Will had been the first to enter the clearing.

"What is it?" Annie had asked upon seeing nine rocks that had been there, undisturbed, for so long that scrub grass had swallowed them. Perfectly placed, they formed a circle twelve feet in diameter.

"A teepee ring," Will had answered. "I found it about ten years ago."

He had stood there, eyes taking it in as if for the first time. Yet Annie instinctively knew he had been there countless times. And she knew his sharing this spot, this moment, with her was significant.

"Just think," he had said after a brief silence, "a hundred years ago, some family lived here for weeks—maybe even months—each year as they traveled through the park."

Annie had watched as Will's right hand swept the landscape splayed out before them: the rolling hills upon which they stood, descending to the flat, arid grassland—filled that day with antelope—that separated the park's north entrance gate from the Roosevelt Arch, two hundred yards to the west, and to the north the town of Gardiner's row of restaurants, gift and coffee shops, whitewater rafting company, and pharmacy.

Beyond, directly opposite them and across the Yellowstone River that bisected the town, another steep and sudden rise of barren landscape. Further west, beyond the Arch, following the Yellowstone's waters as they turned north, the Gallatin Range, stark and magnificent against the blue sky.

"They would have been hidden from sight," Will had explained, "but look…they could spot elk and bison herds—and enemies—miles away. The perfect spot to stay safe and hunt."

He had turned to her then, and added, with a hint of pride, and she sensed even propriety, "And no one knows about it. Not even the park's cultural anthropologist."

"Shouldn't you tell someone, so they can protect it?"

She remembered feeling a bit hurt by the sarcastic snort her question prompted.

"Telling someone, even the Park Service, is the last thing I would do. Not with Jan Mayhue heading up the anthropology division."

"I don't understand."

"Under Jan there has been almost no recognition of the role the tribes played in Yellowstone history. She's opposed to designating the Bannock Trail as a historical trail and has even stated it doesn't exist."

"I thought the Bannock Trail is the most famous trail through the park."

"It *is* the most famous trail. For years, decades—until they were forced onto reservations—the Bannocks and other tribes crossed the park to get to the bison herds in Montana and Wyoming. Wayne Replogle, a former ranger, spent eight years walking the entire route, mapping it out and documenting practically every step of it, and the Bannock have petitioned for historical designation, but Jan refuses. She says there's not indisputable evidence that the route was actually used enough to merit that kind of recognition."

Will had reached for Annie's hand, eyes still fixed to the ring of rocks that a single—or perhaps several—nomadic families had called home often enough to leave reminders of its existence—and for those like Will, its importance—a century later.

"Revealing this site would only bring its existence into the public eye, without affording it any protections it doesn't already have just by virtue of being inside the park's boundaries. When this park gets serious about acknowledging the contributions of the twenty-six tribes who lived and hunted here long before we white men took it over, including the Bannocks; when they actively start protecting sites like this, that's when I'll tell someone about it."

Annie knew better than to argue with Will. Not because he was difficult to argue with and she never won, but because on matters pertaining to Yellowstone, and doing right or wrong, Will rarely erred. He broke rules, but he did not err.

They hadn't lingered. Annie had instinctively shared Will's sense that their visit should be short, and hushed, but as they were leaving, she had kissed Will lightly on his sun-weathered cheek.

"Thank you for sharing this with me," she had said that day.

• • •

Now, as she witnessed the desecration before her, she again turned to Will. Even in profile, the look on his face said it all.

Deep treaded, fat-tire tracks crisscrossed the ring that had remained untouched for generations. Running like spokes of a wheel toward and over each of the nine rocks, several of which had been displaced, most of the tracks stopped immediately beyond the rock, leaving a gap of several feet; and in some cases, even two or three yards. It took Annie several seconds to realize those gaps represented the spots where mountain bikes had been launched by the rock into air before thudding back down to the recently muddied ground, destroying native vegetation and disturbing the earth in the process. Skid marks, along with foot and hand prints, indicated not everyone managed to stay upright.

"There were at least three of them," Will said, his voice flat. "Three different treads."

Both his hands held beer cans, flattened by foot, and several cigarette butts.

"Here," Annie said, sliding out of her backpack and opening it. "Put them in here."

Together they picked up almost a dozen more cans, and countless cigarette butts.

When he fell back to his knees, Annie watched as Will picked up, examined, and then reverently replaced an obsidian chip in the exact spot and position it had been. He had pointed several out to her on their first visit, telling her how the teepee's occupants used the chips as tools.

"I'm sorry, Will," Annie said softly.

As he did that first time they had visited the site, still on his knees, Will reached for her hand.

"I came here to find peace. To find a way to tell you. I had planned to talk to you after the hearing, but I had to get out of that circus."

"They've let you go, haven't they?"

Slowly, Will rose to his feet. He stood six inches taller than Annie's five foot eight, but his dark eyes met hers. She could not tell if she saw more anger or grief in them.

"This time it's final. No reassignments. No leave of absence."

Despite the fact that she'd coached herself not to cry over and over as she searched for Will, Annie's free hand swiped at a tear.

"What will you do?"

Will turned to look out across his beloved valley. Annie let her gaze follow his. And waited for his answer.

None came.

"Do you have a plan?"

She felt, rather than heard, Will take a deep breath. And in the next moment, all of Annie's fears became reality.

"It'd be best if you didn't know."

Terror raced through her. The kind of terror she felt the night she'd come home to find her mother missing, and Archie lying in a pool of blood.

"That must mean you're leaving."

When Will finally turned back to her, he wore a half-smile that Annie would spend countless sleepless nights trying to interpret.

"I love you," she said, reaching for his hand again.

When he didn't respond, she squeezed his hand.

"Look me in the eye and tell me you don't love me."

Raising his other weather- and age-roughened hand, Will brushed her cheek with a tenderness she had rarely experienced from him.

"The last thing you should want, Annie," he said quietly, and with a finality that Annie knew brooked no further resistance from her, "is for me to love you."

"That's not an answer."

Turning away from her piercing gaze, Will let go of her hand, leaned over, and picked up Annie's backpack from the ground.

Eyes turning to the basin below, where a hundred years earlier tribes had traversed its trails and hunted its buffalo, he finally gave Annie her response.

"No," he said flatly. "I don't love you."

8

"ANNIE?"

Annie Peacock's already rocky spirits took an abrupt nosedive at the sound of her name being called.

She had been confident she wouldn't run into anyone she knew on her trip to Bozeman. People from Yellowstone and Gardiner journeyed to their version of the big city every couple weeks for supplies and entertainment, but this was a Tuesday morning. Damn. Why had she decided to stop for coffee in Livingston? If she'd waited a bit longer, she could have stopped at Sola Café in Bozeman, where she wouldn't have to endure the curious glances, the sympathetic comments—especially the sympathetic comments—every time she ran into someone from the superintendent's office or LE, especially Peter Shewmaker—which was multiple times a day given the distance between her house, the Justice Center, and the Visitor Center. To make matters worse, it wasn't just when she was out and about that Annie had to deal with the intense scrutiny. Her mother was the worst culprit, staring across the kitchen table at her with those big, sad eyes. Patting her hand.

The only one who didn't seem to think she was grieving was Archie, who, in his old age, was less apt to jump up every time she entered a room, but his tail signaled he was no less enthusiastic to see her—Will McCarroll or no Will McCarroll.

Thankfully, it had been business as usual at the courthouse; but this morning when she reported to work, Justine informed Annie that the one hearing scheduled for the day had been canceled. Annie's calendar was clear. At first this news—which Justine clearly expected to please her boss—caused Annie a momentary sense of panic. Work had been her therapy, surrounding herself with defendants and out-of-town attorneys who knew nothing about Will McCarroll and his sudden disappearance. Then it came to her. She would head to Bozeman for the day, where no one knew her. Where no one would have reason to look at her with *that* look. She'd decided to take a rare personal day and drive up the Paradise Valley, stop in Livingston for coffee, then head over to the booming, tourist-packed ski town to do grocery shopping and errands.

Driving up the Paradise, Annie had been pleased with her plan. It had come just in time. She literally couldn't bear another day in Mammoth or Gardiner, where even buying groceries, she was sure to run into someone.

It had seemed the perfect solution until she heard her name. Again.

"Annie Peacock?"

Resigned, Annie turned, but the urge to bolt—to blurt out some inane excuse and literally run for the door—disappeared instantly.

"Johnny!"

As it always had, the smile—somewhere between shy and wry—turned her old boyfriend's face into something extraordinarily appealing.

Two years earlier, after over fifteen years apart, she had been in the lobby of the Glacier Park Lodge, where she had gone to present at a judicial conference, when she was thrown off guard by that same voice, those same words—"Annie Peacock?"—spoken in the same nervous tone.

She had turned to stand face to face with Johnny Yellow Kidney.

The two old lovers had subsequently gone through hell together in their efforts to find and save Will, who had been lured into the rugged backcountry in a plot to kill him and prevent him from testifying before a Senate commission on the guns-in-parks law. Now, just as it had that day in East Glacier, Annie's unease melted at the simple sight of Johnny's warm brown eyes. And that smile.

Two years earlier, Annie hadn't known just how to react upon seeing him. But now, with an uncharacteristic squeal of delight, she reached for Johnny, wrapping her arms around him as his long brown arms enveloped her.

"What are you doing in Livingston?"

The smile broadened.

"I've rented a house here."

Annie pulled away, her face a blend of shock and concern.

"You're serious?"

A sudden soulful look, accompanied by, "Would I kid you about that?" gave Annie her answer.

The woman working the counter returned with Annie's latte. Looking over Annie's shoulder at Johnny, she tilted her head and smiled.

"The usual?"

Johnny nodded his affirmation and plopped down a five-dollar bill.

"The *usual?*" Annie parroted, giving him a look straight out of their dating days at the University of Washington.

Almost sheepishly, Johnny nodded toward the hallway outside the little café, where a weathered door announced, in long-faded red lettering: STAIRS.

"I have an office on the second floor."

Handing Annie the latte the barista had just deposited on the counter, he added, "Do you have time to drink that with me?"

"I'd make it even if I didn't."

Johnny led the way to a table at the window, which faced the old Livingston train station. A train rumbled slowly in.

At the next table, a woman in typical Southwestern Montana attire—Chaco sandals, hiking shorts and t-shirt, hair pulled back tightly in a ponytail—sat with eyes glued to her laptop while her toddler rummaged through a trunk full of toys and books, frequently picking one up and hurrying over to share it with her mother.

Annie felt the first small twinge of happiness she'd felt in weeks, especially when Johnny settled in across the table from her.

But as happy as she was to see him, concern for this man—who, she had realized during their ordeal in Glacier's backcountry, she had never stopped caring for—dominated her emotions.

"What's going on?" she said. "What could possibly get you to leave Glacier?"

"Believe me, you couldn't be more surprised at the fact that I'm here than I am."

Despite the charming grin, and though he looked fit as ever in his Badger-Two Med Alliance t-shirt and worn blue jeans, Annie thought Johnny looked "off."

"I've agreed to head up something called the Safe Crossings Project," he continued. "It's to create safe passageways for wildlife and reduce human mortality from wildlife collisions—a lot like a project I was involved in on the Flathead Reservation a couple years ago."

Annie studied him as he spoke. She wasn't buying it.

"What about your work in Glacier? Your wolverine project? Being back on the reservation? It's what you dreamed of...."

The barista's arrival interrupted her. Annie didn't miss the light touch on Johnny's shoulder after she'd deposited Johnny's coffee and bagel on the table.

"Let me know if you need anything else."

Nodding his thanks, Johnny quickly zoned back in on Annie.

"Don't look at me that way," he said with a mischievous grin.

"You still have a way with women."

"What do you mean 'still'? As I remember it, you were the only white girl in college willing to date an angry Indian kid from Montana."

A rush of nostalgia washed over Annie.

"You must have had blinders on."

Johnny's smile vanished.

"Maybe I did. But that's because I only had eyes for one woman."

Then why did you leave me?

The words did not need to be voiced. Annie knew the answer. She and Johnny had already revisited their past—and come to terms with it—that night, two years earlier, when Johnny held her, comforted her—literally risking his own life to save hers—after her horse tumbled off a scree-covered trail in Glacier National Park's rugged backcountry, breaking Annie's leg and leaving her pinned on the steep mountainside by a boulder.

Annie sensed Johnny was reliving their history—recent and not-so-recent—as well.

"Now, Johnny Yellow Kidney," she said sternly, leaning toward him, "tell me what's really behind this news of yours. Because as great as a highway crossing project sounds, I don't buy for a second that you'd give up Glacier and wolverines for it."

Johnny shook his head in amazement.

"You're something, you know it?"

"Talk!"

Johnny proceeded to tell Annie about Tracy Blessings—her visit, her plea for him to become involved, and the tragic discovery of her, lying near death, just off a Two Medicine trail.

"That," he said, "is why I'm here. Why I decided to take this on, at least until Tracy returns, or they find someone else."

Annie sat, silent, for several seconds.

"I remember reading about that van full of kids. It was heartbreaking. And what you just shared makes it that much more so. Is she expected to recover?"

"It sounds like that may take a miracle, but from all I saw and have heard about this woman, miracles aren't so far-fetched."

Annie reached across the cold Formica table for Johnny's hand.

"You are a good man, Johnny. I know what a sacrifice this is for you."

"I'm trying to look at it as a privilege. If we can swing it, and I think we can, thanks to all the hard work Tracy Blessings already put into it, this project will make a real difference. It'll connect wildlife from Yellowstone to Canada, and over, to Glacier. It's a concept we've been way too slow to implement in this country. Imagine being able to drive I-90 without fear of hitting a deer, bear, coyote, or, like Kylie Blessings, an elk?

"I'm actually getting pretty excited about it. In fact, I have a meeting this afternoon with a young engineer who is already doing phenomenal work in this field. I'm told he's a genius."

Her misgivings about Johnny's decision to leave his work in Glacier and beloved home on the Blackfeet Reservation at least partially assuaged, Annie smiled.

"I know how hard it must be for you to leave, but if ever anything was worth that great a sacrifice, this would be it."

"Thanks, Annie. Your approval has always meant a lot to me. This time is no different. Now, tell me about you. And Will. And your mom," he said, then added with a sly grin, "*You* talk now."

As if the words had been waiting to rush out, Annie didn't skip a heartbeat in answering.

"Will's gone, Johnny."

"Gone? What do you mean?"

"They fired him. He got angry about the grizzlies they euthanized and started handing out citations to hikers not carrying bear spray. They'd had enough, and they fired him."

Johnny fell silent. Annie suspected the news was especially poignant for him, having just left—even temporarily—a job he felt the same passion for that Will felt for his work.

"I can't say I'm surprised. I always worried this day would come. The Park Service isn't exactly the most tolerant employer. But I can't imagine Will doing anything but work the backcountry, protecting Yellowstone wildlife…that was everything to him."

"Yes," Annie said, "apparently it was."

It was as much the look on her face as the tone with which she said it. Johnny immediately reached for her hand.

"Oh, I'm sorry, Annie. What an ignorant thing for me to say. I didn't mean it that way."

"He left, Johnny. He's gone. So obviously you're right."

"Where did he go?"

How many times had she been asked that question in the past two weeks?

"He didn't tell me." Annie hesitated. She was not sure whether to go on. But the knowledge of what they had been through together, both over a decade earlier, in college, and even more powerful, two years earlier, told her she could trust Johnny with anything. "I suspect he was protecting me by not telling me."

Johnny's eyes widened.

"You don't mean what I think you mean, do you?"

Before Annie could reply, Johnny answered his question himself.

"Damn. Of course, you do. Of course, that's what he's done."

The two sat, eyes locked, minds in synch. Annie's voice quavered.

"He's out there. I just know it, Johnny. I *feel* it."

Johnny shook his head, braids swaying, in disbelief.

Yet—Annie saw it, despite the fact that she knew he did not want her to—his eyes gleamed with envy. And excitement.

"Damn," Johnny Yellow Kidney repeated softly.

• • •

Will waited patiently.

He had known Emma Day would appear sometime soon. It was probably better that yesterday, such a horrible day—the day he watched the wounded grizzly, a sow, fend off two coyotes who had sensed, literally smelled, her vulnerability—she hadn't come up the side trail that broke off, to the east, about a quarter mile from Chaw Pass.

He had followed the smears of blood on saplings for hours, starting at dawn. He'd tracked enough wounded or injured bears— usually from hunters taking a bad shot—to know that the bear's fat would likely close the bullet hole, making it difficult to see blood on the ground. But it could sometimes be seen smeared on branches as the animal moved through thick brush and forest. Once he'd seen the first smear, mid-morning, he'd experienced both a rush of hope and one of dread. Wolves would be on the grizzly's trail too, perhaps already had.

The question was: how badly was the bear injured? Would he find it already dead, half eaten by a cadre of predators, now part of the Yellowstone food chain—only not due to some natural event? Due, instead, to a gun-happy hiker taking target practice on protected wildlife.

It was the sound of her fighting, a heart-wrenching roar of fury, that had drawn Will's binoculars to the opening where, for over two hours, he watched as the wounded bear fended off two experienced predators. Will's hopes had soared when she succeeded in chasing them away. From what he could see, the sow had sustained a grazing on her rump that had not broken any bones.

She might just be able to survive, if given the chance.

Now, a day later, he watched as another of the bear's supporters, clearly out looking for the wounded sow—Emma Day—alternately appeared then disappeared on her ascent. She was obviously going off trail in her search, otherwise she would have appeared at the next clearing, the one Will kept his binoculars trained on, before now. But she would appear soon, he was certain of that, because her detours would not result in her finding what she was out there searching for.

It had been a cold night. Summer, especially late summer, in Yellowstone by no means meant warm weather. Will's fleece and a down jacket had kept him somewhat comfortable. Wouldn't you know the sow had stayed around the Thunderer, where the population of both wolves and hikers would present a constant challenge in her vulnerable state?

He'd lost track of her yesterday after the coyote encounter. The rock outcropping so high above the floor of the valley offered 360-degree views. He set up his spotting scope on its northernmost edge at first light. He scanned for her all day, until his binoculars picked up Emma Day, trekking onward, up toward Chaw Pass.

At the rate she appeared to be traveling, he'd give her fifteen minutes to arrive.

Grabbing the smaller of his two packs, Will began picking his way off the ledge, toward the trail Emma Day traveled.

9

JOHNNY DIDN'T KNOW WHICH HAD rattled him more—seeing Annie or hearing about Will. And it wasn't just learning that Will had been fired. For some reason, the knowledge that he might have retreated to the backcountry both elated and filled Johnny with dread.

For wouldn't he do the same thing under the same circumstances?

As he literally walked the table-sized desk Tracy Blessings had purchased for the new SCP office—but never had the opportunity to use—up under the window so that he'd have at least some sort of view—not the Absarokas to the northeast, but at least, beyond the trail station, rolling hillsides—Johnny was already having second thoughts about taking the job.

He'd seen the look of shock on Annie's face. Annie, who knew him better than just about any other human being. Despite her words of support, he also saw the doubt in her eyes.

"What the fuck have I taken on?" he said out loud, thinking he was alone.

"Er…excuse me…"

Johnny pivoted toward the open door. A tall, curly-headed, carrot-topped young man stood in its opening. While it had been Johnny talking to himself, the young man seemed to be the one embarrassed.

"I know I'm early," he said, his face turning a shade brighter than his hair. "I can come back."

Johnny stepped toward him, hand extended.

"You must be DuWayne Masters. I guess I'll have to stop talking to myself if I'm going to have my back to the door," he said with a grin. "Because there's no way I'm looking at walls every day when I can be looking at that sky."

"I don't blame you, sir."

"Just call me Johnny." He nodded toward a stack of metal chairs in the corner, which the friendly owner of Katabatic, a brewery downstairs, had given Johnny when he saw him moving the desk in. "Pull up one of those and let's get started."

When the lanky engineer had settled into a chair, his legs extending a good three feet in front of him, Johnny dropped into his desk's swivel chair and turned it to face his visitor.

"Tell me about yourself."

The question seemed to throw Masters off.

"I'm a recent grad student at Montana State," Masters answered. "Have my master's in civil engineering, with a focus on bridges."

"I've been told by one of the board members that Tracy Blessings believes you to be a genius."

Blush renewed, Masters answered, "Hardly. I was a good student. I'm passionate about bridge building. Maybe, when she interviewed me, Ms. Blessings saw that."

"She saw more than that. I'm sorry you don't have the opportunity to work with her, at least not yet, and unfortunately, not at such a critical time in the project. And I'm sorry to make you repeat your introduction. So tell me, how does someone like you become passionate about bridges?"

Masters smiled for the first time.

"My father was a civil engineer. Spent his entire life working for Chicago Bridge and Iron. I used to go out to inspect bridges with him from the time I was a little guy and I just got hooked."

"You grew up in the city, then?"

"No sir. We moved a lot, wherever a bridge needed to be built. Sometimes that was in a city, but more often than not it was in the West, where my dad grew up. Salt Lake, Denver, smaller towns like Moses Lake in Washington and Billings, Montana. If a bridge needed to be built, my dad was there. We lived kind of a nomadic life, but I loved it. And I loved bridges."

Johnny was already beginning to see why Tracy Blessing had made the notes she had about her interview with DuWayne Masters in the file labeled Engineering Candidates.

"We're looking at building bridges that will be a little different than the ones your dad built."

"I understand, sir."

Johnny let the formality go this time. DuWayne Masters was opening up, and Johnny liked what he was seeing.

"But a lot of the principles are the same. My master's thesis was on wildlife crossings. It's not just that I love both—bridges and wildlife. The thing that's so exciting about projects like these is the challenge, the opportunity not only to save lives, connect populations, but the creativity that's going to take."

"Give me an example."

"Well, new ideas, new materials. My thesis focused on building modular bridges—bridges that could literally be manufactured at a plant, like a modular home, and then put together at the site. Then later, if need be—if we find our assessment of the best locations, the ones that would receive the most wildlife traffic, proves false—we pick up and move down the highway. Literally. Lighter bridges. Wildlife don't need heavy steel structures all the time. What they need is width and, for tunnels, height, and most important of all, they need natural ground cover that mimics their natural habitat. Like the Canadians developed."

As he spoke, something caught Johnny's eye. DuWayne had been sitting, legs straight out in front of him, but as he explained his graduate work, shared his passion, he leaned forward in his chair. His pant legs drew higher, and Johnny saw that his right leg was a prosthesis.

DuWayne stopped, mid-sentence, and with no emotion, no sense of embarrassment or indignation at seeing Johnny's eyes directed to his ankle, said, "Lost my right leg from the knee down when I was twelve. In an accident." And then, with complete sincerity, added, "It won't impact my ability to be out there on site, Mr. Yellow Kidney. I assure you."

For once, Johnny was speechless. He rose to his feet abruptly. DuWayne Masters jumped up just as quickly, a worried expression on his face.

"When can you start?" Johnny asked.

"Seriously?"

"Yes. I'm dead serious. In fact, you can help me set your office up today." Johnny strode to a narrow wooden door—the original

102

in the 1921 building—located opposite the wall with the window and swung it open, exposing a room barely bigger than a closet. No window. "If you have time."

"For the love of Pete," Masters said, grinning ear to ear as he stood in the doorway, surveying it as if it were a penthouse suite in the Flatiron Building in the heart of New York City.

"Yes, I have time."

As Johnny patted the young man on the shoulder, he experienced his first sense of genuine anticipation and excitement about this new life that had been forced upon him so suddenly and unexpectedly.

"Welcome on board."

• • •

Will stepped onto the trail, started his descent.

Timing would be everything.

As it turned out, his was perfect.

Less than two minutes down the trail and he heard her, singing to herself. He couldn't help but smile. Janis Joplin, "Me and Bobby McGee." He had to admit it was a good song to alert bears to her presence.

Will raised the sunglasses hanging from his lanyard to his eyes. He had never been a good liar. Come to think of it, he had never been a liar, good or bad.

Seconds later, she came around a curve on the trail.

"Emma."

The young biologist looked like she'd just seen a ghost.

"Will?"

Will found himself unsure of how to respond. He would have to get better at this.

"What are you doing here?" she said. "I thought…"

This part he had prepared for. He'd known it would be essential—the first and perhaps greatest test every time.

"That I was fired?" he said. "Yes, I was. That doesn't mean I can't still hike in the park, does it?"

His tone, equal parts confrontational—which he hated using with Emma Day—and hurt, worked.

Clearly wounded, Emma replied, "Of course not." Then, unable to stop herself, she blurted out, "I can't tell you how good it is to see you."

She followed an awkward pause with the same question Annie had asked him that last day after she'd tracked him to the teepee ring.

"*What are you going to do?*"

Will did not remove the sunglasses.

"I'm taking some time to decide."

Emma's lips pursed, chin quivering. Her eyes welled up.

"I'm so sorry, Will," she said. "And so angry."

Stepping forward, moved by her sweet display of affection, Will placed his arm around Emma.

"It's okay. It's good."

She shook her head.

"No. It's *not* good. Things are all going to hell—those three bison shot and Stucky killing the park wolf and getting away with it."

Will dropped the arm that had been cradling Emma, moved a step back to face her—to be able to look her in the eye.

"What do you mean Stucky got away with killing a park wolf?"

"Stucky brought domesticated sheep onto his property. Wolves killed two of them over the weekend—like he knew that wouldn't happen when he brought sheep into wolf territory? He left the carcasses on his property, then when a different wolf—this one was collared, a study wolf—was drawn to the carcasses, he killed it. And he got away with it. FWP didn't do a damn thing. Not even a citation for leaving the carcasses."

"An autopsy showed the collared wolf hadn't killed any sheep?"

"Yes. And you and I both know what's going to happen next, when the wolf who made the kill returns. Not to mention the danger those domestic sheep represent to the bighorn. Hell, someone already sighted a big wild ram within a hundred yards of Stucky's place." Another stifled sob escaped her. "So please don't tell me it's good that you're gone. It's not good for the bears. It's not good for the wolves, bison, or the bighorn," she said, eyes shining. "And it's not good for me."

Will reached for Emma, placing a roughened hand under her chin to bring her gaze even with his.

"Listen, Emma. You are a fine biologist—and even more important, you are a biologist with integrity and heart, doing work you're passionate about. That means you'll ruffle feathers along the way. But you'll also have your cheering squad and supporters. It takes time."

"You were the only one on my cheering squad."

"I'm still on it."

It was Emma's turn to zero in on Will.

"You're up here looking for the wounded grizzly, aren't you?"

Will looked her straight in the eye, like he'd done with Annie.

"I'm up here for a hike."

If Will told Emma what he knew, what he had seen the day before, the mountainside would be flooded with Park Service rangers and biologists in less than two hours, and shortly thereafter, another shot would ring out and the sow would be dead—killed to avoid the risk of a hiker encountering a wounded bear.

Disappointment ravaged Emma's young face. Will couldn't tell whether it was because she knew he had just lied to her, or at her failure to learn what Will had just learned—that the sow was still alive.

Knowing how strongly Emma disapproved of the park's policy to eliminate bears who deserved a chance, he could not burden Emma with having to make the decision he now—no longer a Park Service employee—had no trouble making.

Actually, one that he would never have had trouble making.

But he had sought Emma out for a reason, and now he would put her to another test. "What do you know about the bison investigation?"

The transformation in Emma's expression should have embarrassed Will. "You wanted to run in to me today, didn't you?"

"Yes."

"What do you need?"

"The name of the lead investigator."

"That's all?"

"That's enough. I don't want to get you involved."

Emma's silence was short-lived. "Cliff Utzinger. He's been working the investigation hard, but I hear he's got nothing, that he's reached an impasse."

"Cliff still stationed up at Tower?"

The nearest ranger station to the Lamar, where the bison had been killed, was located just south of the Tower Falls junction.

"Yes…"

The way her answer trailed off told Will that Emma realized what was at stake.

Will suddenly felt ashamed of himself for putting his young friend in this position. He was about to tell her so when Emma Day reached out and put an index finger on his lip, silencing him.

"Next week the Tower seasonals leave," she said.

Yellowstone summer staff began departing right after Labor Day, the schedule for which depended upon where they were stationed, with the areas of highest visitation being the last to depart, leaving a skeletal crew of year-round employees, who then assumed a wider range of tasks.

"Cliff will be out doing field work again."

About the only thing Emma Day hadn't done was hand Will a key to the facility. Will had no doubt that if she had one, she'd have given it to him right then and there. As a bear biologist, however, Emma's office, when she was in it, which was rarely, was located in the Yellowstone Resource Center. She had not been issued a key to any of the ranger stations.

But that wouldn't be a problem. Not for Will.

10

JOHNNY STOOD, SILENT, FOR SEVERAL seconds before lightly tapping on the door's frame.

DuWayne Masters turned his head. His lanky body followed as he swung the chair Johnny had traded with him—which allowed DuWayne to push away and rise from his desk more easily—to face his visitor.

Johnny had already grown fond of the toothy grin greeting him. "Morning, Boss."

It took no more than three or four steps for Johnny to cross the office, which was decorated with pictures of wildlife and wildlife crossings from British Columbia and the Netherlands, and the most recent addition, a gift from Johnny, a poster from the People's Way Partnership on the Flathead Reservation.

Plopping the fresh edition of the *Bozeman Daily Chronicle* on top of a hundred-plus-page highway crossings manual issued by the Federal Department of Transportation, which Masters had been reviewing, Johnny grinned back.

"You're a celebrity."

DuWayne picked up the paper to see his own image—same chair, office, and posters framing it—staring back at him from the front page of the area's largest newspaper.

"Holy mackerel," he said. "I figured we'd get a little piece at the back of the science section."

Johnny watched in silence as Master's eyes skimmed the column on the front page, then turned several pages to find another two columns devoted to the subject.

"It's a great interview," Johnny replied. "You're now officially the rock star of highway crossings."

Lowering himself into a chair at the side of Masters' desk, Johnny added, "Seriously, you did an outstanding job of explaining why we need this project—the data—without coming across as a scientist so absorbed in his own work that he's out of touch with the real world. We need local support, and between the fact that the reporter obviously liked you, your passion, and the information you provided, you just did the project a big favor."

Eyes gleaming, Masters replied, "Thanks, Johnny. I lucked out getting that reporter. She's an MSU grad, and she was obviously pro-wildlife. I just told it like it is."

His expression grew more somber as he went back to skimming the article in his hands.

"I honestly can't see how people won't buy into this. I mean, we're saving human lives as well as wildlife. And that foundation award will lessen the state and federal money we need."

Johnny's grin faded.

"Believe me, there will be opposition and conflict. We had plenty of it on the reservation. Not with tribal members. As desperately as they could have used the money the tribe allocated to the People's Way Partnership, almost no one opposed its contributions to the project. But we needed federal funds, too. That's what we took plenty of crap for. I just want you to be prepared for the letters to the editor and online comments the article—and maybe even you—are sure get in the next few days. Don't get drawn into it. Let me handle the PR. You just keep doing what you do best, and that's…"

Johnny stopped cold, turning toward the sound—a scratching that had been blending into the background noise until it suddenly grew louder.

He could not see DuWayne's eyes, his look of concern, as his boss stood and walked toward a cardboard box sitting on a TV tray against the back wall of the small room, but he heard the springs of DuWayne's chair squeak as the engineer stood and followed, sheepishly, behind.

The box had originally come from Amazon.com, but it was clear its contents weren't what had originally been delivered. Johnny noticed small holes punctured across the top half of the box, and a screen—looked like one from the window in Johnny's side of the office—literally lying over the top of the box.

"What the…?"

As he stepped up to get a look inside, DuWayne said, "I'm sorry about taking the screen off your window. I promise I'll buy a new one. I just wanted him to get a little light.…"

Johnny peered down into a swirl of green—leaves and branches cut short—until he saw movement. A small head—that of a prairie dog—raised frightened eyes to him.

"I found the little guy on the road yesterday," Masters said hurriedly. "He'd been run over, but only his tail. He was stuck, flailing around. He would've been hit again in no time."

Frightened, the small animal had turned to retreat into the branches Masters had apparently put in the box. As he did, Johnny saw the damaged tail as he darted back into the cover.

Johnny turned to Masters and said, "Good work."

Masters smiled broadly.

"You don't mind?"

"Of course not. I'm just a little confused," Johnny replied. "You sure you don't have any Indian blood in you?"

Masters let out a laugh that echoed out the door and into the hallway. Then he grew serious.

"When I was a boy, ten years old—actually the week before my tenth birthday—my father took me with him to surrender my dog to the pound.

"He had lived his whole life—we had had him about three years—outside, and he was supposedly my dog. My dad said I wasn't taking good enough care of him. I'll never get over that. I've never stopped thinking about him. He was a Lab mix of some sort, a really quiet, nice dog. I think I've been trying to make up for that my entire life."

Johnny felt a lump in his throat—a rarity for a man who had to deal with animals dead or dying on a daily basis. He'd always had a special love for dogs, which had caused untold grief for him growing up in Browning, where the few dogs that ended up in shelters were often the most fortunate. It had been one of the reasons he was relieved to move to East Glacier when he was hired to work out of Two Medicine. The East Glacier community banded together to take care of homeless dogs—taking them in, feeding them, inviting them along on walks—as the pups led a life wandering from one garage, one porch, one storefront, to another.

"That's how you became interested in wildlife crossings?"

"I think so. Yes. Who knows? Maybe some of these little guys will benefit too. My wife and I live just west of Nineteenth Street, where all the development in Bozeman is taking place at an insane rate. All the fields that have been filled for a hundred years with these little guys are being churned up. It doesn't seem to bother anyone. Becca and I sit and watch them from our patio every evening. They're fascinating. The community structure, that alone—how can we just uproot them? Or worse, excavate their habitat during winter, after they've hibernated, which is done all winter long in Bozeman—the rush to build is so strong.

"These little guys are good for the earth. We're just wiping them out on a scale that's unconscionable.

"After we bought our house and realized what was going on, we felt ashamed for moving in. The dense development over our way may be better than urban sprawl, but can't some efforts be made to relocate the wildlife that we're displacing? No one's even addressing it. I've stopped and talked to bulldoze operators, called their bosses. I wrote the city commission. No response. No one cares."

Johnny was not only touched by the genuine angst and compassion he was witnessing in this serious young engineer, he was suddenly struck by the realization that the world he lived in, that of Glacier National Park, and the issues he dealt with there in one of the earth's last wild places, were, oddly enough, not that different than those in an urban environment.

"You're right," Johnny said. "The work you're doing, the message it sends, will even trickle down to benefit prairie dogs and ground squirrels. Hell, let's make that one of our priorities."

During their conversation, Johnny had already noticed drawings on the table behind Masters' desk. Now the redhead reached for them.

"Actually, that's one of the ideas I'm incorporating into these crossings. Ground habitat that's natural for prairie dogs and other rodents."

Paging through the roll of mechanical drawings, Masters slid one out.

The young engineer from Rock Springs, Wyoming, had come alive. Passionate, intense, he rolled the map out on top of his desk, placing a bottle of water, a plant, and a book on three corners, then reached in his pocket for his wallet, to place it on the fourth.

Dozens, perhaps hundreds of pencil marks—words, symbols, arrows, lots of arrows—adorned the brown paper.

"This is my big vision of things," Masters said. "It's evolving, but this will give you an overview of the Safe Crossings Project. Fifty-two will be underpasses—did you know they cost about a tenth of what an overpass costs? And they're effective. Hell, you know that from your project on the Flathead Reservation...."

The words came out at a rapid-fire pace.

There were symbols for everything. Grass, lights, fences. Foxes, moose, elk, bear, smaller creatures.

Arrows indicated passageways, movement corridors.

Accompanied by the sound of the prairie dog scratching and chewing on the box behind them, the words flowed out of DuWayne

Masters' mouth like the Yellowstone River on the map—during spring runoff—as he explained the detailed blueprints to Johnny.

Sitting there, watching his new employee, Johnny was reminded of when he was first hired as a biologist with Glacier National Park. All those years he'd lived off the reservation, attending school, being miserable and without identity, longing for the only life he had previously known—the wild places and wild animals he'd turned to as a somewhat troubled juvenile; the family his Blackfeet friends and community were to him—had paid off. He saw in Masters the same joy and enthusiasm, the same high Johnny had experienced riding the trails of Two Medicine or Cut Bank Creek, setting out his first wolverine traps and fur snares.

Somewhere between the natural grasses Masters described as he pointed to the floor of the underground tunnels—which would encourage use by small mammals—and the subliminal lighting that would draw larger animals, hopefully top predators like the grizzly, to the tunnel's mouth or the bridge's base, Johnny found his own excitement for the Safe Crossings Project starting to catch up with that of DuWayne Masters.

As he got up to leave, Johnny placed a hand on Masters' shoulder.

"I'm happy to have you on the team."

A bright flush spread over DuWayne's face. He stood and extended his hand.

"Mr. Yellow Kidney, Johnny, I have never in my life been happier. Never. We just learned my wife's pregnant, I'm finally earning some money, which allowed me to go out and buy a brand-new high-tech car last week." His laugh was that of a young kid at Christmas. "You can't imagine these new cars, *everything's* computerized. Hell, they can parallel park for you." He quickly grew serious again as he finished, his eyes trained on Johnny with undisguised admiration and gratitude. "And I'm working on my dream project, in a place I absolutely love, with a man I admire and greatly respect."

Johnny swallowed against the lump in his throat.

"And tomorrow," he replied, "another big article comes out about this project. Only this time it's not local. That *New York Times* piece is going to put you on the map, my friend. You'll be building highway crossings all across the Rockies when you finish this one. And buying your wife her own new car."

A shit-eating grin spreading across his pale face, DuWayne Masters shook his head.

"Life just doesn't get much better than this, does it?"

• • •

The Tower Falls ranger station stood dark, framed by a pastel-streaked, sun-just-setting sky that, under different circumstances, would have caused Will to halt in order to experience one of those rare moments of his life in Yellowstone where things actually felt right.

But not tonight.

He'd approached the station from the east, away from the north loop road that connected Cooke City to Mammoth, sheltered by trees until the last hundred yards, where the chance of being seen from the road leading north out of Canyon was unavoidable, but still far preferable than the north, with the busy traffic leading back to park headquarters from the wolf and bison watching in the Lamar.

For a brief minute he had no choice—other than to break a window in the back, which he would have been tempted to do had it not been for the memo he had received just before being fired about the park considering installing window alarms—but to risk being seen when he opened the cabin's front door.

Reaching into his front pocket, he withdrew the key, one of many he'd had duplicated before being sent to Glacier the year he'd testified about the guns-in-park ruling. One of the many he had not returned to Peter Shewmaker when he instructed Will to turn in all his keys.

An extended horse trailer, pulled by one of the guiding businesses on the periphery of the park, approached from the Lamar, weighted down with a dozen saddled, sweaty horses.

Moving slowly up the hill, a line of vehicles stuck behind it, its cowboy driver honked the horn, waving out the window at Will. Not exactly what Will wanted, but there was little to no interaction between guides and Park Service employees, and at least the trailer blocked Will from sight of the vehicles lined up behind it. Lowering the ball cap that now replaced his felt ranger hat, he stepped onto the wooden porch, hugging the log wall to stay shaded by the roof's overhang as he moved to the front door.

With one more look around before entering, he slid the key into the slot, holding his breath for fear they had changed locks. The door swung open with a creak.

Nothing had changed in the three months since his early summer visit to Cliff Utzinger to discuss the first mauling. Now Will crossed the room, wasting no time, to Cliff's desk, turned the computer screen so that its lights faced away from windows on two walls, and, holding his breath, logged on using the password he and Cliff had joked about: backcountrygestapo.

The screen came alive; ironically, with a picture of the Grand Tetons as background.

Will went to the document icon, clicked, and began scrolling down the list of folders and files.

Bison investigation.

Clicking on the folder, Will did not take his eyes off the screen.

A list of a dozen documents appeared. The first, a Word document, was entitled "notes."

There was one more Word doc, entitled "interviews." The rest were PDFs.

Will clicked on the PDF labeled "Bison 1 photos."

He had seen the big old bull bison lying there, lifeless, on the side of the road that morning he'd been called to Swan Lake Flats to help. The scanned photograph, in its starkness, was even more difficult to look at.

Of course, that day the adrenaline had been running strong, as had the anger.

Now it was more a determination—a steely, hardened determination—that drove Will.

It wasn't until the third picture, taken literally from the ground, that Will saw what he hadn't seen that day. The hole left by the bullet.

It was on the top of the bull's head, just off center. In disbelief, Will scrolled down to Bison 2.

There, the very last of seven photos. The bullet wound. Back of the neck.

Bison 3. The female.

She must have been the last to get hit. She'd had time to turn to run.

Several bullet holes riddled her buttock area. One hole dead center, top of the head.

Hands shaking now, Will opened the first Word doc and skimmed the notes to see if Cliff Utzinger had picked up on it. But he saw nothing other than the ordinary investigative notes taken upon arriving at a crime scene, with a few notes clearly written by Cliff later, after his own review of the documents.

Witness statements. Over twenty of them.

The first call had come from a visitor from Utah who saw the lifeless bodies, thought the bison were just enjoying the sunny morning. He had stopped to show his kids, take some pictures. But the big animals never moved.

He called 911.

Other vehicles began stopping. Soon law enforcement had arrived.

No one had seen the actual crime. No sign of any suspects. Neither Cliff nor any of the other investigators, including Will— before he had been abruptly called off the scene to meet with Gonzalez and Shewmaker—had seen any suspicious behavior in those they had interviewed, all of whom told similar stories of, at first sight, believing the three bison were sleeping in the sun.

The bison had to have been killed at night. Swan Lake Flats was a busy thoroughfare during summer days, but by nightfall, visitors were either nestled in tents or RVs at campgrounds, or well on their way to motels at one of the gateway communities.

Nagging thoughts racing through his mind, Will clicked the Bison Investigation file closed and was about to turn off the computer; but just as he scrolled to the Power Off icon—actually his index finger poised over the mouse to click it—he froze.

The file immediately below the Bison Investigation file had caught his eye.

Bighorn Sheep Deaths.

Emma Day had mentioned sheep dying. Will clicked on the file.

It consisted of one document, an email dated that morning.

From Public Affairs. Marked *Confidential.*

Will had received such emails before. Public Affairs was charged with communicating not only to the public, but to the park employees. Their goal: minimizing negative publicity, especially in the form of conflict, for Yellowstone.

Thirty bighorn sheep, 13 from the Gardiner herd, 17 from the Tom Miner herd, have died from pneumonia. All lambs dead. Autopsy results expected today, but current theory is pneumonia, contracted from newly introduced local domestic sheep. No public statements should be made until further notice from this office.

The fire of the all-too-familiar rage began to flicker somewhere deep inside Will. His hands visibly trembling, Will shut Cliff Utzinger's computer down.

Daring a look first out of each window, Will headed toward the door, reached for it. Then, suddenly, hand already encircling its knob, he turned back to look at Utzinger's desk.

A local phone directory—the kind Will saw on doorsteps in Gardiner, where they'd been dropped, and where they remained untouched sometimes for weeks, only to end up at the town dump, a disgusting waste of paper—sat on its corner.

With a new urgency—though the darkened sky perhaps warranted less, not more, caution—he crossed back to Utzinger's corner of the ranger station, opened the book, and skimmed to the page he was looking for.

Ripping a sheet from the back of the book, he scrawled a number on it, then shoved it in the pocket of his jacket.

Finally, as quietly and unobtrusively as he had entered the ranger station thirty minutes earlier, Will McCarroll exited, and disappeared back into the trees.

11

THE PHONE ON THE PASSENGER seat of his truck beeped to life just as Johnny passed the billboard on Highway 89—a truck-sized photo of perpetually smiling, right-wing state senator Liz Conway, now a candidate for the U.S. Senate, under which ran the slogan:

Less government means more income for Montanans

Shaking his head in disgust at the sight of the woman who, as a puppet for the oil and gas industry, was leading the charge to desecrate his peoples' most spiritual and sacred lands, Johnny reached for the phone.

"Johnny?"

Annie's voice had always pleased him immensely. It had an airy, fragile quality to it that she had always managed to keep in check in person. After they broke up, in college, he used to lie in bed thinking of it, trying to recreate it in his imagination.

"Hey," he said now, his grin audible in his voice. "Did you get my message?"

"Yes, I did. Just now. I'm sorry I didn't notice I had one last night. Are you still heading this way today?"

"I'm on my way down the Paradise right now. Meeting my young engineer down past Emigrant, to look at possible crossing sites. If you're available for lunch, I thought I'd drive down to Gardiner when we're through. Or come up to Mammoth."

"My only hearing's first thing this morning, so I could be free for a late lunch, say one o'clock. Why don't I meet you in Gardiner, at the Sawtooth? We can eat outside. It's a gorgeous morning, isn't it?"

"It is now," Johnny replied. "I'll see you at one."

As he lowered the phone in order to see the end call button on its face—he hated these damn smart phones—he heard her voice again.

"Johnny…"

He pressed it to his ear.

"I've been hearing there's a bad accident down by Yankee Jim. Just to warn you."

"Someone probably hit an elk. They're on the move. I won't get down that far till after I meet with DuWayne, so I'm sure it'll be cleared by then."

"Okay, be careful."

"Don't worry."

He had just rounded the first bend when he saw the flashing lights heading his way, toward Livingston. Johnny pulled the truck over to the side, waiting for the emergency vehicle to pass.

Ambulances on the reservation were a rare thing. Accidents were not.

Sitting there, he offered a prayer to the Creator, asking for whoever was inside not to be in pain or fear, praying for the EMTs and doctors to be wise, kind, and skilled.

Pulling back on to the highway, Johnny's momentary solemnity lightened as he proceeded down the valley. The Absaroka Mountain Range to the east stood magnificent and bold, rising dramatically, to heights of 13,000 feet from the ranchlands dotted with cattle and horses grazing peacefully. The jagged, wild peaks, some still covered with snow, along with the dazzling waters of the Yellowstone River running parallel to the highway, never failed to amaze and comfort Johnny.

Almost as pretty as Glacier. Okay, maybe just as pretty.

He had come to be grateful for this intrusion on the life he loved back in Glacier. He had reconnected with the only woman he'd ever loved, Annie Peacock, in a land as special—in a different way, but he could not deny its unique beauty, the spiritual power of its wildness—as that he called home.

And he had come to realize the significance of the Safe Crossings Project, and his role in it.

And who could complain about a job that required him to drive down the Paradise Valley on a morning such as this, to meet with one of the most talented and genuinely good persons he'd ever had the privilege of working with, and a rancher who had shown some receptivity to allowing a safe crossing on his property?

DuWayne had told him to look for a herd that consisted of horses, cattle, llamas, and goats on the east side of the road, then turn in a quarter mile south under the archetypical wood arch that announced the name of practically every ranch along both sides of the well-traveled byway to Yellowstone.

A single word had been carved across it. *Irie*.

When he caught sight of a dozen miniature horses grazing the fence line adjacent to the highway, Johnny slowed. A group of standard-size horses had started racing across the open expanse, which was dotted with llamas and the occasional cow. Johnny flipped his blinker on and turned into the narrow gravel drive, which was blocked by a metal gate. He stopped, got out of his truck, and strode to it.

DuWayne had told him the gate would be unlocked. After eyeing the livestock to be certain he had time to pull through safely, he gave it a push.

It didn't budge.

In the distance, toward the Yellowstone River he'd been paralleling since leaving Livingston, he could see just the roofline of a barn—beyond where the road rose, then fell, and headed toward the river. No other buildings were visible.

DuWayne's first screw up, Johnny thought as he lifted his cell phone to place the call.

The phone rang four times, then went to voicemail: DuWayne saying please leave a message and he'd get right back.

Someone—probably a ranch hand who hadn't been informed of the arrangement—must have come through after DuWayne arrived and locked the gate. Johnny decided to walk in.

As he turned toward his truck to shut the engine off, he heard another motor—louder than his truck's—and pivoted back to face the barn.

A cowboy-hatted figure wheeled his way over the crest of the hill on an ATV, lifting his hand in a friendly wave. Johnny leaned against the front grill on his truck and waited.

Bringing the machine to a halt at the gate, the leggy cowboy climbed off nimbly, and, smile on his leathery face, called out, "I'd been keeping an eye out for you but then one of the lambs got stuck between a stall door and the wall. Took me a couple minutes to free the little bastard."

Approaching the gate, he extended his hand over its top rail, looking a little confused as he eyed Johnny.

"Nice to finally meet you, DuWayne," he said in a voice so raspy Johnny was certain he'd see the outline of a can of chew in one of his back jeans pockets.

Johnny tried not to smile at the friendly rancher's confusion. DuWayne had reported the two of them having several phone conversations during negotiations for the Safe Crossings Project to acquire a conservation easement on Irie.

DuWayne Masters sounded distinctly pale skinned. The rancher obviously hadn't expected to see an Indian on the other side of the gate this morning.

"Actually, I'm Johnny Yellow Kidney. I'm working with DuWayne. I thought he'd said you and he were planning to meet first, then I should join you, but looks like I beat him here."

"You thought right," the rancher replied. "He was supposed to be here almost an hour ago. I waited at the gate for fifteen minutes or so, but morning's my busiest time, so I went on back to the barn to muck out stalls and just kept peeking outside once in a while— until that little lamb got himself stuck. DuWayne didn't seem to like the kind of fella who'd be late, at least not from our talks on the phone."

"That's *not* like him," Johnny replied, eyes scanning the highway. "And not like him to not call me if he *is* going to be late."

If the inconvenience disturbed the rancher, he did a good job of hiding it.

"I can show you the stretch of land I might be willing to donate to your project."

Johnny studied him. "*Donate?*"

The rancher broke into a smile.

"I was kinda saving that to surprise the young fella. Yes, I'm inclined to help you out. I'm sick and tired of seeing dead deer and elk along that highway. Last year, a grizzly was hit and killed.

"And then there's the people. Course they're almost all tourists, headin' to the park. Folks around here know you gotta keep your eyes scanning non-stop—not be looking at some goddamn phone—and practically crawl down this road from dusk till sunup."

"That's fantastic news," Johnny said. "I'll let you deliver it to DuWayne. Surely he'll arrive any minute. Why don't we wait for him to take a look at that stretch? He's the expert, in terms of whether it'll meet his specifications."

"Suits me," the rancher replied. Simultaneously, both men turned toward the highway, waiting for another vehicle to turn in behind Johnny's truck, the silence broken only by passing RVs, pickups, SUVs and the rare sedan—all of which bore out-of-state license plates. And, behind them, the occasional whinny from the spirited horses.

Still side by side and facing west, the two men fell into an uncomfortable silence.

"You Crow?"

"Blackfeet."

The rancher nodded, staring out across the valley, toward the Gallatin range that bordered its west side.

"Pretty country up there."

"Yep," Johnny replied. "This isn't too shabby either."

"No, sir," the rancher said. "It's not."

It had quickly become clear to both men that small talk wasn't going to be enough to make the time pass—or DuWayne Masters appear.

"I tell you what," Johnny said. "Why don't you get back to work, and I'll take a little drive and keep tryin DuWayne's phone. If you see him before I talk to him, tell him to give me a call. I'm just heading down the road a little. I'd like to see that cattle guard your ex-governor put in to allow the park buffalo some space."

"Schweitzer. Yep, he snuck that cattle guard in under the radar." The rancher's chuckle sounded even more gravelly than his voice. "He's about the only one of our politicians who's ever been willing to stand up to the livestock interests that control this state. Livestock and hunting. It's down the road, about fifteen miles, just past Yankee Jim."

"See you soon," Johnny said.

He climbed back into his truck, a nagging, unsettled feeling taking seed in his gut. Turning onto the highway to Yellowstone, he eased the truck into the morning Yellowstone tourist traffic.

Reaching for his phone, he pressed the redial button.

• • •

Will knew the old building—and the park's priorities, including who would attend such a meeting—well.

He snuck into the back of the Albright Visitor Center, waited in the wings of the theater, just off stage, listening as Max Oldenham, the park's bighorn biologist, presented his lecture, one given to all new interps and law enforcement.

"Our latest figures show that we have a robust population of five hundred in the park," the biologist reported.

A young man in uniform, sitting in the front row, raised his hand.

"What about the sheep that just died? Won't that decimate the bighorn population in Yellowstone?"

"Far from it. First of all, those sheep were in the Gardiner Basin. There's very little mingling between that herd and the park herd."

"Excuse me," the young man persisted, as older, more experienced rangers in the audience either raised eyebrows or masked their smiles of pleasure at the novice's boldness—and the consequences that were likely to follow. "But isn't there *some* mingling? After all, the herd at Rescue Creek is only a few miles away. Bighorn roam way farther than that."

Oldenham took a deep breath.

"There's always dieoff. Predators, inner-breeding, disease— they all take their toll, but we're not overly concerned about the animals just north of the park."

Clearly satisfied with his answer, he decided to elaborate further. "Actually, sometimes a die off is a good thing. Those animals with resistance to disease are the ones who survive. They rebuild their population and it's that much more resilient."

Will could hear some mumbling. He saw several heads shaking in disapproval.

"Typical Park Service bullshit," he muttered under his breath. No longer so pleased with the response he was getting,

Oldenham cut the discussion about the domestic sheep and bighorn short, returning to standard park protocol and dry presentation.

Almost no one came forward to discuss the topic with Oldenham after he finished. As Will watched the group file out of the small theatre, and Oldenham gathered his notes, Will stepped out of the shadows.

Oldenham looked startled.

"Will."

Eying the door to the lobby of the visitor center as it closed behind the last ranger, Will approached.

"Still towing the park line, I see."

Max shook his head.

"I've got a family to feed, Will. You, well, you must have had the luxury of saying what you believed. I don't always have that. I can't afford to be fired."

"Tell me, Max. What's the park going to do about the mingling of Stucky's sheep with the north Gardiner bighorn?"

"What can we do?"

Will stood there for several seconds, debating about whether to give his old colleagues a straight answer. But Max wasn't a bad guy—and he was right. Look what speaking up did for Will.

Max had young children to support, and, according to park rumors, a wife with serious mental health issues.

So instead of lecturing the lecturer, telling him that the park should pressure Stucky to get rid of his sheep, cite him for violation of the Lacey Act, Will simply replied, "That's what I thought," then hurried out the back entrance of the building.

12

AS JOHNNY TRAVELED SOUTH ON Highway 89, more flashing lights appeared, this time in his rearview mirror, heading his way. He slowed, looking for a place to pull over on the shoulderless highway, then, as the fire truck neared, he pulled onto the grass lining the highway and came to a stop as it raced by.

He couldn't read its home base but knew from its size it was from a nearby city—most likely Livingston. He'd passed a volunteer fire department in Emigrant just minutes earlier, but Johnny knew from life on the reservation that small volunteer fire departments could afford small customized fire trucks, at best. On the rez, often the volunteer firefighters had only their own pickups, with barrels of water kept on hand in the back at all times.

This time when he pulled onto the highway, Johnny did not ease in to the sixty-mile-per-hour speed limit. Pushing the gas pedal down, he had almost closed the distance to the fire department's truck—until a baby elk stepped gingerly onto the highway, followed by its mother—at which point Will braked dramatically, losing sight of the fire engine as it rounded a bend.

The cow elk and her yearling safely crossed, Johnny picked up speed again. He reached for the phone but then thought better of it. He wasn't sure of the road ahead, as he had only been to Yellowstone once before, a biology conference on the "island syndrome" experienced by both Yellowstone and Glacier, one that especially impacted both parks' grizzly bear populations. That had been a decade ago.

He knew 89 took a couple serious turns after Dome Mountain Ranch—which the biologists at the conference had actually visited, as it was the most wildlife friendly property outside the park—near where Annie had said the accident occurred. After a curve of road that hugged an abrupt bend in the river and cradled a long building bearing the banner *Yellowstone Retreat Center*, the highway straightened out for miles, allowing Johnny to pick up speed. His gut tightened fifteen minutes later, as he approached a line of vehicles whose brake lights told him they were merely inching along. The line extended all the way from the curve half a mile ahead, which he knew to be the start of Yankee Jim Canyon, to Dome Mountain, where Johnny joined it.

By the start of Yankee Jim, the line of cars had come to a standstill. Many of their occupants stood outside, on the shoulder of the road, staring south, into the twisting canyon, or visiting amongst each other.

Pulling his truck off, onto the shoulder, Johnny reached for the NPS jacket on the passenger seat and climbed out. Sliding his arms into the jacket bearing the well-known emblem on its right upper arm, he jogged forward, passing dozens of cars, RVs, and trucks, all with engines turned off.

No one was going anywhere anytime soon.

When he rounded the curve on foot, Johnny saw a cavalcade of emergency response vehicles, lights flashing. The action was all directed toward the river.

A line of firefighters ran the fire truck's hose forward and over the guard rail, which had been almost flattened at the point the highway turned dramatically east, just entering the canyon.

Law enforcement had converged from both directions. Five vehicles were parked at odd angles, blocking traffic going north and south. The Park County sheriff and two deputies stood in conference with two Yellowstone law enforcement rangers. Another Park Service law enforcement official stood, taking pictures, over the rail. In their urgency, someone had apparently recruited a couple interpretive rangers to further barricade onlookers.

As Johnny approached, one of them, a young woman in uniform, held her arms out on either side, as if she were guarding a particularly agile point guard moving the ball up the court.

"Go back to your vehicle, sir," she directed Johnny.

Johnny turned his shoulder just enough for her to see the patch on his jacket.

"Oh…"

She looked to her partner, who appeared just as confused about how to deal with the fact that Johnny apparently worked for the Park Service, too.

Striding by both, silent, Johnny headed for the LE at the guard rail, avoiding the Park County sheriff, who would be the least receptive to his presence. Park Service LE tended to stick together.

Nodding as the LE looked up, Johnny tried walking right past him, to the guard rail, but the officer reached out an arm to stop him.

Several fire fighters had begun the descent to the raging river below. Yankee Jim Canyon was known to provide the greatest thrill for rafters and kayakers on the Yellowstone River. That thrill had cost its share of lives. So much so that local outfitters almost always pulled their rafts out just prior to the canyon.

"Whoa," the forty-ish ranger said, eyeing Johnny with serious interest.

"I'm Park Service," Johnny said. "I was supposed to meet a friend up the road, but he didn't show. Just let me take a look at the vehicle...."

"Don't recognize you."

Johnny reached into his pants pocket, then extended his hand with his card, saying, "Glacier, biologist."

The LE ranger wasn't impressed.

"The vehicle's not visible from here, and I can't let you climb down there. They're trying to get that car pulled up before the rapids sweep it downriver."

His words stopped Johnny cold. He literally shook his head to dislodge the image the ranger's words had created in it. He hadn't noticed the tow truck parked behind the fire engine but now he saw several men wearing Paradise Towing jumpsuits emerge from behind it and climb over the rail, heavy-gauged steel cables in hand.

The LE must have felt some sympathy for him, as he stopped taking photographs and closed the distance between Johnny and him.

Voice lowered, he said, "For what it's worth, the occupant's already been removed. Ambulance took him to the Yellowstone airport. He's being airlifted to Seattle."

He.

That's all Johnny heard. "Did you see him?"

"No. I was interviewing witnesses when they finally cut him out of the vehicle."

"What did the witnesses say?"

The ranger took a deep breath. It was clear he was struggling with how much to divulge at the same time that a sense of Park Service camaraderie, coupled with empathy at seeing how distressed this biologist from Glacier was, made him want to help.

"The car's brakes seemed to have failed. Several witnesses reported him passing them at high speed, honking as he approached and flashing his lights, as if to warn them. He couldn't make the turn at that speed."

Johnny could feel his heart begin to race. He eyed the road beyond the bend.

"Okay," he said, "Thanks. I'll keep moving."

The ranger nodded. He'd already figured out what Johnny was thinking.

"You might be able to get a glimpse from up ahead; there's a pull-out just before the cattle guard."

As Johnny strode farther south on Highway 89, passing vehicle after stalled vehicle—this time headed north as they departed Yellowstone or Gardiner—their drivers clearly growing impatient, several called out to him, assuming from his jacket that he was part of the response team.

"What's taking so long?"

"Hey Ranger, what's the story?"

"How much longer we gotta sit here?"

Head down, ignoring them, Johnny had just come within sight of the pullout the LE ranger mentioned when a deafening *SNAP*— the unmistakable sound of metal coming apart—reverberated through the canyon.

Sprinting to the pullout, Johnny cleared the guard rail like the seasoned track star and hurdler he'd once been, scurried down the hillside, rocks flying beneath his boots, and pivoted north, toward the bend in the river, just in time to see a crushed vehicle, still half-secured by one of the two steel cables attached to the tow truck, break free into the wild rapids, sending the car—a brand new silver sedan—flying downriver.

• • •

"You're looking pretty chipper this morning," Justine said to her boss as Annie slipped out of her judicial robe and dropped into her desk chair.

Annie turned a smile her way.

"Seriously? You can tell that in the thirty seconds you've watched me come in from that hearing? Maybe I'm just happy to have it over with. I swear, that kid's attorney from Cody is a pain in the rear end."

Standing squarely in front of Annie's massive, document-strewn desk, Justine planted hands on both hips.

"You know I know it's not that. Come on. Come clean. Why are you dressed up today? And you did your hair."

Annie's dark coloring usually succeeded in hiding any hint of embarrassment, but now a blush brightened her cheeks.

"You're something else," she replied. Then, when Justine did not attempt to make a move—or remove her piercing gaze from Annie—she continued, "Okay, so maybe I did try to look nice today. I'm meeting a friend for lunch."

Justine wasn't about to let it go at that. She stood there, giving Annie the look she'd given her on countless other occasions, when Annie was, as Justine put it, "holding out" on her.

They hadn't yet felt the presence standing at their door.

A creak of the building's wooden floor gave him away. Both women turned to see Will McCarroll starting down the stairs to the first floor, just outside Annie's door.

Annie jumped up, darting for the stairwell.

"*Will.*"

Justine quickly disappeared into the courtroom through the door behind Annie's desk.

Already halfway down the stairs, Will stopped, and slowly turned to face her.

Annie was shocked by his appearance. He'd lost weight, and his usually impeccable uniform that hung so beautifully on his fit frame had been replaced by a Patagonia jacket that appeared not to have been washed in weeks. Still, the sight of him dizzied Annie. As quickly as she could, she closed the distance between them, grabbing him by the arm, knowing the courage it had taken for him to appear and that only a physical connection would keep him there— prevent him from bolting.

"Please, talk to me," she said.

Staring into his eyes—those eyes that had filled her with a sense that finally, in the end, all was right in her world—it hit her.

Will had become like the animals he'd protected all those years.

He tried to pull his arm out of her grasp.

A security guard had heard their voices and now appeared at the bottom of the stairwell. He had seen Will many times before when he visited Annie, but it was clear that without his uniform, he was unrecognizable.

"Your Honor? Everything okay?"

"Yes, John," Annie answered. "Everything's fine."

She felt Will stiffen. She could literally feel his resolves to free.

"Please," she repeated. "Talk to me. Tell me where you've been. What you're doing. I've been worried sick, and I miss you."

"I just went to Max's lecture on bighorn. Decided to stop by and say hello...."

His voice drifted off. He had always been incapable of small talk.

Quietly, plaintively, Annie said, "I love you, Will."

That got to him. She could see it.

His eyes finally met hers, mirrored the pain there. "I love you too, Annie."

When she loosened her grip on his arm, he turned and descended the stairs.

Eyes blurred by tears, Annie watched him walk away.

• • •

Staring dead ahead, Will strode toward his old Jeep, which he'd parked behind the Chittenden building to avoid anyone from headquarters recognizing it and coming to look for him.

Seeing Annie had rattled him like nothing before.

Then he realized that actually wasn't true. Not even close. Rachel, Carter....

He blotted the thoughts—the images of his wife's and child's bodies on the Pebble Creek trail—out of his mind, as he had become practiced at doing for almost three decades now.

Will was just climbing into his car when he saw the lean, dark-haired figure, head down, crossing the lot, heading in the direction from which Will had just come.

Instinctively, without a moment's hesitation, Will yelled, "Yellow Kidney," shutting the open Jeep door and standing to his full height.

Johnny turned, clearly surprised. Impossibly, his brown skin looked ashen.

"What are you doing here?" Will called as Johnny closed the distance between them. Johnny grabbed Will by both shoulders, then wrapped him in a big bear hug.

"Shit, Will. It's good to see you."

"What's going on? What're you doing here?"

Johnny shook his head slowly, as if trying to clear it. He was obviously rattled.

"I just came from an accident at Yankee Jim. A young guy who works for me. It was his car. I couldn't see it good enough, haven't had it confirmed yet, but I know it was him. I was supposed to be meeting him at a ranch up the Paradise...."

He was rambling. None of it made sense to Will.

"He's on the wolverine project? Why would you be meeting at a ranch in the Paradise?"

Johnny's reply only heightened Will's state of confusion.

"No, he's a civil engineer."

Johnny must have finally recognized the bewilderment on Will's face, as he said, "Hell, Will, my life's taken as big a turnaround as yours. I took a leave of absence from Glacier to head up something called the Safe Crossings Project. It's based here, in the Greater Yellowstone."

"You left Glacier? Your wolverine work?"

The disbelief audible in Will's voice clearly hit a nerve with Yellow Kidney. He took a deep breath.

"Two months ago, the woman who started the project, a Seattle reporter named Tracy Blessings, came up to East Glacier to recruit me to help with the tribes, get them on board. Like I had with the People's Way on the Flathead Reservation. I was a jerk to her, Will. I told her I wasn't interested, then I let her go out hiking that afternoon. Never even thought to warn her not to go alone."

Will was having trouble digesting all of this—Johnny's story, and, even as shocking as the news that he'd walked away from the wolverine project was, what any of it had to do with his being in Mammoth. Still, he could see his friend's distress and instinctively wanted to help ease it.

"Hell, Johnny," he said, "we all know that no matter how many times we warn them, people hike both parks alone, especially in an area as busy as Two Med. But I don't get what that has to do with giving up your project. What happened? Did she get injured?"

"No," Johnny said, his eyes finally meeting Will's. "Shot. She got shot."

"Holy shit."

"Right there at Two Med. Where the Guns-4-All nightmare went down."

Just hearing the name of the gun rights group—the memories and emotions from two years earlier it stirred—almost had a physical impact on Will.

"Guns-4-All is connected with this?

"That's the current theory—that the Blessings shooting was a reminder that even though the group's founder is in prison, Guns-4-All is alive and kicking. But the cops are being quiet about it. No one's sharing anything at this point, so it's just a theory."

Ignoring the emotions spinning somewhere in the back of his mind, Will instinctively went into practiced-investigator mode.

"I still don't see you taking a leave, or how being down here is necessary to get the tribes involved. You've got more reservations up your way than we have here."

Will detected a slight startle in Johnny that he chalked up to the distress his friend was obviously feeling about the accident he'd just seen.

"The tribal liaison job was what Tracy Blessings had in mind when she came to talk to me," Johnny replied, "but she's been in a medically induced coma ever since the shooting. They talked me into taking *her* job, heading the Safe Crossings Project up—until she gets out and is strong enough to take over again. Our initial focus is establishing a corridor between Yellowstone and Glacier.

"I hired a young MSU graduate student, DuWayne Masters, to be my engineer. We were supposed to meet this morning to talk to a rancher about an easement for a wildlife crossing, but he never showed up. For some reason, he passed right by the ranch, and ended up in the river at Yankee Jim."

Will had seen far more stunned tourists or hikers than he'd ever be able to forget, people who had narrowly escaped injury in the backcountry but watched as their companions—or in some cases, family members—fell to their death, took a fatal step into one of the park's hot springs, or dared to violate the park's dictate that they stay fifty yards away from wildlife.

Johnny wore that same expression now.

"DuWayne's being airlifted to Seattle right now," Johnny added. "The Harborview trauma unit."

Eyes closed, he took a deep breath.

"He's such a great kid, Will. I'm used to this kind of tragedy on the rez. I never expected it here."

Any sadness or angst Will had been feeling after seeing Annie took a back seat at seeing Johnny's grief. Johnny had not only become his friend two years earlier, each had risked his life to save the other.

They had become brothers, in the truest sense of the word.

Still, Will wasn't Johnny Yellow Kidney—a man capable of spontaneously enveloping an old friend in his strong arms upon seeing him. Aside from Rachel, and then—after decades of dulled, or no, *deep* personal connections—Annie Peacock, Will simply didn't have it in him to display such emotion.

"I'm sorry," he said. "I wish I could do something."

"Thanks, man," Johnny said. "I've been worried about you, too, Will. I ran into Annie in Livingston, and she told me what went down. You doing okay?"

"I'm fine. I'm good."

An awkward silence had developed between the two men at the mention of Annie.

Will reached out a hand to shake Johnny's.

Johnny grasped it, and then held on to it after Will had loosened his grip.

"Will," he said, "after the meeting with DuWayne and the rancher this morning, I was supposed to meet Annie for lunch."

Each man met the gaze of the other, and in that instant, Will knew.

He took a deep breath, allowed Johnny the brief reassurance of his continued grasp, before saying, "I hope your young friend makes it."

Then Will McCarroll turned and walked back to his car.

13

EMMA DAY HAD STAYED ON the Thunderer too long. Now, as she descended the last quarter mile of the trail, she wanted to break into a trot but even though the almost-full moon lit the trail well, she knew a misplaced step on its rocky surface could cause her to tweak her ankle again, which had finally healed. Instead, she lifted her two-way to her mouth and began talking into it.

She had not pressed the button to actually engage the radio.

It was an old trick her college roommate had taught her. While Emma had been a serious student at the University of Montana, one who rarely went out at night and if she did, always with a friend or two, her roommate was a partier who thought nothing of walking home from the bars on the Hip Strip—Higgins Avenue, a mile off-campus—on the bike trail along the Clark Fork River. On more than one occasion, she reported to Emma that she felt she was being followed so she lifted her cell phone to her ear and loudly carried on a conversation with her fake boyfriend, who—according to the conversation—was about to meet up with her on the trail.

Now Emma kept up the one-sided conversation and turned on her flashlight.

Despite the precautions, Emma's epidermal nerve endings screamed at her.

By the time she got to the pull off, where she'd parked, and put her key in the ignition, she had broken into a cold sweat. She reached for the knobs on the car's control panel, turned on the heat.

The tap on her passenger window came close to making her heart stop.

Emma flipped on the headlights at the same time she put the car into reverse and, despite telling herself not to do so, looked sideways toward the window.

"Oh my god," she cried. "Will!" She rolled down the window.

Will looked as ashen as Emma felt.

"Shit, Emma," he said, breathless, as though he had been running. "Thank god you're okay."

"What do you mean?"

"She was following you."

"Who?"

"The sow. The wounded grizzly." His chest heaved with his deep breaths. "I was just down the Soda Butte; I'd been looking for her when I saw you come off the trailhead and cross the creek. She came into the clearing about twenty seconds later, on your trail."

As the realization hit Emma, she involuntarily shuddered.

"She'd followed me down," she exclaimed. "It was *her*. I felt her behind me."

Both fell silent for several seconds, digesting what had just happened—as well as what had not just happened.

"Will, what are you doing out here? You haven't been out here ever since I last saw you, have you? That was two weeks ago. At least."

She could see Will struggling about coming clean.

"No, I haven't been. We've been all the way down to the lake and back."

"We?"

"I've been trailing her. She left the Thunderer the day after I ran into her. She'd had several near encounters with hikers and one serious incident with wolves. That drove her down to Lake. I thought she'd head into the Thorofare, where she stood a chance of being able to stay put and fatten up before hibernating—to just heal. But damn if she didn't decide to come back up here.

"I'd lost track of her three days ago, just north of the Thunderer. I was just about to bed down when I saw your car and, with how late it was and you not in it, I was worried about you."

Emma remained silent, trying to digest it all. He could see the wheels turning in her head, the debate about whether to go right to her superiors with what Will had just told her.

"Emma, you have to keep this to yourself. Get them to close the trails again, but don't say it's because of Two Coyote. She's on the move again. She's just passing through. I feel it."

"Two Coyote?"

The expression on Will's face was new to Emma, something she'd never seen there before. Embarrassment.

"The first time I found her, she was fending off two coyotes," he replied, eyes steady on Emma.

"It was wolves next," Emma said.

"Yes," Will replied. "That's why she left the Lamar. And she'll leave again, Emma. Trust my instincts. Find a way to give us a little time. She can survive, I know she can. The wound was mostly superficial and it's pretty much sealed now. She'll be going into hibernation in a couple more months, where more healing will take place. We have to give her a chance. I'll try to get her to head north, into the Absarokas. No hikers, fewer wolves. You can do that, can't you?"

Emma studied Will before answering.

"I can try," she said half-heartedly. "Will, I'm worried about you. This isn't safe."

Will's face took on the steely look of determination Emma had seen once before, when a gorgeous grizzly who had been raiding apple trees along the Yellowstone, just outside Gardiner, without human interaction, went one step too far and broke into the garbage transfer station that, for years, Will had been demanding the Park Service or town of Gardiner bear-proof. Emma had been the one to tell him the bear had been put down. Both knew that her bosses had deliberately kept their plans from Will, and then been too cowardly to be the ones to tell him of the innocent bear's fate.

"I'm fine, Emma," he said. "Never been better."

Emma studied him.

"Let me give you a ride home."

Will laughed.

"I'm home, Emma. And there's nothing for you to worry about. Just keep this quiet. Give Two Coyote and me a couple weeks to finish business here."

• • •

"Hey, Johnny," the raven-haired barista behind the counter at the Montana Cup called out.

Johnny Yellow Kidney looked up from yesterday's edition of the *Livingston Enterprise*, where he was reading a story about the recent die-off of bighorn sheep just outside Yellowstone National Park.

Ever since running into Annie there, he'd been having lunch at the small coffee shop just down the sidewalk from the door that led to his second-floor office, but this was the first time the pleasant young woman working the counter had called him by name. He had wondered if she might be part Indian, maybe Assiniboine or Lakota.

She met his curious gaze now, nodding toward the front window that looked out on Park Street, Livingston's equivalent of every town's Main Street.

"Just saw the sheriff walk by. I bet he's headed to your office.

He came in here yesterday looking for you."

Johnny jumped up, spilling his coffee across the tabletop and newspaper in his haste. He started toward the stack of napkins on the counter.

"Don't worry about it," the girl said cheerfully.

The powerful winds that gave Livingston the nickname "West's Windiest Town" hit him the moment he opened the door, almost taking it off its hinges. He stepped onto the sidewalk just in time to see the door to the building that housed his office hesitate, caught between the force of the hinge and that of the wind, then shudder close.

Several long strides and he'd opened it again.

"Sheriff," he called to the imposing figure halfway up the stairs.

Rocky Goodwin turned.

Goodwin had been Park County's sheriff for as long as anyone could remember. His calm demeanor, rivaled only by his reputation as a relentless investigator—one who, to the chagrin of his deputies, often took over their cases when he had a personal or emotional stake in them—had won him reelection a record number of times.

For some reason—Johnny suspected it might have something to do with his being Indian in a county not particularly known for its hospitality to native peoples—this had become one such case.

A man of few unnecessary words, Goodwin nodded, then stood silent in the hallway behind Johnny as he opened the door to his office.

Stepping inside, Goodwin pulled the door shut behind him.

His gaze swept the office, coming to rest on the door Johnny had kept closed the past four days.

"That the kid's spot?" Johnny nodded.

"Please, have a seat."

Goodwin lowered himself into the chair that had seen only one other occupant since Johnny had moved the Safe Crossings Project in. DuWayne Masters.

"Well," Goodwin said, the slowness with which he spoke belying the urgency which Johnny knew the sheriff felt almost as keenly as did Johnny, "we've eliminated the possibility that your young friend swerved to avoid an animal. My tactical teams scoured every skid mark on that highway and there are none, old or new, that match his vehicle's tires. That's a tricky spot in the road. People get to driving fast down the valley—the road's mostly straight and they're in a hurry to get to the park and get to hell out of the cars they've been in for days to get there—and they don't slow down when they see the warning signs before Yankee Jim.

"Or they get a call, or text, and don't even see them till it's too late."

He reached into the pocket of his brown sheriff's department jacket, withdrawing a can of snoose and then, never taking his eyes off Johnny, grabbed a pinch of tobacco between two fingers and pushed it into the side of his mouth.

The long pauses were enough to drive Johnny crazy, but he remained silent.

"We've also gone over all his phone records, and he hadn't called or texted anyone in the twenty-seven minutes before the crash. He'd had a short conversation with his wife, who says that he called and said he was about a mile from Irie Ranch. That's the only activity on his cell."

Another long pause. This time Johnny couldn't help himself.

"What about something medical? Could he have had a stroke or something?"

"We've looked into that. The doctors at Harborview say it wasn't anything medical."

"So there are no answers?"

"Hold on, young fella. I'm not done," he replied, reaching for a toothpick he'd just spotted on Johnny's desk. "We've narrowed it down to something mechanical."

"But it was a brand-new car," Johnny declared.

"Exactly. And not just any new car. One of those fancy ones with all the computers. I'll be the first to admit that stuff is way out of my league, but I've hired a consultant. Guy who used to develop computer systems for automobiles down in California, but then he realized he could make a shitload more money hiring himself out as a consultant."

"Does he have any ideas yet?"

"He suspects the system went haywire. Witnesses said they saw Mr. Masters flashing his lights to warn them as he raced up behind them and that when he passed them, he looked panicked."

Johnny closed his eyes. He couldn't bear to think DuWayne had foreknowledge of what was going to happen. He had told Johnny he visited Yellowstone regularly, so he would have known those roads, that stretch in particular. The thought that he had some warning, which an engineer with DuWayne's training and expertise surely must have had, sickened Johnny.

"Oh god," he muttered.

"Yep, oh god," Goodwin echoed. "This expert, he's got some other theories that he's going to look into."

"What kind of theories?"

"Too early to know," Goodwin said as he rose from the chair.

He stayed put momentarily, looking around the office.

"So what're you gonna do without your engineer? Close down shop?"

"Ironically, I got a call just this morning from DuWayne's professor. He's actually coming over from Bozeman tomorrow afternoon to meet with me. Says he has an idea. The doctors haven't let me talk to DuWayne yet, but the minute they do, I'm flying over to Seattle to tell him not to worry about things here. Till then, I'm waiting to hear what the Safe Crossings Project board wants to do. We're having a conference call tomorrow afternoon, after I meet with DuWayne's professor, to discuss a plan."

"Well, I'd better get back to work," the sheriff said, his tongue probing for a trace of tobacco lodged between his front and canine teeth, "and let you do the same."

14

WILL HAD BEEN WATCHING HER sleep through his spotting scope, from his vantage point on the outcropping high above the Soda Butte, for several hours, until he'd seen the flash of light—sunlight reflecting off something, most likely sunglasses or binoculars—down trail.

Hikers on the trail.

Apparently, Emma had no luck getting them to re-close the trail to the Thunderer. That now left him two choices. But judging by the day—unusually warm for early autumn and a cloudless sky, which would mean, even if he were successful in deflecting the approaching hikers, who he estimated would take at least an hour to reach the spot in the trail near the clearing in which she slept— he would be forced to choose the option he least wanted.

It would be their first real encounter.

He had watched her lift her nose in the air, turn her head, stand on her two hind legs, rising to the height of a horse trailer, and sniff again.

She knew he was following her.

But each time it had happened, he had withdrawn, given her more space, and she had never followed him. The other night, seeing her behind Emma, had stunned Will into reality.

It was time to get serious.

He unsnapped the leather strap holding the can of bear spray in its holster.

Then he unsnapped the holster to his gun.

Twenty yards away from her, he clapped his hands and stepped into the clearing.

"*Hey, Bear.*"

Her head rose immediately, but the rest of her stayed put. He could see freshly dried blood on her left hindquarters. Something had ripped the wound open again.

He clapped again and she rose, facing him squarely.

Will raised his hands over his head, making himself larger.

"Hello, Two Coyote," he said, as if to an old friend.

Her nostrils flared as she took in his scent.

"You have to leave now."

She jumped to her feet but did not advance. He could not read her eyes.

The bear spray would be his first defense, but if it didn't work...

He held his hands to the sky, reaching higher.

"You must go. Back down to the lake. To the Thorofare. You'll be safe there."

Slowly, she rose onto back feet the size of giant frying pans— to her full height. Will had only seen her do this from a distance, through his scope or binoculars.

He had been charged by bears more times than he could count, felt the adrenaline rush before they'd either stopped—a bluff charge—or been stopped cold by the red-hot spray, but this—the sheer size and power of the magnificent sow…he had never seen anything quite like this.

"Leave, Two Coyote, leave," he said calmly, hands still held high, as he began to walk backwards.

He knew he should spray her, scare her away from this place, this mountain that had summoned her home.

But he could not. Not when she didn't charge, not when she didn't even bluff. Not when instead, she lowered her massive front paws to the ground, then slowly—as Will backed away—turned in the other direction, and with one last look over her shoulder, ambled into the trees, a lopsided gait favoring her wounded hind leg.

Heart and head racing, Will realized that left just one option.

The only thing he could do right now to protect her.

Once she had disappeared and he had waited several minutes to make sure she hadn't circled around him—a tactic Will had experienced firsthand from another grizzly sow the previous fall—he headed toward the trail below.

Toward the path traveled by the two-leggeds heading Two Coyote's way.

15

JUSTINE STROLLED TO THE RAILING in front of the bench, where Annie sat reviewing the case before her.

"Case number 2943, Stucky versus Yellowstone National Park," Justine called.

A portly man in an ill-fitting black suit stepped forward.

Annie looked up and recognized him.

"Mr. Moody, I don't see the defendant in this courtroom."

"Good morning, Your Honor. My client, Mr. Stucky, fell ill this morning and could not attend. I am authorized to enter his plea."

Annie hesitated. She had halfway expected a shenanigan of this sort from Stucky. He'd been in her courtroom before.

"Very well." She lowered her eyes to the cause of action. "Your client is charged with three violations of the Lacey Act, which makes it illegal to transport wildlife outside of Yellowstone National Park."

Annie could see the smile growing on the attorney's smug face as she read the charges, one for each wolf Stucky had killed.

"How does your client plead?"

"It's quite obvious how he pleads. No wolves were transported out of your park. Your Honor."

"The State contends that the gut pile your client left on his property lured three wolves there."

"First of all, you have no idea if those wolves came from within the park."

"I see here that at least one was collared."

"Then there should only have been one charge. And then you'd have to prove where that collared wolf came from just before the night he was shot. In self-defense.

"Secondly, the wolves left the park freely. No one, especially not my client, *transported* them. Your Honor."

Annie had had enough.

"While I appreciate your giving the prosecutor advance notice of your client's defense, we still have the formality of a plea to deal with. I ask you again, Mr. Moody: how does your client plead?"

"Not guilty," Moody replied, almost jovially. "My client pleads not guilty."

"Very well, the court clerk will set a date for trial, and the two of you can work out deadlines for discovery. This hearing is dismissed."

As Moody was heading toward Justine, who sat at her desk in the corner closest to the bench, Annie could not resist. Perhaps it was Will, who had been haunting her dreams and waking moments. Johnny had told her about running into Will in the parking lot of the Chittenden House.

Perhaps it was in some way to appease Will, to lessen any hurt he had felt upon hearing that Johnny was there to have lunch with Annie.

"Why is it your client feels bison who leave the park should be hazed and sent to slaughter to protect his property, his livestock, from a disease that bison in the wild have never transmitted, but the reverse is not true—that his sheep should not be allowed to endanger wildlife that belong to the whole nation and are cherished by the whole world?"

Moody stopped cold and turned to her with a look so evil and hostile that Annie almost regretted her words.

"I assume you're talking off record here," he replied, "and that you're referring to the bighorn sheep that have died in the vicinity of my client's ranch."

"You know the answer to both," Annie shot back.

Moody's entire demeanor—the earlier sense that the proceedings amused him—had transformed. Posture rigid, bloated belly aimed her way, he moved slowly toward Annie and the bench.

"Private property rights should and will always be superior in the eyes of the law. Mr. Stucky is a proud citizen of the state of Montana, whose heritage is all about private property rights. It's a matter of justice. And my client—and I—will always fight for what's right. For justice, tooth and nail."

Annie did not flinch. She saw the security guard step forward, from the back of the courtroom, and wave him away.

"I repeat, you've been dismissed, Mr. Moody. And I would suggest your client not fall ill for another hearing. I would also suggest that you meet each and every deadline for disclosure so we can move this case forward and serve the justice you so honor and fight for."

• • •

Perhaps it was because Johnny's impression of professors had been formed two decades earlier, at the University of Washington, but when the man wearing a ball cap, t-shirt, and jeans walked into Montana Cup, Johnny assumed he was a fisherman who'd just flown in, eager to catch the last big rainbow trout of the season. At first glance, Johnny even took the long tube the man carried under one arm to be a fly rod, and silently marveled at the paranoia of a big-city dweller so worried about leaving his rod in his vehicle that he carried it into a Montana coffee shop.

It wasn't until Johnny glanced outside and saw the white truck bearing the MSU/Western Transportation logo—the same logo he'd seen on DuWayne's jacket—parked at the curb that he realized the identity of the man who now approached him, wearing a friendly and easy smile.

"Professor Easton," Johnny said, rising to his feet as he extended his hand.

"Please, call me David," Easton replied, accepting Johnny's greeting with his own firm hand.

As soon as Easton had settled into the chair opposite him, Johnny asked the question foremost on his mind.

"Have you heard anything new about DuWayne?"

Easton's expression alone—without any words to accompany it—was enough to compound the grief and angst Johnny had been feeling for three days now, ever since the accident.

"I just got off the phone with his wife," the MSU professor and engineer replied soberly, "as I was driving here. She's still in Seattle. DuWayne will be there indefinitely."

Both men fell silent, neither meeting the gaze of the other, for several seconds.

"I'm here for DuWayne," Easton continued. "He doesn't want his accident to delay the project. He feels strongly about that."

"He's speaking now?" Johnny asked hopefully. The last he had heard, in one of his daily calls to Harborview Hospital in Seattle, DuWayne had been unable to talk.

"Not exactly, but he and Charla have developed a means of communicating. She said he seems to understand everything and they've developed a code where he squeezes her hand 'yes' or 'no,' or just to let her know he's heard her. They're able to have conversations that way." He looked at Johnny again. "He told her doesn't want the Safe Crossings Project to die or be delayed. He wants you to replace him."

Johnny's heart sank. He had seen how much the Safe Crossings Project meant to DuWayne. In typical fashion, DuWayne was now thinking of the project, thinking of Johnny.

Still, he couldn't imagine the passionate young engineer wanting anyone else to take the helm, and how long finding the right person would take.

When Easton cleared his throat, Johnny realized he wasn't done speaking.

"I know how much this means to DuWayne," Easton continued. "I've never seen a student so excited about work he was doing after he graduated. And I want DuWayne to be the one to drive this project."

Easton's words only served to add confusion to Johnny's intense disappointment.

DuWayne was unable to speak, would be hospitalized indefinitely, didn't want the project delayed, but here was his professor saying he wanted to honor DuWayne's wishes at the same time that he wanted DuWayne to be the master engineer.

"I don't understand how that's possible," Johnny replied, brow creased in confusion. "I have a call tomorrow morning with the project's board in Seattle. We'll be making a decision about whether to proceed, and how to proceed. If we decide to proceed, I don't see how it could be any way but without DuWayne."

"No," Easton replied firmly. "That's not true."

He reached for the tube he'd arrived with, which now sat on the table in front of them.

Standing, he began extracting its contents, unrolling them, using every available item on the table—salt and pepper shakers, a ketchup bottle, a ceramic cup holding sweeteners—to anchor them.

Johnny recognized them immediately as architectural drawings. *Familiar* drawings.

When Easton was done, he looked up at Johnny, his eyes filled with passion, and something else. Fear.

"This is DuWayne's project. His safe crossing."

He turned his gaze downward, back to the papers.

"And it's brilliant, simply brilliant."

Johnny stared at the papers, too. He recognized the symbols, drawn by the precise, pale hand.

"I'm afraid I don't understand," he said.

Easton lifted his eyes. Again, they held fear.

"I can do it. I worked with DuWayne on this project. He was my student for three years. The best student I've ever had—academically and character-wise. Taken together with the drawings

164

he showed me the day before his accident, when I dropped in to his office at his invitation, I'm confident we can move the Safe Crossings Project forward. And on time.

"And it will be DuWayne's work. Not mine. I can execute it, even run things by DuWayne, with his wife's help, to keep him involved on a daily basis."

As close to speechless as he could remember ever being, Johnny shook his head slowly, pondering the impossible.

"I don't understand. This is a full-time project. How can you possibly take this on while you're teaching?"

"Hell," Easton replied, "I retired at the end of the spring semester, and it's already driving me fucking crazy. I've got the time, and I've got the motivation. Please, let me do it. Let me stand in for DuWayne."

Johnny took in a sharp, hopeful breath.

"I'd need for him to give this his blessing."

"I just spoke to Charla," Easton replied. "Told her what I want to do. She was sitting right next to DuWayne's bed, holding his hand."

Johnny felt himself tearing up at the thought of the young couple, fighting for DuWayne's life in a hospital 700 miles away, trying to hold on to hope.

Easton saw how his words were affecting Johnny. He went on. "Charla said he squeezed her hand emphatically." He paused.

"*Yes.* DuWayne said yes."

Johnny stared at the drawings made by DuWayne and imagined his excitement as a young grad student, his pride at the work he had done.

Then he looked up at the expression on the professor's face. When he did, he realized that what he'd taken to be fear was not fear.

It, too, was hope. Desperate, fervent hope that Johnny would agree with this unusual proposal.

"This is unbelievable," Johnny said quietly. "Of course. I'll recommend to the board that we proceed immediately. In honor of Tracy Blessings, and in honor of DuWayne."

To secure their agreement, cast it in Montana-style cement, David Easton reached his right hand across the table to grab Johnny's, knocking over the salt shaker in the process.

"Thank you," he said. "Thank you."

Johnny grasped the hand back.

"I'm the one who should be saying thank you."

As if needing to break the intensity of the moment, Easton began methodically removing the anchors holding the drawings in place on the table, placing them back precisely in their previous spots.

"Charla told me something else when she asked DuWayne about my filling in for him," he said, eyeing the top drawing one more time.

Bent over the table, his age showing in the slope of his shoulders, the swelling in his knuckles, and the bend to his arthritic fingers, he looked back up, into Johnny's dark eyes.

"She said a tear fell from DuWayne's eye as he squeezed her hand to say 'yes.'"

Sliding the papers back into the tube with a practiced hand, Easton's eyes held their own tears.

"Believe me," Johnny said, nodding his head, "*that* is thanks enough."

• • •

His mud-encrusted Jeep sat on the side of Papesh Road, just above Highway 89. Even without his binoculars, the view below afforded him all the information, all the details, he would need.

The long, gravel driveway was lined now by a three-rail fence— reinforced between rails by a wire grid that had not been there before, to keep the herd of sheep in check. No sign of bighorns. The Gardiner Basin herd. Later, come fall and winter, they would be visible 24/7 from right where his Jeep sat on down to the highway. They would, as they had since the road was built in the early 1920s, venture across to the rich grass on the property below, just outside the new fencing.

He simply stood there, leaning against his dirty Jeep, staring down at that piece of property, with a hatred reserved for fanatics.

The house was just visible, most of it hidden by the cottonwoods lining the river.

Half a dozen signs littered the fence. *Montanans for Economic Progress. Make Montana Great Again. Liz Conway for U.S. Senate.*

Time after time when driving by, Will had been tempted to stop and rip them off.

Just beyond, the Yellowstone River, slowed now by the hot summer, still provided enough thrills for the five rafts—each loaded with tourists and a guide—floating down the river. Screams erupted when they disappeared behind a stand of trees on the banks of

Stucky's property, and he knew they had hit the riffle just after McConnell.

Wait till they got to Yankee Jim.

Damn, what a shame about that young engineer.

The sun had started its descent.

A helicopter passed overhead on its way to the airport, its runway less than a mile south, toward Gardiner, its roar and the air it stirred causing a herd of mule deer to disperse. Cattle and horses that grazed the land just north of the park year-round merely raised their heads or went on grazing. The domestic sheep—the first in the Gardiner Basin since Yellowstone's establishment, and new to the area—scuttled about but quickly settled back in to grazing as well.

Will had taken photos and notes.

He knew how the park's investigation would go. Hell, Yellowstone—the National Park Service—was a partner to the Interagency Bison Management Plan that had sent over eight thousand wild bison to slaughter since its inception in 2000, under the guise of protecting local cattle from brucellosis. A disease that had never been passed from bison to cattle in the wild. Once Yellowstone bison left the park, their management was turned over to the Department of Livestock—the same agency that looked after the interests of the ranchers and cattlemen. The grass upon which their cattle grazed was often heavily subsidized federal land.

The Park Service cooperated yearly in this grasslands war that was supposedly about disease prevention.

What the hell kind of serious investigation would the Yellowstone bighorn biologist be able to conduct, much less present publicly?

Jobs were on the line, the line that everyone in the five agencies, regardless of their titles, knew they could not cross by standing up to livestock interests. The line that the new administration and state politicians had clearly drawn.

The bighorn were doomed. The Gardiner herd, which intermingled with the park herd, would be exposed to every disease the newly introduced domestic sheep carried—which, now, from what Emma Day had reported to Will, included pneumonia. Pneumonia would spread like wildfire, killing bighorn lambs first, then ewes, the big bulls last, but kill them it would.

All because of Stucky's sheep. Maybe it wasn't too late.

Will stood on the hilltop, stewing, until the helicopter had landed and now, took off again, heading northeast, toward Livingston and the Crazies.

Minutes later, Stucky's pickup truck pulled into the long driveway—and it came to Will. The solution.

Anger rising in every fiber of his body as the realization hit him, Will watched Stucky get out, stride like a bull to the gate, lift its latch, and enter the pasture where his new sheep grazed.

Will stood there, taking more pictures, thinking, working through it all in his mind, until Stucky disappeared into his house and the sun had set.

Then, headlights off, he rolled down the hill, turned left onto 89, and headed toward Mammoth.

16

PETER SHEWMAKER LOOKED UP FROM his desk at the knock on his door.

Surprised to see Emma Day, his well-honed sixth sense told him the new bear biologist's appearance spelled trouble.

Rising to greet her, he managed a tense smile.

"Come on in."

Emma stepped inside. Declining the chair he offered her opposite his desk, she looked uncomfortable.

"What can I do for you?"

Standing several feet from where Peter had dropped back into his chair, behind his desk, Emma hesitated.

"I don't know, Peter. Maybe I'm seeing ghosts where none exist, but I wanted to talk to you about Will McCarroll."

That's all it took. She had Peter's attention.

"What about him?"

"You know about the grizzly that young punk, the outfitter, took target practice on, don't you?"

"Yes. What does this have to do with Will?"

Emma took a deep breath.

"I ran into will the other evening. I was coming off Chaw Pass. I'd had this feeling I was being followed, but I thought it was a lone hiker I'd passed earlier, a man. When I got down to the trailhead and started crossing the open area to where I'd parked, Will called out to me, to warn me. That bear was following me."

"Did you see it?"

"No. I never did. But Will had seen her."

"We don't know if it's a sow or male," Peter replied.

Emma seemed to hesitate.

"Will knows," she said. "It wasn't the first time I've run into him up there since the bear was shot."

Peter shook his head the way a parent does upon learning his kid's been getting in trouble in class.

"I'm sorry, Peter," Emma was quick to say. "Maybe I should have come in sooner, but Will told me he's just up there hiking, and he certainly has the right to do that.

"But I'm worried about him. I think he's living up there. I think…"—she hesitated again—"I think Will's protecting the bear."

Peter sighed.

"We're getting reports of someone scaring hikers off that trail, and out of campgrounds anywhere near there."

Emma moaned.

"You think it's Will?"

"Who else would put fake wolf tracks around tents at 3k3 to scare them off the Thunderer?"

Emma may have been new to Yellowstone, but she had spent enough time in that part of it to know that 3k3 was a backcountry campsite—which hosted bear poles and bear-proof garbage cans, and for which campers had to register and get a permit—on the Thunderer Cutoff Trail.

"We need to close those trails, Peter."

"No, we need to get Will out of the backcountry. And to euthanize that bear before someone gets hurt."

It only took Peter a second to realize he'd hit a nerve. His sixth sense told him this was important and that he'd better not scare the young biologist off, which, from the look on her face, seemed a strong possibility at any second.

Softening his tone, he followed up with, "I'm sorry, Emma. With the bison investigation and the firestorm over that, and wolves getting shot, it's been a rough couple weeks. Will's antics are the last straw."

Emma took a deep breath.

"Will said the sow went down to the Lake area, and that he's sure she'll go back. From what I've seen and heard of him, no one knows this park's wildlife, especially bears, better than Will. Can't we just close the trails for a little while? See if he's right?"

Peter's eyes went to his window. A late-afternoon storm was moving in, hovering over Electric Peak.

Emma Day was right. No one knew the instincts and behavior of Yellowstone's wildest animals better than Will. And with the fame Will had acquired over the past few years—both in saving the alpha female of the Druid pack and in testifying against the guns-in-parks law before the Senate Commission—no one stood to bring more attention to the recent troubles Yellowstone, and those charged with running it, were experiencing.

"How long does he want?"

"Two weeks."

Peter shook his head.

"That's too long. This is our last good weather; we're breaking records for this time of year."

"How long then?"

"Three days," Peter replied. "Four, tops. That's it."

Emma turned away, but not before Peter saw the glint—excitement? relief?—in her eyes.

"Oh, and Emma," he called after her as she stepped into the hallway, "if Will has anything he'd like to share about the bison killings, please let me know."

Emma froze momentarily. Then she glanced back at Peter and—wide-eyed—nodded her head.

She knew better than to say more.

• • •

Johnny had moved from his front office looking down on Livingston's Park Street to the back office—DuWayne's office— for the call.

He wanted to *feel* DuWayne on this call. He hoped that, through his voice, the other participants would also feel the young engineer's presence and spirit.

At precisely nine a.m., Johnny picked up his cell phone and dialed the 888 number, then, when prompted, entered the code to join the call, and again when prompted, identified himself.

"Johnny Yellow Kidney."

There are four participants on this call, a mechanical voice informed him.

"Johnny, welcome."

Bob Heyka's familiar, usually cheerful voice sounded subdued, somber.

"Thanks, Bob," Johnny replied.

"We've already got four of the project's board members on the line."

Heyka's announcement was followed by several "Hello, Johnny's," and a "Nice to meet you, Johnny" from an unfamiliar voice.

"Now we're just waiting for our Canadian member, Michael Kornberg," Heyka said. "Let's give him a couple minutes."

An awkward silence followed. Less than a minute later, Heyka broke it.

"Well, let's just go ahead." He coughed—not a cough that hinted he was ill, but more one that, to Johnny, indicated the head of the Safe Crossings Project board was uncomfortable.

"As you know, another tragedy has occurred. Ten days ago, DuWayne Masters lost control of his car as he was driving down Highway 89, headed to Yellowstone."

Johnny cleared his throat.

"Um, Bob, just to clarify, DuWayne was headed to a ranch about thirty miles north of the park when he ran off the highway."

"I know that area," Heyka replied. "Yankee Jim is so close to the park that I assumed that's where he was heading. He'd emailed that he was meeting with a rancher to talk about a safe crossing easement. When I heard where he went off the road, I assumed he'd been heading to one of the ranches in the Gardiner Basin."

"No, Irie Ranch is in the Paradise."

"So why was he down in the Basin?"

"That's what we don't know," Johnny said in answer. "He drove right by the ranch where we had the appointment. I was supposed to meet him there. I expected him to be there when I already arrived. He'd texted me he was on his way."

There was another short silence.

"That's very perplexing," Heyka said.

"The police are investigating. There were reports of DuWayne being unable to control his car. That he was honking and flashing his lights to warn drivers ahead of him."

Another voice, female, entered the conversation.

"Oh my god, that's terrible. What could that have been?"

"They're looking at several possibilities," Johnny replied. "I'm in regular contact with the Park County sheriff and his office. I'll be sure to keep you informed."

Johnny could feel the mood of the call take an even more somber turn.

"According to the hospital, DuWayne's still in serious condition," Heyka said. "They can't predict when, or even if, he will be able to return to the job. I set this call up to discuss how to go forward without him."

This was Johnny's opportunity.

"I have news I'd like to share about that."

Heyka cut Johnny off.

"Please, Johnny, if I may…. As I say, I originally set this call up to discuss our options for going forward." He paused. "But I received more bad news yesterday. Devastating news, really."

At that very moment, a beep indicated another caller had joined the call.

"Michael Kornberg here," a distinctly Canadian voice said, adding "I apologize for being late."

"Michael," Heyka said. "Happy you're here. I'm afraid you've joined us just as I was about to share more bad news—as if young Masters' accident weren't bad enough."

The suspense on the line felt palpable to Johnny. He took in a deep breath as Heyka continued.

"Our new president has apparently gotten his way. Yesterday I was informed that the federal funding we'd been granted for the Safe Crossings Project—the funding that Tracy Blessings worked so hard and passionately to acquire—has been cut."

Johnny heard at least one gasp, that of the female.

"Cut how much?" she asked.

"All of it."

"Oh, no."

Another caller, male, uttered "That son of a bitch."

"Unbelievable," Johnny said, his voice reflecting the irony he felt. "I'd come to this call with some positive news. DuWayne's former professor, the one who'd overseen his master's project—a safe crossing for wildlife—came to me yesterday and offered to take over for DuWayne."

All Johnny could think about was the way Easton had described DuWayne squeezing his wife's hand to tell her he wanted Easton to step in for him, to ensure that the Safe Crossings Project became a reality.

All he could see in his mind's eye were the tears Easton had described in DuWayne's eyes.

Johnny felt close to tears himself, enough so that he couldn't bring himself to share more. Especially now, when he knew all the others on the call felt a disappointment as keen as his. They had all known Tracy Blessings. And, according to Bob Heyka, during his first meeting with Johnny, many had been close to her daughter, Kylie, as well.

Johnny wasn't the only one feeling pain.

The entire group fell into a silence—which the Canadian lawyer quickly broke.

"Tell him he's hired."

"What?" Johnny replied in disbelief.

"What?" Heyka echoed. "Michael, maybe you missed what I just reported. Our federal funding's been cut. Immediately. Nothing, not a penny more. That leaves the grant you acquired for us from a Canadian foundation and a few individual donors, none of whose generosity can keep this project running." He paused, then added, "Johnny, I'm afraid we may not even have enough to give you a proper thirty days' notice."

"Notice means nothing to me," Johnny answered. "I can wrap things up without pay. It's never been about money."

"Notice is not necessary," Michael Kornberg persisted cheerfully. "Compensation *is*. And Mr. Yellow Kidney, please go ahead and accept the kind offer of this professor you met with. I'd say even offer him a bit of a bump over what you may have already offered him."

Johnny's head swam, and from the silence of the rest of the group, he assumed the others were experiencing the same confusion.

Heyka had basically just announced the termination of the Safe Crossings Project, yet the Canadian lawyer was telling him to go ahead and hire Easton.

Heyka had had enough.

"Michael, please confirm that you heard my announcement about our federal funds being cut."

"I apologize for joining the call late, Bob," Kornberg responded, "but I was in a meeting with the Canadian prime minister. I did, indeed, hear your announcement."

"And?" Heyka replied, clearly frustrated.

"And like many of our longstanding allies, the prime minister was already quite unhappy with your new president," Kornberg announced. "Talk of the wall being built, the travel ban, the United States' withdrawal from the Paris Accord. Now the imposition of tariffs on Canadian steel and aluminum…" his voice drifted off as though he were trying to maintain control. "Your president's behavior at the G7 was reprehensible, but his personal attacks on the prime minister were the last straw. The last straw."

The silence on the phone line could literally be felt by all on the call as they waited, knowing Kornberg wasn't done.

"But all of those things, matters of world importance, took place on the political stage, and the prime minister will, of course, with his usual acumen and tact, and with the blessing of the Canadian people, deal with them. The environmental stage is where we can, and must, move forward immediately, with or without your president. Delisting of Yellowstone's grizzly bears, the green light for the Dakota Access pipeline…. It's clear your president has no respect or regard for the Earth and its inhabitants—*all* of its inhabitants.

"Canada welcomes your grizzly bears and wolves. We signed on to the Safe Crossings Project because we believe a civilized nation takes responsibility, takes proactive steps to ensure that its wildlife continue to exist and flourish. That's what the Safe Crossings Project is all about."

Not a sound could be heard from others on the line.

"I just left the prime minister. Apparently, someone in the White House gave one of our staff a heads up about the U.S. federal funding for this project being cut because of the movement in your country to take back federal lands from the public." Kornberg paused briefly, skillfully. "Needless to say, it's been clear that same disregard for public lands translates to disregard for your wildlife.

"The prime minister wants me to inform this board that Canada—and Canada alone—will step up and finance the Safe Crossings Project."

Johnny startled at these words.

The female voice uttered a quiet "Oh my god."

"We intend to use this project as an example to the world," Kornberg continued, his voice holding an unmistakable note of pride. "We intend to let the world know that when it comes to the environment, and living up to our responsibilities to protect and preserve the natural world, Canada stands for everything your president and his base do not."

Johnny had begun offering a silent prayer of thanks to the Creator as he continued to listen to Kornberg.

"They were working on the press release as I left the meeting. You can expect an announcement that Canada will step up where the United States failed to meet its obligations and promises later today or tomorrow. The prime minister wants to move forward quickly, with urgency. He told me he envisions a grand opening ceremony, lots of publicity and fanfare."

"This is unbelievable," Bob Heyka said. "What a godsend. Please convey our deeply felt gratitude to the prime minister."

"I'll do so," Kornberg said. "Mr. Yellow Kidney, this new chap—the young man's professor—how soon is he available?"

"Immediately," Johnny replied. "He's eager to get started. He's already reviewed DuWayne's plans and specs. And he's been in touch with DuWayne through his wife. She assured him that DuWayne passionately wants the Safe Crossings Project to go on without him, and without delay."

"Well, you can tell all of them the prime minister is eager as well. You've got a blank check, my friend. And you will have any assistance you may need from out Canadian safe crossing engineers, who—I'm sure you're aware—are world renowned for their recent wildlife crossing innovations."

It was clear the Canadian lawyer was taking great pleasure in his duties this day.

"What is it you Americans like to say? Let's roll?"

Bob Heyka's laugh was echoed by several others on the call. "Yes," he replied. "That's a famous and meaningful saying in this country.'

"Brilliant," Kornberg answered. "Let's roll."

17

AS HE DROVE NORTH AND rounded the curve hugging the hill that housed the Yellowstone Bend Motel, the cowboy-hatted driver of the truck waited for one more set of headlights heading south—toward Gardiner and the entry gates to Yellowstone—to pass, then, with the miles ahead of highway pitch black, he flipped off his lights. He'd just passed the annual fall rodeo, which drew every rancher in the Gardiner Basin and most of the town of Gardiner, as the anthem blasted from the Gardiner high school band and cowgirls waving flags circled the arena on horseback.

It was still going strong. He had time.

Slowing, he turned left, into the long driveway. The trailer behind the truck rattled as it moved slowly down the graveled passageway. Had anyone been home, windows open on this unexpectedly warm autumn evening, it would have ended his mission; but tonight the house sat black as the highway. The Basin was such that locals never bothered to lock doors or turn on lights when they left. One looked out for another—except on nights like these, when the whole town attended a basketball game. Or the annual rodeo.

Soon, weighted, the truck would move more quietly.

Thirty minutes later, his job finished, he pulled back onto 89. Boldly, he passed right back by the rodeo grounds, lacking any concern about the "baa"ing coming from the trailer. It simply blended in with the noise coming from the rowdy two- and four-legged rodeo crowd.

18

INSTINCTIVELY, WILL'S HAND SHOT OUT of the sleeping bag at the familiar sound—branches made brittle by a hot, dry summer breaking underfoot.

Hand poised over two objects lying side by side next to his down bag—a can of bear spray and a Glock 9mm—Will waited.

He hadn't seen her now in almost a week, had begun to believe she'd returned to the Thorofare.

Could he be wrong? Was Two Coyote still wandering the mountain—the trail—where she'd been wounded?

Gripping the bear spray, he silently, slowly curled his upper body, almost imperceptibly, to get a glimpse in the direction of the brush that some living creature was now moving through, in his direction.

Lying still like that, all he would see at first were feet. Either two or four.

He was prepared for either.

But this time he was wrong. This time it wasn't feet that told him the nature of the being approaching.

"Will?" a voice called from some twenty yards down the trail. Then several seconds later, closer, "Will McCarroll?"

Bolting upright, he let out a sigh before calling out, "This way."

Before he'd slid completely out of his bag, Emma Day stepped through the thick brush separating the dirt on which he'd slept for days now from the trail.

She looked sheepish, apologetic.

"I recognized your bag, hanging from the pole at that last campsite."

Brushing his hands through his unruly hair, then reaching for the metal bottle sitting on a tall rock next to his sleeping bag, Will squirted its cold water on his face.

"I figured I'd accomplish two things at once. Keep anyone from using that site, while I made sure my food was out of reach."

Emma smiled.

"Mission accomplished. We've been hearing that campsite's always in use. It's driving Teddy mad."

Stationed at the Albright Visitor Center, Ted Williams served as the park's backcountry ranger charged with issuing permits for campsites. Williams was known to keep meticulous track of the permits in order to ensure he'd never issue more than one per bear pole.

The comment made Will smile.

"So," he said, surprised at how pleased he felt to see the young biologist. He'd been living alone for days now, hadn't had a conversation with a single soul—at least not a two-legged soul. "What brings you looking for me?"

Emma's large round eyes grew serious.

186

"I had a talk with Peter. Asked him to close these trails." She hesitated, as if building her courage. "I told him I'd seen you, Will. I'm sorry. I feel like I've betrayed you, but I've been so worried. I went in there to ask that he close the trails, just like you asked me to do, but I did more than that. I told him you were out here."

Will grew silent, but he did not avoid her eyes when she turned them on him. He could see the guilt and remorse they held.

"That's okay, Emma. Peter's actually been pretty good about putting up with my shenanigans. I figured he'd be hearing about some of them."

Emma Day broke into her first smile of the day.

"I like the fake wolf prints."

Will chuckled.

"I suspect Peter and Gonzalez don't share your appreciation. I knew it was a matter of time till they sent LE out here to find me and cite me with enough violations that I'd be banned from the park." His eyes, still crusty from what little sleep he'd managed to get, scanned the sky—a brilliant blue, even at this early morning hour. "I was already thinking I'm going to have to move on. Head down to the Thorofare looking for her."

"You haven't seen her, then?"

"Not for four days. If she's still on the Thunderer, or anywhere near Chaw Pass, I'd be surprised."

"Well, you've got three more days to look for her here."

"Peter agreed to close the trails?"

"Yes. I asked for two weeks. He gave me three days."

"That's fair. If I can't find her, or signs of her, in three days, I'll head down toward the lake."

Will looked around. Soon he would need to sneak into the bushes to relieve himself and was trying to scout for a spot that wouldn't embarrass either of them.

"Maybe she's not going that way," Emma replied.

The statement startled Will. The young biologist had always deferred to his judgment when it came to her charges, the park's bears. Especially its grizzly population.

He turned back to her, a scowl deepening the lines in his weathered face.

"What do you know?"

"Two things," Emma replied. "Trevor called me into his office at the Resource Center the other day to talk about bad press we're getting over the recent maulings and euthanasias. He's concerned about the wounded sow. Says she's a formula for more bad publicity, more tragedy."

"That's why they need to keep these trails closed."

"He told me something else, Will. It's why I came up here this morning. I couldn't sleep. Today's my day off, but I had to find you and tell you."

It was the first time Will realized that Emma was wearing jeans, and that the shirt she wore under her fleece jacket was a t-shirt, not the park-issued long sleeves.

"What did Trevor tell you?"

"He believes that sow is one of two grizzly cubs that were transplanted by the Park Service from Glacier National Park about ten years ago. Their mother drowned, and Superintendent Sweeney asked to take them."

Will finished the story for her.

"The Lake Sherburne cubs," he said, eyes wide as he remembered. "Those two cubs were inseparable that first fall. They were taken down to Lake, where winter's a little milder. Then we found one cub dead in the spring, looked like he'd starved. The other had survived but lost enough weight that she'd slipped out of her collar. We found it in the campground across from the empty hotel. No one's ever known what happened to her since. We assumed she didn't make it either."

Both Will and Emma fell into a brief, thoughtful silence.

"So that's why she went to Lake," Will finally said. "And that must be where she's gone again now."

Filled with a sudden sense of urgency, Will bent to the ground, threw a couple items of clothing into his sleeping bag, and started rolling it up.

"Three days should be more than enough, Emma," he said, slipping into his boots. As he laced them, he looked up at her. "She'll have cleared these trails by then."

Head down now, as he tied the double knot he'd perfected decades earlier, it jerked back up at Emma's next words.

"I don't think she's headed to the Thorofare, Will."

Slowly, Will rose to his full height and looked Emma Day squarely in the eye.

"What do you know?"

"We've heard reports of a wounded grizzly heading up the Absarokas. Hikers staying at Pray saw her. Of course, it could be another bear, but…"

"Damn," Will said. Then he repeated it. "Damn."

Now it was Emma's turn.

"What?"

"Then that's what she's doing."

"What," the biologist stuttered, "what is she doing?"

Will shook his head in amazement. It all suddenly made sense. Wounded, she'd disappeared, gone down to the Thorofare for a while, but in the end, a stronger instinct may have pulled her back, and might now be driving her north. He couldn't help a small, sad smile.

"If it's her," he said, "that's what she's doing."

He finished his thoughts out loud.

"Two Coyote's heading home."

19

ANNIE HAD DELIBERATELY WAITED UNTIL Eleanor Malone finished her dessert of huckleberry ice cream. Standing, Annie walked over to the stove—the one she had purchased after Eleanor's kidnapping.

The night Annie had walked in from a trip to Bozeman to find her mother missing, an empty teakettle sat smoking—the water to make it whistle long gone—on a burner turned on by Eleanor earlier, after she had eaten her dinner alone. Her evening ritual, dessert and then tea. Not dessert and tea. Dessert and *then* tea. Annie had known the moment she entered the house—through the back door that led to the kitchen—that something was wrong; horribly, horribly wrong. Finding Archie bleeding and locked in the old piano room adjacent to the kitchen had confirmed that, as had Annie's frantic race upstairs in search of her mother; but even though Eleanor was found days later and rescued, and Archie eventually recovered, Annie found she could not bear to look at that stove. Or listen to a teapot whistle.

She had purchased a new stove, and now used a garden-variety pan to boil water for tea.

Still, as she walked to both now to make tea for her mother, the memories rushed back. She had learned with time, however, and with help from the park psychologist, how to banish them temporarily from her thoughts, knowing they would soon return.

Tonight, however, she had something else on her mind.

Back still turned to her mother, she said nonchalantly, "Mom, there's Bingo tonight up at the church."

When Eleanor didn't respond, Annie glanced over her shoulder to where Eleanor sat at the dinner table. Eleanor was smiling.

"He's back," she said. "Isn't he?"

Annie always tried to anticipate her mother's reactions, but she hadn't expected this. Steaming cup in her hand, she turned and crossed back to the table beneath the window, where the two of them took their meals. Where, until two months earlier, Judge Sherburne had filled the third chair.

"What do you mean, Mom?"

"Yes, of course I'll go to Bingo," Eleanor replied. "I knew he was back. When I saw how you'd changed into that pretty shirt before dinner, I knew Will had returned.

"Of course, I'll go to Bingo," she repeated.

The expression of pure joy on her mother's face stunned Annie, silenced her momentarily.

She placed the tea in front of Eleanor and lowered herself into her chair.

"Will's not back, Mother," she said quietly. "I don't think he's coming back. Ever. My friend Johnny is coming over tonight. Not Will."

Eleanor lifted the steaming cup to her lips. Annie thought she was going to cry.

Without taking a sip, Eleanor placed the cup back on the table, took a deep breath, reached over and placed her hand on top of Annie's.

"I like Johnny. He's a good man. I'll go put a jacket on. I can walk to the church."

"I don't want you walking anywhere. I'll take you."

Eleanor squeezed her only daughter's hand.

"Okay, let's go."

Johnny had been waiting in the driveway, still in his truck, when Annie pulled back in after dropping Eleanor off at the last stone building on Military Row—the name for the structures the military had constructed in the late 1800s, when they were called in to keep law and order in the new Yellowstone National Park.

His warm smile as he stepped out of the truck, his lean, sinewy physique and neatly bound ponytail helped Annie put out of mind her mother's words, her disappointment that it wasn't Will coming over to see her daughter.

"You're early," Annie teased, glancing at an invisible watch on her thin wrist.

"I'm right on time," he laughed, wrapping a relaxed arm around her shoulder, as they stepped onto the porch.

As he had the first and only other time he'd visited Annie's house—the day he'd witnessed the car of DuWayne Masters being pulled from Yankee Jim, the same day he'd run into Will outside Annie's office—Johnny paused, turned to look at Minerva, the famous hot spring that drew thousands of visitors a day to the lower boardwalk area.

Annie's eyes followed his.

Minerva's geothermal waters glistened in the glare of the setting sun, which, combined with the colorful bacteria that thrived in their near-boiling temperatures, created the Yellowstone equivalent of a psychedelic light show.

"She's coming back to life," Annie said, her voice reflecting the wonder she still felt upon looking due east, just fifty yards from the Stone House. "Sometimes I still pinch myself to be living here, where I can literally see the changes on a daily basis. Judge Sherburne used to sit in his recliner and look out the window all day."

Annie sensed the grin on Johnny's face to be equal parts pleasure and melancholy.

"Back to life," he said quietly, eyes still fixed to the waters. "It gives you hope, doesn't it?"

Annie turned to study him.

"You're thinking of your friend, aren't you?"

Johnny stared straight ahead.

"I was. Yes. But also of us."

"What do you mean?"

Now he turned to meet her gaze.

"Who would have thought that we'd end up here, together again? In Montana?"

Annie understood only too well. And she knew that perhaps she should give an answer that reflected this understanding.

But they were still on uncharted ground. And Annie's feelings for Will had not changed. She feared they never would.

And so she did not.

"Technically I live in Wyoming," she teased.

Annie had always loved Johnny's laugh. How pure and uninhibited it was, how it lacked any trace of self-consciousness. And now, she also loved the acceptance it indicated for her decision not to delve into their relationship—into the mere fact that she had called and asked him to visit tonight.

"*Technically*," Johnny replied. "I'm just happy to be here."

Silent, Annie grabbed his hand and led him through the front door.

• • •

The sun had already begun its descent behind the Gallatins when Will took the soft right turn off Highway 89 onto the East River Road. As he glanced in the rearview mirror, a dip in the majestic range allowed the day's last rays to be caught in its reflection, nearly blinding him. When he looked back again seconds later, over the supplies he'd crammed into the back of the Jeep, he was surprised to see a truck, maybe a quarter mile behind him, make the same turn, and then, immediately behind the truck, two other vehicles.

It was rare to see traffic on the narrow road this time of night.

Must be a wedding or some other event at Pray.

Pray Hot Springs Resort was an unusual breed of resort. Most the lodges or motels down the Paradise Valley catered either to the extremely wealthy or to the average Joe tourist. Its pool fed by a hot spring and a five-star restaurant made Pray a candidate for the rich, and they had plenty of options—including lodge-like cabins sitting high on a ridge overlooking Yellowstone Country—to satisfy their need for luxury and privacy; but over the years, the owners had worked hard to ensure the locals, especially kids, could enjoy Pray, too. It was a popular spot, one Will had been to many times, but not by choice. Will's experience at Pray over the years always resulted from being called out to back up the local sheriff.

Pray could be a little crazy. Especially after an evening event.

Will glanced in the mirror again.

The make of the second vehicle behind him, clearly a new and high-end vehicle, made him that much more sure that Pray was the venue for a happening. The Mercedes van appeared to be traveling in tandem with another of the same make. Will's LE experience told him the older model truck directly behind him had nothing to do with the pricey vans. Probably a worker headed back to a little rented cabin tucked away somewhere in the foothills after a day working at minimum wage in one of the Gardiner stores that catered to tourists.

His thoughts turned to the mission at hand. It would be like looking for a needle in a haystack. But if she had followed her instinct to avoid the trouble brewing for her if she stayed in the park—or if Emma was right and Two Coyote was the cub transplanted years ago from Glacier and was now following her instincts to head home—the route she'd likely take would coincide with the location the hikers had reported a wounded bear. And if she continued on that route, heading north and, ultimately, to Glacier, she would start by following the Absarokas.

The trail Will planned to set up camp along was one of several, but after nights of going over and over it in his mind, he had followed Trevor Nolan's vehicle to the Gardiner garbage transfer station and asked him what route he would take if he were a grizzly headed north.

196

Startled, Trevor had looked at him momentarily like he was crazy, then answered, "The Emigrant Creek trail." After a few more exchanges about the need for Gardiner or Park County to bear-proof the transfer station, Trevor had uncharacteristically shaken Will's hand and parted with the words, "Be safe."

Maybe he was crazy, Will thought now, but if so, he'd done crazier things. He was convinced Two Coyote had left—or, his greatest fear—been killed. He'd brought enough supplies to last a couple weeks. Besides, he'd wanted to check on the sheep.

By the time he'd reached the turn off to Pray, the truck behind him had turned its lights on.

One headlight, the left, remained dark.

As Will whizzed by the turn-off for Pray, the truck turned right, into the resort entrance. Seconds later, the two vans did, too.

Less than a mile later, just after the paved road turned to gravel, it hit Will.

The night he'd sat on the hill above his spread and watched Stucky return home from work, he'd noticed from the lights shining down his long gravel driveway that the left light appeared to be dimmed.

That had been several weeks ago. If not replaced, it would likely be dead by now.

Stucky was many things, but one thing he was not is a person who would strip down to shorts in public to soak his bloated belly in a hot springs pool filled with kids and local revelers—or attend a pricey function at Pray Hot Springs Resort.

With the lightest touch on its brakes, the right wheels of Will's Jeep lifted slightly off the gravel as he pulled into an abrupt left U-turn.

• • •

As she sat at the end of the couch closest to the window, under which she had placed the recliner years earlier, the night Will had brought him to the Stone House, Annie smiled at the sight of Johnny looking so relaxed and at home in it that he had pushed back to accommodate his long legs.

"What's so funny?" he asked, reaching for her hand with a quizzical grin.

"That was the judge's recliner," she answered. "No one's sat in it since he died."

Johnny bolted forward.

"Oh man, I'm sorry. You had just told me about that. I'm such an idiot...."

"No," Annie said, grabbing his extended hand. "Stay there. Please. I was smiling because it makes me happy to see you there."

Johnny eased back into the recliner, but this time kept it upright.

"Tell me about him." Annie's smile became wistful.

"He was something else," she said. "By the time I met him, he'd already had the stroke—that's why I was hired. But he was a legend here in the park. He was a hero to so many."

"What made him a hero?"

"His passion for this place. He always ruled by the law, but if there was ever some leeway, some precedence, he came down on the side of this park—its animals, its landscapes, and its people. He pushed the envelope, and a defendant found guilty in his courtroom always got an earful. People still quote him."

Annie could feel Johnny's eyes on her, felt bathed in his grin.

"Give me an example."

She couldn't help but smile back.

"Well, my personal favorite was when he sentenced this slick-looking New York attorney who was speeding and drunk when he hit and killed a grizzly bear to 'a two-week vacation at Yellowstone's version of the Ritz.' Which of course was the park's jail back then—a steel cage inside a brick box, with six beds and two exposed toilets. His comments like that would show up in papers across the country."

"A couple made their way up to Glacier," Johnny replied, clearly amused. "That must have been a hard act to follow."

"It still is. But what a gift he became to my mother and me. He may not have been able to speak by then—he could say a few words, and slowly his speech was becoming clearer—but I never had trouble understanding him. What he was feeling, what he wanted me to know. His mind was as sharp as ever.

"I honestly don't think my mother would be alive today if it weren't for the judge. He was the one who put the pieces together, figured out that she had been kidnapped by members of the Church of White Hope."

"They were trying to get you to resign, weren't they? They wanted you off the bench?"

Annie nodded.

"I'm no Judge Sherburne, but I guess I'm thought of as being too pro-environment, especially by the extraction industry that was using the Church as a front."

She paused, her thoughts instinctively turning to Will, to the irony that Will had despised Annie for allowing bison to go to slaughter—the hardest and most wretched decision Annie had ever been forced to make from the bench. And it hadn't just caused a rocky start to their professional relationship—Will as a backcountry ranger, bringing those he arrested before her in the courtroom; even after they'd fallen in love, Annie sensed he'd never forgiven her for her decision that she had no choice but to follow the letter of the Interagency Bison Management Plan.

"They thought they could scare me off the bench by kidnapping Mother."

She grew silent, her thoughts returning to that horrid day she'd watched as law enforcement unearthed the newly disturbed grave at the cemetery on the old Gardiner Road to find a metal box.

Inside was Eleanor Peacock's ear.

"They almost succeeded," Annie continued. "After it all ended, after we found Mother, and we asked the judge to continue living with us, the two of them became like this old married couple. Practically inseparable. It was the sweetest thing."

Sensing the melancholy that the memories still caused Annie, Johnny's face lit with the mischievous smile she knew from their college days.

"What do you think the Judge would do with the culprits who stole Stucky's sheep?"

It worked. Annie burst into laughter.

"Oh my god, imagine the quotes we'd get from that case."

Her giggling continued as Johnny sat straight up, donned a judicious face and deep voice; hand raised in the air, wielding an imaginary gavel.

"The defendant is found guilty as charged. Thirty-day sentence will be suspended." He bent forward, turning toward the imaginary defendant. "Now, how about joining me for dinner?"

Annie realized at that moment that she couldn't remember the last time she'd actually laughed. A good, self-surrendering laugh. The kind Johnny had always been capable of eliciting from her.

At the same time, there was nothing frivolous or lacking in depth about Johnny. She'd come to believe that growing up on a reservation, where tragedy was so commonplace, had given him wisdom and sensitivity—and the means of coping—that made him who he was.

Now he reached again for her hand.

"I'm sorry you lost him. But happy for you that he came into your life. And your mother's. Sometimes the Creator works in mysterious ways."

"He does indeed."

Annie felt Johnny's eyes on her as he said, "I heard an interesting rumor tonight, at the Yellowstone Grill."

Suspecting just what he had heard, Annie bought a few seconds to prepare herself by replying, "What was it?"

"I heard that folks believe Will's living in the backcountry, up near the Thunderer."

Annie sighed.

"Those aren't just rumors."

"I didn't think so," Johnny said. "And the bear? The wounded grizzly?"

"I can't get much in the way of answers from anyone I talk to in law enforcement, but the young bear biologist told me it's true too. Will's obsessed with protecting her."

Johnny shook his head.

"What a guy."

Annie couldn't respond.

"You're still in love with him, Annie," he said, squeezing her hand. "Aren't you?"

Annie turned her warm, dark eyes on Johnny and, as she had when Johnny told her he was leaving Seattle, the University of Washington, to move back to the reservation, she did not try to avoid letting him see the pain in them.

"Yes. I'm still in love with him."

Johnny inhaled a short, sharp breath.

"Where does that leave us?"

"I don't know," Annie replied. "I may never see Will again. I have this horrible fear, this horrible feeling...."

She shook her head as if trying to clear it from her mind.

"Well, you don't have to know. I know...I know that I've never stopped loving you. Not since I fell in love with you in college."

Tears streamed down Annie's cheek as he continued.

"But I also know that Will McCarroll saved my life. He's my brother, in a more real and powerful way than blood could ever make us brothers. And I know that some loves aren't meant to be anything more than caring, anything more than friendships."

He let go of her hand, leaned toward Annie, and cupped her chin in his hand.

"So don't worry about me. Worry about that crazy ranger of yours."

Finally, Annie let out a laugh.

Cheek still damp, she smiled and said, "You know it was Will who stole Stucky's sheep, don't you?"

Now Johnny burst into laughter.

"Seriously? How do you know?"

"Some things you just know."

"Maybe it's a good time for him to be out of touch with the rest of the world."

"What do you mean?"

"That Stucky sounds like a bad character to me. I've seen all the signs on his property. He's part of that Alliance, and they stand against everything Will's devoted his life to. I read where back East, they've become violent. That they bombed a monument to Thoreau. And it looks like there's a movement here, too. There are flyers posted all around Livingston for a quote-unquote *convention* they're holding this weekend. And according to the president of our board, who has high-level friends, they're responsible for our federal funding being cut for the Safe Crossings Project."

"Oh no, that's terrible. What will happen now?"

"Canada just stepped up. They're going to fund the entire project." Johnny took in a deep breath. "That means we can move forward quickly now. DuWayne already acquired easements for the first crossing, near Livingston."

"Johnny, that's incredible!" Annie cried.

"It is, isn't it?" Johnny replied. "The Canadians are so much further along in their wildlife crossing engineering than we are. They have modular units already constructed, and they're sending one to us. Right away. They're willing to delay a bridge they had planned for British Columbia to allow us to get started. After all the shenanigans with our president, the prime minister wants this to happen, and fast."

Annie could hear the excitement in Johnny's voice.

"We hired DuWayne's former professor at MSU, David Easton, to oversee installation. We just finished excavation. We're even hoping DuWayne can be back for the next crossing, in the Shields

Valley. Easton is already working with the Canadians on the plans. Now that we have the funding, we can really move forward quickly."

Johnny paused, as if he were still processing the new developments as he shared them with Annie.

"One of the prime minister's first requests was for a high-profile grand opening," he continued. "I don't blame him for wanting to rub the president's nose in the fact that Canada is paying for a project to protect *this* country's wildlife."

Johnny grew serious.

"And citizens," he added. "We can't forget how this all started. With the death of Tracy Blessings' daughter on the highway. And all the tragedy that has unfolded since."

Annie reached for his hand.

"No, we can't forget that. But right now we—*you*—have something to celebrate. While our officials are hell bent on removing protection from Yellowstone's grizzlies, I read recently that British Columbia just banned hunts. Canadians consider hunting grizzlies morally reprehensible."

"My people do, too," Johnny replied.

From the day she met him, Annie had seen the pride Johnny took in being Blackfeet, in his traditional heritage.

"Your people," she said, locking eyes with him, "value our wolves, our bison, our grizzlies. Your people recognize the gift they are."

Johnny smiled at the emotion in her voice.

"Many of your people do, too," he said. "Most importantly, *you* do. It's one of the reasons I fell in love with you, Annie."

Almost reflexively, Annie dropped her gaze, unable to see the pain that love had caused Johnny. But when he placed a hand under her chin, gently forcing their eyes to reconnect, Annie saw no resentment, no anger.

In those deep, dark eyes, Annie saw only kindness. Only love. "I'm headed up there tomorrow for the modulars' arrival and installation," Johnny said. "I'll have to stay there through the grand opening." He paused. "Would you be my guest for the grand opening? Maybe even come a couple days early and we could go over to British Columbia?"

Suddenly overcome with emotion, Annie squeezed his hand.

She sensed that Johnny could read what she was thinking: how important the new crossing would be to Will. To the animals he spent his life protecting.

How of all the ceremonies and events he'd been forced to attend over the years, this is the one he wouldn't want to miss.

"I would be honored," Annie said softly.

20

WILL PULLED HIS JEEP INTO the main parking lot, which was, as usual, crowded with SUVs, pickup trucks, and, for Pray, an unusual number of new-model sedans. The first part of the lot gave him a view of the narrow road that climbed the hill directly above the resort's main buildings. He could see dust kicked up from recent travel, but not the vehicles themselves. He continued forward and parked at the far south end of the building complex.

Getting out of the Jeep, he crossed to the Pray Grill, which overlooked the swimming pool, eyeing vehicles parked on that side of the building as he did so. Lots of pickups, but none running, so no way to tell in the dark if one had a burned-out headlight.

No sign of the two luxury vans.

Instead of going into the café, Will rounded the adjacent saloon—on the southwest corner of the complex that housed the café and hotel—where there were two more rows of parked cars. Again, no sign of the vehicles he'd seen turn down the Pray road in his rearview mirror.

Several people Will did not recognize stood smoking cigarettes or talking quietly outside the hotel's main entrance.

Keenly aware of his rumpled clothing, Will opened the door to the vestibule, lifted his ball cap, and ran a hand over his hair—thinning some, but still wild and plentiful at the age of fifty-six—then stepped inside the lobby, which was teeming with activity. That—the activity—did not come as a surprise, but the age, dress, and demeanor of this crowd, though lively, was different; not the normal chaos of children with parents chasing after them, or couples escaping for a night alone, or small groups of friends out for dinner, or to party. This was clearly an event of some sort that had rented the resort facilities for the night.

As he slipped inside, Will's gaze was drawn to the back hallway, where he saw two well-dressed men and a woman with long dark hair, drinks in hand and backs to him, disappear through the swinging door that had been propped open. He knew from experience the hallway led to an outside exit at the back of the compound. Fleeting as the sight was, something about one of the men caused Will to begin working his way across the crowded room toward the door.

Until a hand on his shoulder stopped him.

"Ranger McCarroll?"

Will turned to face Sam Calhoun, owner of one of the most popular—and dangerous—bars in Gardiner. Will had been called to The Wild Gander more times than he could count, most recently when a patron had his finger chopped off on the bar itself for snitching on a local ring of elk-antler poachers.

Still eyeing the hallway, Will replied, "What's going on here, Sam?" as a woman, this one younger and dressed in business attire, disappeared into it.

Will could see Sam was enjoying his night away from work. His breath reeked of alcohol.

Sam nodded his head toward the crowd milling around the lobby, most of whom had broken into small groups and appeared to be engaged in serious conversation. Several seemed focused on literature or brochures of some sort that were being read aloud or handed around the group.

"It's a local get-together of like-minded citizens," Sam answered drunkenly. Will recognized the terminology immediately as that used by ultra-conservative and anti-environmental residents of Montana who were banding together to upend everything Yellowstone stood for. "Before the legislative session starts next month."

"You mean a local Alliance convention?"

Distracted by all the women in the crowd—many of them in their early- to mid-thirties or forties—Sam clearly failed to catch the sarcasm in Will's voice, and the fact that the group's recently adopted name was supposedly a secret known only to its members.

"Yep, something like that," he answered. "That's why I was surprised to see your boss here. I mean, a liberal appointed him, didn't he?"

Will visibly startled at this news.

"You mean Peter Shew—" he began to reply, shocked to think Peter would get involved with the local right-wingers, when suddenly it clicked for him.

The man who appeared familiar. The dark, slicked-back hair, broad shoulders, pricey-looking jacket.

It had been Al Gonzalez, superintendent of Yellowstone.

Sam was too far gone to notice any reaction in Will's expression. "You here to provide security?" he asked as he finally tried to focus glazed eyes upon Will, and the fact he wasn't in uniform.

"Maybe undercover?"

His brow creased in puzzlement.

"Hey, how come I haven't seen you driving around town for a while?"

Will observed another female member of the group disappear into the hallway.

"Yeah," he said, now eager to lose Sam. "I'm undercover. Listen, there'll be sheriff's deputies out there tonight, so I hope you got a room here. You better not try to drive back to Gardiner."

"Yeah, yeah," Sam nodded, "you're right."

His gaze moving to the front desk, where several female convention-goers, who looked easily as tipsy as Sam, had apparently come up with the same idea. "Maybe I'll even get lucky," he added, before making a beeline toward them.

While Will's attire would've fit in most days or even evenings at the resort, he could feel the attention he was drawing, which would soon mean someone else recognizing him.

Right now, that was the last thing Will wanted.

Pivoting quickly, he left the lobby through the front entrance he'd passed through just minutes earlier.

Outside, a stiff wind and threatening skies had moved the smokers and loiterers elsewhere. Pulling on the visor of his cap, head down, Will rounded the compound to the back side.

The principal buildings at Pray—the hotel, saloon, café, and pool to the south and store/coffee shop and a strip of motel rooms to the north—sat at the bottom of a gulch encircled on three sides by serious foothills. Directly behind the hotel and pool compound stood an oversized barn and a corral, in which several horses still munched contentedly on their evening serving of alfalfa hay, no doubt after carrying inexperienced riders along the trails that networked the entire Paradise Valley.

The barn, horses, and a garden that supplied fresh organic vegetables to the restaurant just meters away provided some measure of camouflage for Will as he headed toward his destination: the sound of voices, raised in song, coming from the second—and higher—of two hills behind the resort, both of which housed rows of the resort's most coveted cabins.

Small lanterns lit the stairs cut into the hillside to allow guests easy access from the offerings of the resort to the privacy and luxury of the structures sitting high above the valley floor. Will had only responded to the most exclusive row of housing—on the top hill—once, as a backup to the Park County sheriff, when a New York magazine executive's wife reported $200,000 in jewelry missing after she left their cabin unlocked—an insurance-fraud crime that turned out never to have happened.

But that now provided him a sense of the setting above. He moved due south, just under the ridge, until the first hillside forced him to start climbing. As he did, the two teepees that sat just below the highest ridge came into sight. A campfire burned out of control between them, circled but largely ignored by at least a dozen people moving about, some singing and swaying, others gathered in small groups.

The combination of fire, wind, singing, and clouds that moved across the moon so rapidly they allowed the spectacular mountains—Gallatins to the west, insanely jagged and towering Absarokas immediately east and even brief glimpses of the Crazies to the north—to appear and disappear in an instant made for an eerie feeling as Will agilely climbed the steep, rocky slope that led to the first row of cabins above the resort. He paused briefly behind an antique caboose car at the end of the row. Usually vacant, it had apparently been put to use for the event, as one of its windows stood open.

Ducking in and out of the shadows, Will reached the north end of the row of cabins and was about to cross the small dirt road that switch-backed up the hillside when ahead, about fifty meters, he saw a stopped car, lights on. A security guard stood at the driver's window. As the driver and guard talked, a man and a woman suddenly exited the cabin closest to them, which was brightly lit on both floors, and approached the car.

The man instantly looked familiar to Will. *Gonzalez.*

After exchanging only a few words with the couple, the guard waved the car through, then flagged it into a small outcropping on the road to park. Will watched as its occupants climbed out of the vehicle.

Mentally chastising himself for not having the foresight to take his binoculars with him when he left his Jeep in the parking lot, Will suddenly reversed course and headed back to the caboose. He had seen camping gear on the bed in the room through the open window.

Minutes later, high-end binoculars in hand, he was back at the same spot. The woman had disappeared. Gonzalez now stood talking quietly to three men, while in the foreground, the guard waved another car through.

Will lifted the binoculars, adjusted the focus.

Senator Eugene Simms, the conservative politician from Nevada. After succeeding in convincing Nevada's conservative populace to elect his hand-picked candidates in the last election, Simms had forced the sale of 1.9 million acres of Nevada desert that had belonged to the state's citizens since statehood was granted in 1864. That success lifting his wings, he had recently started an organization called American Lands for Profitable Enjoyment.

Will watched as the senator patted one of his companions on the back, saw them lift their heads in laughter. When another car coming up the hill caused the group to look north, in Will's direction, Will turned the binocs on the companion.

"Holy shit," he whispered.

Robert Clay, of the infamous and ungodly wealthy Clay dynasty. It was a fluke that Will would be able to identify him, as Will wasn't someone who kept up on the political or news scene, but he had been assigned to protect Clay when he visited the park four years earlier due to threats made by radical environmentalists who believed Clay's visit was not, as he claimed, as a tourist, but instead signaled the start of a scoping project—its goal being to eventually drill for gas, oil, and gold under the park's surface.

Will had despised the man on first sight and kept his distance, only ensuring that the park-pampered business tycoon remained safe.

Now he watched as Gonzalez and his three male companions disappeared into the back door of the large, well-lit cabin. The guard remained in place.

Head reeling from the thoughts racing through it—Gonzalez, Simms, and Clay, all at some kind of secret meeting just outside Yellowstone—Will had only moments to evaluate his options.

The guard and ongoing activity meant he would have to retreat, climb the foothill to the south, and approach the cabin from that direction.

By the time Will made his way up the south hill, everyone seemed to have moved inside the cabin, where some kind of gathering was obviously taking place. He could see the guard, who now sat facing the road on the open tailgate of his parked pickup, clearly screening for any newcomers.

Will waited, and when a large, rapidly moving cloud obscured the moon, he scrambled down the steep, vegetation-less hill. Just as he reached the ridgeline upon which the lit cabin sat, its back door opened.

The only source of cover were the two teepees.

Will sprinted behind the one closest to him. When he heard footsteps headed his direction, he dropped to the ground, lifted the buffalo hide covering the wood frame of the teepee, and rolled inside.

21

INSIDE THE RICHLY FURNISHED LOG cabin—whose walls were crowded with the heads of trophy animals—over a dozen well-dressed and manicured men and women mingled, helped themselves to a colorful array of appetizers at the food bar, or stood waiting for a tuxedo-clad bartender to serve them their drink of choice.

One woman, however, shied away from conversation. Tonight, uncharacteristically, the coarse-looking politician, who was recently featured in a campaign ad showing her shooting a drone out of the sky, wore a tasteful black dress and two-inch heels, giving her already imposing stature a slight boost. Nodding curtly at any attendees who looked to be approaching her, she mostly kept her eyes glued to the cabin's back door.

When it opened and the group of three men entered, she raised her hands and clapped loudly, in a manner that clearly signaled a call for silence.

No one, it seemed, cared—or dared—to disregard the signal.

"It looks like we're all here," she said, forcing an unnatural smile. "If you'd please take a seat, we can get started."

With the exception of the three newcomers, who remained standing next to her, in front of the vast stone fireplace, everyone scurried to find a spot.

"Thank you all for coming," she started. "As most of you know, my name is Liz Conway. I'm one of the founders of the Alliance for Economic Progress and currently a state senator." This time the smile she managed, along with a cutesy wink, was sincere. "And as most of you know, I'm running to become Montana's first female United States senator!"

The applause was immediate, followed by those seated around the vast living room rising for a standing ovation.

Nodding her pleasure, Conway held her hands up in a modest protest, but allowed the clapping to go on.

Two of the men standing behind her reached out and patted her proudly on the back.

"Enough, enough," she protested. "Enough about me. I'm so pleased with tonight's turnout, such a lovely evening. We have two days of fun events planned, during which this carefully selected group will meet from time to time. More on that before we adjourn. I promise to try to get you back to the ballroom in time to enjoy the band, and our surprisingly large local turnout. But for now, we have important work to get started on, and I'd like to introduce these gentlemen who are here to ensure that we do, indeed, accomplish our goals."

She turned to the men standing behind her.

"I'd like to start by introducing Senator Eugene Simms from the state of Nevada. As you all know, Senator Simms is responsible for groundbreaking legislation that will force the feds to turn over federal land to the State of Nevada. We have him to thank for breaking that barrier and providing a model for the rest of us. Senator Simms…"

Simms stepped forward to another round of applause reverberating throughout the structure.

A polished public figure, he commanded a different level of attention than Conway.

"Thank you," he said to the room at large, then turned back to Conway. "And thank you, Senator Conway, for your support and initiative in moving our important agenda forward."

Turning again to those gathered on plush leather furniture or standing against the wall, where a slightly opened window allowed a light breeze from the west to enter, he continued.

"What we accomplished in Nevada is unprecedented; however, environmental groups and bleeding-heart liberals are hell bent on stopping the public land transfer movement. They are determined to allow lands rich in resources to lie fallow while the citizens of this country suffer, and governments face budget crisis after budget crisis. While citizens go without health care and infrastructures break down, we are supposed to be worrying about wolves and bears and—this is one of their key words—'ecosystems,' who they've shown over and over they can't even manage sensibly.

"It's ludicrous and personally, I believe it's not only shameful, it's a sin."

Heads nodded while more than one "Amen" could be heard.

"We now have a national crisis on our hands, especially here on Western hands and lands, and we need to take immediate steps— perhaps even drastic steps—to stop this crisis from worsening and get this country back on track. What lies on and beneath these federal lands are resources capable of turning this crisis around. Capable of restoring the greatness of this country. But they will lie unmanaged and untouched in federal hands.

"This meeting, and others like it across the country, is the start. It's up to us, all of us; it's up to the states to take control and save America. Save *Americans*. Not wolves. Not bison. And certainly not man-eating grizzly bears."

A voice from the room could be heard muttering, "Exactly. That's why that Safe Crossings Project is bullshit."

Simms was on it in a flash, eyes scanning the group.

"Who said that? Raise your hand, please."

A young man who looked more like a Montana fly fishing guide than a politician raised his right hand.

"Please," Simms said. "Introduce yourself and repeat your comment. I'm not sure everyone in the room could hear it or understands it."

Seeing the young man, Conway's face contorted with confusion. And concern.

Looking immensely pleased with himself, the young man stood up.

"My name's Eli Walters," he said. "I'm a hunter and advocate for a local elk foundation. I came here tonight as part of the Alliance, but when I saw people like the superintendent of Yellowstone and some of our local politicians heading up the hill, I followed. And I'm glad I did."

Silence prevailed for several seconds, as Simms and Conway literally put their heads together in a rushed, whispered discussion.

When Simms broke away, he said, "Mr. Walters, would you like to expand upon your comment? Something about the Safe Crossings Project?"

"I sure would. The last thing we need is our federal lands and money being used to build bridges and underpasses that allow our elk, wolves, and now, grizzlies, since they're losing protection they never should have had in the first place, to walk safely out of Yellowstone country. We hunters are already dealing with enough hardships. The fires in Montana have destroyed over a million acres. That's a million acres of habitat. Do you know how hard it's going to be to find elk this year, let alone what your odds will be if you have a wolf tag? Or—worse—a grizzly tag?"

His comments resonated with many in the group, who either talked quietly among themselves or sat nodding their heads in agreement.

Simms and the others at the front stayed silent, simply observing the response.

"Thank you, young man," he said when it quieted down, "not for crashing a private meeting, which you should be careful about, especially these days," he added, shaking his index finger at him good-naturedly, which met with numerous chuckles, "but for letting us know we'd better be a little more vigilant. And more importantly, thank you for sharing your sentiments about another left-wing, environmentalist-based project that this country, this region, simply does not need and cannot afford."

"You're very welcome, sir," the hunter said. Nodding at the rest of the group, he added, "And thank you for letting me have my say. I'll go now and leave you to your business."

As he exited the door, he paused, looked back over his shoulder, and added, "You people are our only hope. You are our heroes."

This time the applause was thunderous.

Before it died completely down, a smiley-faced Simms cleared his throat.

"That was powerful. I want to add, however, that thanks to our new president and the encouragement of Mr. Clay and myself, any federal funding for the project the young man's talking about has been cut."

A male voice yelled out, "But Senator, didn't you see today's announcement from Canada?"

Taken off guard, Simms visibly bristled. He'd had enough surprises for the night.

Conway, too, looked startled. Immediately, she stepped back, grabbed the phone she'd left on the fireplace mantel, and began tapping keys on it.

Resorting to his oft-used strategy, Simms replied, "Of course, I've seen it. And it doesn't trouble me at all. Now, let's move on. It's now…it's my pleasure to introduce a man who not all of you may know, but believe me, he's had an impact on your life on a daily basis. Ladies and gentlemen, please welcome CEO of World Extraction Inc, the largest oil and gas production company on the planet, Mr. Robert Clay."

"Thank you, thank you," Clay said, stepping forward. Then, turning to Simms, he added, "I don't mean to correct you, Senator Simms, but your kind introduction omitted the fact that WEI is also the biggest mining—with a focus on gold—conglomerate in the world." Turning back to his audience, he continued, "And, seriously, folks, let's not forget what mining our precious metals can do to help this crisis; to help folks like you, and your constituents who are just trying to get by. Just trying to make ends meet."

Another hand flew up, this time belonging to a heavyset man in his late forties.

"Sir, Mr. Clay. I'm a state representative from Park County. I have to tell you, sir, that gold mining here is already a huge controversy. And the environmentalists have our senior senator on board. Our governor, too. Of course, they're both Democrats."

This seemed to irritate Clay.

"So what's your point?"

Startled, and clearly rattled, the man stammered, " I just thought it was relevant."

Clay let out a belly laugh that startled even Simms. Conway just smiled, clearly amused.

"Believe me, it won't be relevant for long," he replied. "Our movement is gaining momentum, huge, huge momentum. Thanks to Americans like you and local chapters of the Alliance, like this." His eyes scanned the rest of the group. "Any other questions?"

No one seemed inclined to risk the same fate as the state representative from Park County.

"Okay, then, it's my great pleasure and honor to introduce a very special guest who flew all the way here from Brazil to join us." He winked at the crowd. "As you might guess, in light of the current historic progress this country is making in terms of protecting our borders, especially from our neighbors to the south, it took just a little help to ensure that my executive vice president of WEI's operations in South America did not experience any delays at the border. Ladies and gentlemen, please welcome Señor Raul Javari."

Lukewarm applause greeted the dark-skinned, dark-haired man, who had stood silent and without expression until now, as he stepped forward and nodded in acknowledgment.

Clay, looking irritated at the reception his EVP had received, made the decision to spare him from questioning.

"I think over the next couple days' discussions, we will all find the input Señor Javari has to offer to be invaluable as we welcome him as a partner who stands to strengthen our movement not only here in our great country, but potentially expand it on a scale that we've never before imagined possible."

He looked over at Conway, who got the cue.

"Okay, then," she said in a businesslike tone, "all of you have received the tentative schedule of sub-committee meetings. Word of these meetings is not to be shared with anyone. In the event we schedule additional meetings, or change meeting times, you will be notified via text, so keep your cell phones on you at all times."

Her eyes searched the group and came to rest on the superintendent of Yellowstone.

"Now, with the exception of Superintendent Gonzalez and the gentlemen already up here, the rest of you are free to go. Enjoy the special dinner and entertainment we've taken great pains to plan for you."

• • •

The footsteps that sent Will scrambling under the edge of the teepee paused only briefly, near the teepee's opening, before retreating back in the direction of the cabin.

After half an hour of silence, Will belly-crawled toward the door flap, which hung loosely open and faced the cabin in which he'd seen the three men disappear.

He could see the truck the guard had been sitting on, in the same location. But no guard. From where he lay, he was unable to see the cabin itself. Assessing his position, Will decided that the other side of the teepee's opening might provide an angle of vision that would allow him to see more.

Rolling sideways, he crossed the patch of light entering the teepee from the campfire, moon, and cabin's exterior floodlights.

The cabin came into view.

At first the figure was lost in the shadows, but then it moved ever so slightly, and Will's eyes riveted on him.

The guard.

He was standing up against the cabin, directly below an open window.

Will watched him stand there, silent, barely moving, for a quarter hour. Then, suddenly, the guard darted out of the shadows, into the light, and toward his truck.

As the back door to the cabin opened and men and women flowed out, the guard nodded casually, wishing several a good evening.

For several seconds, Will dared to hope the distraction of those departing the cabin would be the opportunity he needed to slide back under the teepee's bison hide and take off down the hill.

But while some of those exiting the cabin climbed into vehicles that headed down the steep drive, a steady stream started down the steps on foot, heading toward the resort's main buildings.

At the bottom of the stairs carved into the hillside, several stopped to talk.

Will noted that Gonzalez, Simms, Clay, and his companion were not among those leaving through the back door.

He quickly realized that he would have to stay put and wait for the house to empty, and the guard to leave, before making a run for his Jeep parked below.

Will watched for several minutes as the guard walked to the top of the steps to peer down in the direction of the resort. Seemingly satisfied, he proceeded to walk a half circle around the cabin, eyes scanning every direction.

Then, to Will's relief, the guard opened the cabin's back door, and with one glance back over his shoulder, disappeared inside.

22

"WHAT THE FUCK?" SENATOR SIMMS turned blazing eyes on Liz Conway. "What the hell was that jackass talking about, and why wasn't I informed?"

The house had emptied of the bartender and other meeting participants, and now only Conway, Simms, Javari, Gonzalez, and Clay remained, scattered about the furniture the others had occupied minutes earlier.

Satisfied that the rest of the group had joined the activities below, the guard stepped inside and now stood, silent, in the back corner of the room, next to the back door.

"Don't look at me," Conway cried. "I'm not your assistant. I didn't know anything about the Canadians' announcement either." Sarcasm tinging her voice, she added, "It's been a slightly busy day for me. I didn't exactly have time to be glued to my phone or computer."

At that, she tossed her phone onto the rough-hewn coffee table, held up by sawn-off antlers.

"There," she said. "That's what he was talking about."

Seated closest to the table, Gonzalez reached for the phone and, after adjusting his glasses, began to read aloud.

"This is from the *New York Times*. The Canadian government today announced its intention to fund a troubled environmental project for which Canada had previously agreed to provide minimal funding, but whose U.S. federal funding had recently been cut. The Safe Crossings Project, begun by well-known American legal analyst Tracy Blessings of Seattle, Washington, has struggled with multiple recent tragedies. After her daughter died when the bus she and other teens were riding in collided with an elk on Interstate 90 as they returned to Seattle from Yellowstone National Park, Blessings turned her grief into action to ensure other families would not experience the same loss. The Safe Crossings Project was formed to construct bridges and underpasses for wildlife to be able to bypass highways, including the interstate that Kylie Blessings died on. Shortly after the project's founding, Ms. Blessings was found unconscious in Glacier National Park. She had been shot. The investigation into her shooting is ongoing, as Ms. Blessings remains hospitalized and in a coma. Under the previous Administration, the project had the support of the U.S. government; however, with the new Administration in place, and a third tragedy, in which the project's civil engineer was seriously injured in an automobile accident, the White House recently pulled all funding.

"Today, through his spokesman and lawyer, Michael Kornberg, Canada's prime minister—the country's first indigenous leader— announced that Canada will provide all the project's funding, which is estimated to be in the millions."

Gonzalez shook his head in dismay as he lowered the phone enough for his eyes to sweep the rest of the group.

"And listen to this," he said, lifting the phone back to eye level. "Plans are in the works for a grand opening ceremony that Kornberg claims, quote-unquote, will make Canada, Canadians, and the rest of the Safe Crossings Project partners proud, and let the world know that despite recent strains in their relationship, Canada is committed to strong leadership when it comes to environmental responsibility and being a good neighbor."

The group fell into a brief, stunned silence.

"How can I just be learning this?" Simms said when Gonzalez tossed the phone back on the table in disgust. "Why wouldn't I have been given a heads up so we could have stopped it? The whole point was to shut down the project by getting federal funding pulled. And we did that."

"Those fucking Canucks," Clay added. "This makes us look terrible. Weak and ineffectual."

"I agree," Simms replied. "And it won't please the president to hear what the prime minister inferred about his leadership and responsibility."

Javari cleared his throat and in perfect English, but a thick accent, announced, "My president has been under attack as well."

No one, however, paid him any attention.

When Conway leaned forward to retrieve her phone from the table, drawing Clay's attention again, he seized on the moment.

"You said you could handle this."

"My god," she replied sharply. "With everything that's happened so far, who would have believed the fucking project *wouldn't* shut down?"

Clay glanced back at his own phone, where he'd been frantically Googling for information.

"Look at this. They've already issued a formal thank-you to the Canadian prime minister; a joint statement saying, 'It's unfortunate our new president took deliberate steps that jeopardize Montana's citizens and the state's precious wildlife, which bring millions of tourists to our state, providing essential income our citizens rely upon.'"

Conway shook her head.

"And from what I'd heard, they've already obtained most of the easements they need, and according to my sources, the property owners who've already signed on have all agreed that title to the easement will be held jointly by the property owner, the federal— not state—government, and the Safe Crossings Project. The only exception I've heard is with the tribes. The head of the project's Blackfeet, and he made sure the tribes get ownership when it expands to the reservations." She shook her head in dismay. "So this'll actually increase the amount of federal property—prime federal property—in Montana."

"More federal lands," Simms said in disgust.

"And, of course, most of the passageways animals use when they leave the park are on federal land," Gonzalez said. "The only good news is that once we get those lands turned over to the state, we can make passage so difficult with projects like the Antelope Mines that the animals never even make it to the crossings these people are trying to build."

"That's too uncertain," Simms said adamantly, "and too far down the road. Projects like this Safe Crossings send a message that your state doesn't care about the historical mining industries—gold and silver—that made Montana great. Oro y Plata. The Treasure

State motto. It makes a mockery of our movement, at a critical time. And it sure as hell damages our base. We have to stop it."

No one paid any attention when the guard moved silently across the back wall of the room and disappeared into the kitchen, beyond which was the cabin's only bathroom.

Gonzalez spoke again, quietly and with a tone that brooked no nonsense.

"Yes, we have to stop it."

"I agree" Conway said. "I'd hoped that Stucky's bringing the domestic sheep in would scare the Canadians off—when they heard our bighorn populations were dying from the pneumonia the domestics transmitted to them. Their biologists are paranoid about that type of thing." She grew quiet, thinking, then added, "What about parvo? Parvo would do it, wouldn't it? All we'd have to do is go and round up a bunch of dogs on the Crow or Blackfeet reservations. Hell, any of our reservations. Then turn them loose in the park. That would make the Canadians think twice about our wolves ending up there."

"Parvo's not an option. At least not anymore, with the Canadians stepping in. It would take time," Gonzalez answered. "And the goal we've all agreed upon is to not even let the Safe Crossings Project get off the ground."

"Nobody expected it to move forward after Tracy Blessings was shot," Conway said, throwing a scathing look Clay's way. Turning to Simms, she added, "Your idea to get the federal funding cut seemed unbeatable."

The room fell quiet.

It was Javari who broke the silence.

"In my country, I know what we'd do."

Everyone but Clay shot him a quizzical look.

"In my country," he continued, "the miners go in and eliminate the obstacles."

"What do you mean?" Conway asked.

Javari smiled.

"Wipe them out."

"Who?" Conway persisted, clearly confused.

"They call them the Lost Tribes," Javari responded cheerfully, the note of pride in his deep voice unmistakable. "The uncontacted tribes. We have the same problem you have. We, too, have *los liberals* trying to protect the lands. Only in Brazil, it's the tribes and the lands they have occupied for centuries, not the animals, they are protecting.

"Those lands are vast, and they are rich, as your lands are rich. My country is poor, very poor. And those lands where only one hundred or so small tribes live stand to make the federal government and companies like WEI very profitable, and that money—how is it you say?—rains down on the rest of us.

"In my country," he continued, "that's what we would do. We would destroy them."

Several voices spoke in unison. "*Destroy who?*"

Javari smiled.

"The crossings for the wild animals, of course. We would destroy them. Bomb them."

Silence fell over the room again.

"He may have a point," Clay said. "Hell, they've been bombing back East and gotten away with it."

He turned to Conway, who still held her phone in hand. "Does that article say anything about a timeline? Where the project stands?"

Conway scrolled down, skimming the *New York Times* article, then shook her head.

"No."

Javari, however, wasn't quite finished.

"Didn't the article say something about a grand opening?"

Eyes met across the room, but again, no one responded to Javari, or even dared voice what the Brazilian was suggesting.

"I dunno," was all Simms would say, shaking his head.

"I like it," Clay said. "The grand opening...We might even be able to make it look like one of the alt right groups back East was responsible. I think I have connections that could accomplish that."

"It's desperate," Conway offered. "But it definitely would make a statement. We wouldn't look weak anymore, would we?"

"We have to do something," Gonzalez said. He paused, then added, quietly, "And frankly, I feel like I've already taken enough heat without Yellowstone's wolf packs being wiped out."

"What do you mean?" Clay asked.

"The bison killings, two grizzlies euthanized, the bighorn. Hell, firing McCarroll. Those didn't exactly reflect well on me. The fucking National Parks Association just named me worst Park Superintendent in the park system."

"Yes," Simms said, nodding his head in commiseration. "I know it hasn't been easy. We need to give you credit for the hits you've taken, Al."

"I was willing to do it. For the greater good..."

As a successful businessman, Clay had never needed—nor in his opinion, stooped to honing—the diplomatic skills of a practiced politician, like the one sitting next to him.

"Cut the bullshit, Gonzalez," he broke in. "You know damn well you're going to be well rewarded. We don't go back on our promises, not if you keep yours. Once this is over, your bank account and title—a high-level job in the new Administration—will sound a lot more impressive than head of a national park that no longer exists—or, at the very least, has been cut in half."

Gonzalez bristled at being called out.

"I've put three decades into getting where I am," he said. "My reputation was gold before this group started turning Yellowstone upside down."

"I don't know that I'd call it gold," Clay replied, nodding his head, his eyes intense. "When you asked to meet with us, we did our homework. We discovered you and your wife were living beyond your means. What you've put up with for us since then has been penny ante compared to what you stand to gain."

"I'm still getting beat up," Gonzalez replied heatedly. "*USA Today* just raked me over the coals for firing McCarroll."

Conway appeared amused by the friction, while Simms, holding a straightened right arm forward, as if to ward off evil, was determined to defuse it.

"Enough. Divisiveness isn't going to get us anywhere. Especially this weekend, when we have a lot to accomplish."

Jumping on the opportunity to change the direction of the conversation, he homed in on Gonzalez.

"What's the latest on McCarroll? Didn't you say he'd pretty much disappeared last time I talked to you?"

Still visibly angered by the exchange with Clay, Gonzalez let out a bitter half-laugh.

"Disappeared? I know damn well where he is. Emma Day, our bear biologist, just reported to Peter Shewmaker that McCarroll's living in the backcountry, up near the Thunderer. He's..."

The sudden creak of the back screen door opening stopped him mid-sentence.

"*Not anymore he isn't.*"

All heads turned to that corner of the room, where two men had just stepped inside the cabin.

The guard.

And, hands cuffed behind his back, Will McCarroll.

23

"I FOUND HIM LISTENING OUTSIDE the window," the guard announced, nodding toward the back wall of the cabin.

The leather flap on the belt holder of his handgun stood open, indicating he'd recently drawn the weapon.

Of the entire group, all of whom had now jumped to their feet, Gonzalez appeared the most startled.

"Who is this?" Simms said, beelining toward the two, then grabbing the neck of Will's t-shirt and twisting it, forcing Will to face him.

Blood dripped from above Will's left eye.

"I'll tell you who it is," Gonzalez said, staying where he'd been seated. "Senator Simms, let me introduce you to the famous Will McCarroll."

While the name was lost on the Brazilian, it was not on Conway, Simms, and especially Clay, who looked ready to implode.

Turning to the guard, Clay demanded, "What's he heard?"

The guard nodded at Will—who, staring ahead, remained silent—and replied, "We'll have to ask him."

"I want answers, and I want them now," said Clay, coming eye to eye with Will as Simms stepped aside.

"What are you doing here?"

Will did not blink, even as the blood reached his eye, seeping into it.

"I came for the event."

"So why were you outside the window?"

Will trained his eyes on Gonzalez.

"When I walked into the lobby, I saw my former boss heading out the back door." He paused. "My curiosity got the best of me."

"That still doesn't answer my question. Why were you up here, outside at the window?"

"That's the best answer you're going to get."

Clay turned on the guard with a vengeance.

"You came highly recommended to us. We were told there's no one better. Now look what we're dealing with."

"Mr. Clay," the guard replied, without a hint of apology in his voice, "I don't know who this character is. Apparently, some of you do, but I can tell you: he's no run-of-the-mill party crasher.

"The only way he got anywhere near this place tonight was by scaling the hills south of here, then slipping down a steep rocky slope in the dark. He's no amateur, believe me."

Gonzalez had joined the group at the back of the room.

"That's an understatement. He's the best law enforcement officer Yellowstone's ever seen," he offered. "And a royal pain in the ass."

He had avoided eye contact with Will until now, but finally, looking straight into Will's steely gaze, Gonzalez asked, "Why are you here, McCarroll?"

Will met Gonzalez's gaze without flinching.

"I'm a private citizen now, Superintendent. I don't answer to you anymore."

"You might want to rethink that," was all Gonzalez said.

"Get him out of here," Clay ordered the guard, with a jerk of his head toward the door. "Now."

He reached inside the pocket of his sports coat.

"Here's my key. I'm in the big house at the far end. Make sure he's secure. And don't screw up again. You hear?"

Grabbing the key, the guard swung Will around by the shoulder, answering, "Yes sir." Then with 200+ pounds of muscled force, he shoved Will out the door hard enough to send him to his knees.

Once they'd disappeared and Conway had closed and locked the door behind them, Gonzalez shook his head slowly, eyes closing briefly, as if trying to ward off the sight of Will McCarroll.

"This is bad," he muttered, under his breath. "This is really bad."

• • •

After the guard disappeared through the back door with Will in tow, while the rest of the group engaged in urgent discussion, Gonzalez stepped outside, into the quickly cooling night air.

Lifting his phone, he pressed "3" on its speed dial. A male voice answered on the first ring.

"Good evening, Superintendent."

"Shewmaker, what the hell is Will McCarroll up to?"

"Pardon me?" Peter Shewmaker replied.

"McCarroll. I'm at an Alliance fundraiser at Pray, and McCarroll showed up. Don't try to tell me he's aligned with the Alliance. I won't buy it."

A brief silence followed.

"I can't answer that, Al," Shewmaker replied, then, after a brief hesitation, added, "but I know someone who might be able to. Emma Day, our bear biologist."

"Call her."

"I will, sir, but at this hour, I can't promise she'll answer."

"Then keep calling until she does. And get back to me."

"Will do."

24

HANDCUFFED TO A CHAIN THE guard had wrapped around the base of the toilet, and then, as added security, around Will's waist, Will spent the night locked in a windowless bathroom on the second floor of the house Clay had rented.

After the door closed, leaving Will in total darkness, he heard a heavy piece of furniture being pushed up against its other side.

Neither man had spoken, with the exception of when Will tried to shoulder the guard down the steep stairs to the first floor.

The guard's "You stupid son of a bitch" was followed by a punch to Will's gut.

Alone in the dark, the conversation Will overheard as he stood outside the window of the cabin in which the meeting of high-level park, government, and business officials was taking place, kept repeating itself, like a reel, in his head.

They were talking about bombing the grand opening of the Safe Crossings Project.

Johnny Yellow Kidney would be there.

And so, Will suspected, his thoughts going back to the day he'd run into Johnny at the courthouse…so might Annie.

Will had to get free. He had to warn Annie and Johnny.

But that would clearly not be easy. The guard knew what he was doing. No amount of struggle or force loosened the chain's hold on Will.

Will finally fell into a light, restless sleep, his head resting against the toilet seat. He awoke before the morning's light crept under the crack between the door and the wood-planked floor.

Soon he heard conversation downstairs. While he could not make any of it out, he had come to recognize Clay's and the guard's voices.

When the door slammed shut, Will called out.

"Guard. Hey, guard."

A creak on the stairs told him his captor had stepped onto one of the lower stairs. Then silence.

The next thing Will heard was the front door opening again.

And then shutting.

Both men had left the house.

25

DRESSED IN JEANS, A RED, white, and blue striped long-sleeved v-neck, and a buckskin vest whose fringe shook with her every hand gesture, Liz Conway stood proudly at the front of the restaurant at Pray Hot Springs, which had been turned into a conference room, rows of folding chairs filling the space usually occupied by elegantly set tables. It was standing room only.

"Good morning," Conway called out with a wave, before stepping up to the podium's microphone. "I hope you all enjoyed the extravagant breakfast bar we arranged to make sure you have stamina for what we have planned for you today!"

Laughter and a few shouts of "Yes!" and "Thank you!" greeted her.

"I can't tell you how pleased I am to see this amazing turnout for the first annual meeting of the Western chapter of the Alliance for Economic Progress!"

Polite applause rippled through the room.

"We may be little old Montana, but the world has taken notice of us, hasn't it? And with your support for the Alliance's agenda—

everything from fighting big government to cutting your taxes, health care reform, border security, and, our highest priority, the transfer of public lands to states—the Montana chapter of AFEP is helping to lead the charge. And the change."

As the response grew more enthusiastic, Conway paused like the seasoned pro she was to allow more applause. She used the opportunity to make eye contact with members of her audience, many of whom she recognized from past gatherings, protests, or simply social media. She was taken aback, however, by the number she did not recognize, and the presence of several American Indians, scattered throughout the room.

"Again, I'm delighted by the attendance today, and the diversity represented," she declared. "We will get started with the great agenda we have for you in just a few minutes," she continued, "but first, I have an announcement to make. One that calls for celebration. The Montana Department of Environmental Quality has just approved the Antelope Mines application for mining gold literally just above where we now sit: on Emigrant Peak!"

Expecting cheers to rock the room, Conway was shocked when, along with applause and cheers, one by one, at least twenty of those seated in front of her rose to their feet.

With them came signs:

Leave Yellowstone Country Alone

No Mining on Sacred Lands

Some, including a couple of the Indians, had the audacity to raise fists in the air as, in unity, they began to chant.

"Hands off Yellowstone country, hands off Yellowstone country."

Conway was not alone in being taken aback by the protesters, several of whom now stood, raising handmade signs they had kept hidden until that moment.

Several of the attendees Conway recognized, or knew from working together, rushed one particularly angry-looking protester.

Seated in the back row, Gonzalez had been reading his program's description of the morning session—A New Agenda: Taking Back Our National Monuments—when the protest broke out. Dropping the program to his lap, he turned his attention to the signs and shouts.

Just as he did, the phone in his blazer's pocket vibrated. Pulling it out, he pressed a key to light its screen.

A text. From Peter Shewmaker.

Call me

Standing, Gonzalez slipped out the back door of the room and into the hallway. Several other convention-goers stood just outside the room, talking on their phones, texting, or visiting amongst themselves.

Continuing down the hall to an exit door, Gonzalez stepped outside, into brilliant morning sun.

He pressed the phone icon above Peter's text. Peter's voice answered within seconds.

"Al."

"What did you find out?"

"It's the grizzly sow that was shot up on the Thunderer," Shewmaker replied. "Will's been obsessed with protecting her. Just yesterday morning Emma Day saw Will and shared information we'd received about a wounded sow heading north, sighted by hikers on the Emigrant Creek trail. That's in the hills just above Pray."

Gonzalez shook his head at the irony.

"I know where the fucking Emigrant Creek trail is," he replied.

"Al...?" Shewmaker's voice was hesitant.

"What?"

"I have to ask. What are you doing at a gathering of the Alliance?" He paused. "I mean, they're all about getting their hands on public lands.…"

The question didn't throw Gonzalez.

"That's exactly why I'm here," he said sternly. "To find out what the hell these dimwits are up to."

The brief silence that followed worried him.

"But don't they recognize you?" Shewmaker replied. "Don't they wonder?"

"Okay," Gonzalez said, lowering his voice to just above a whisper. "Keep this to yourself. I've gotten the key players to believe I may be considering going over to their side. That I could support some of their agenda. I told them the only way I'd show up is if there was strict screening. No press. No one outside knows I'm here." He thought for a moment, then, voice filled with irony, added, "Except, of course, now McCarroll.

"So keep this call to yourself. No one—do you hear me?—no one knows I made it."

There was just the slightest hesitation before Shewmaker replied.

"I hear you, Boss."

• • •

Robert Clay often ignored his phone, but he had watched Gonzalez depart the room. Now, when the phone vibrated, he picked it up.

Simultaneously, across the room, others reached into pockets or briefcases to view the text.

Meeting in 5 minutes. Critical.

One by one, Clay, Javari, and Gonzalez stood, then slipped silently out the back door of the room.

Conway remained standing at the front. Her suede vest lacked pockets, and her freshly washed jeans had been too tight to slide her phone in a back pocket that morning, so she was not yet aware of the text. But she had seen the others slip out of the room.

"Enough, enough," she yelled at the protestors. "While I respect the fact that everyone in attendance may not agree on every issue in our proposed platform, which we will be approving this weekend, I would urge you to sit down for now, and voice your objections at the appropriate committee meetings. And Grady," she said, pointing point at the apparent leader of the three who had rushed the Indian, "get your hands off him." She didn't intend her next words to carry across the microphone. "I don't need this shit."

While the Alliance members obeyed, the protestors remained standing. When one raised a hand to speak, Conway ignored it.

That didn't stop the petite, attractive brunette whose sign read *Not In My Backyard.*

"The Antelope Mine doesn't just hurt wildlife," she called out. "It will negatively impact Yellowstone tourism. Isn't that what this group is all about? Prosperity? Jobs for this region? Yellowstone employs two-thirds of the people living in this valley."

Voices had begun yelling, "Sit down!" and "Who let them in?" when another sign-holder—a tall, stately man sitting directly behind the woman—raised his voice to be heard over them.

"The roads to that mine will tear up and scar Emigrant Peak. And think about the wildlife. Wolverines den up there."

Usually drawn to confrontations like these—her quick wit and sharp tongue rarely meeting their match—Conway couldn't help being distracted by the knowledge something had obviously happened to draw the others out of the meeting.

Lifting her hand to silence the shouts of both sides on the Antelope Mine issue, she declared, "I'm going to call a short recess to allow all of you to decide if you're going to dedicate this time to accomplishing our important agenda, or" she glared at the attractive brunette, "use it to protest."

She strode toward the restaurant's side door, head down, but turned back just before opening it.

"I trust that you will choose the former."

With that she exited.

• • •

Gonzalez stood waiting just inside the cabin.

"Where's Liz?" he asked each of the men as they entered.

"She's handling a protest about the Antelope Mine," Clay answered. "This better be good, Gonzalez. That's one of my subsidiaries. I would like to have stayed and gotten a sense of what to expect from those fucking protesters."

"Look," Simms said, pointing outside, toward the teepees. "Here she comes now."

Phone in hand, Conway emerged from the top of the steps at a run.

Once inside, she echoed Clay's thoughts.

"I'm so pissed off right now," she said. "Half the crowd down there are here to protest the mine and AFEP. Who the fuck let them in? I never even thought to screen attendees."

She fell into a chair, uttering, "This better be good."

Before the others even considered sitting down, Gonzalez began.

"Will McCarroll left the park to follow a wounded grizzly sow he's been obsessed with. He's spent most of the last month in the backcountry tracking her and trying to protect her by keeping hikers out of any areas she's in. Yesterday he got word that a wounded grizzly was sighted on the Emigrant Creek trail." He nodded toward the east. "That's just above the resort. That has to be why he came to Pray. He thinks it's his grizzly."

Visibly astonished, Simms was the first to respond.

"You mean, his showing up here had nothing to do with our meeting?"

"That's what it looks like. I saw the guard on my way up here and he told me he'd just found McCarroll's Jeep. It was loaded with camping gear and supplies. I think McCarroll either *planned* to park at the resort and head out from here, or that all the goings-on drew his attention and he made an unintended stop. I now believe it was a total coincidence, but that then, knowing McCarroll as I do, what he saw piqued his curiosity. Especially when he saw me."

"Shit," Simms said. "And who knows what he heard last night? Talk about planting parvo in the park was bad enough. Then we started talking about a bombing. That kind of information can't go anywhere." Clearly shaken, he added, "I mean *nowhere*."

"I agree," said Gonzalez.

Simms had begun working himself into a state of panic.

"Now look what we're dealing with. A famous Yellowstone ranger being held prisoner. Talk about a can of worms. How do we get out of this one?"

"Well, we'd better find a way," Clay chimed in, "especially since it's my cabin the son of a bitch is locked in right now."

Javari had learned from the earlier meeting that his input was not invited, but now he cleared his throat.

"You get rid of him," he said.

For once, all eyes turned to the Brazilian. "What do you mean?" Gonzalez replied.

"Kill him," Javari said nonchalantly. Then, almost as an afterthought, he added, "Or have him killed."

Gonzalez let out a short, bitter laugh.

"There's a small problem with that. I just talked to his former boss, Peter Shewmaker. I swore him to secrecy about the call, but he's not only a highly ethical lawman, he's had a longstanding relationship with Will. He may be willing to honor his promise not to mention that call under some circumstances, but not if he hears of anything even remotely suspicious happening to Will." He paused, then, added, almost to himself, "I could kick myself for calling him."

The room fell into silence.

It was Conway who broke it.

"Can we capture that grizzly?"

Simms physically startled.

"And then...?"

"If Will McCarroll's been known to follow her, to have contact with her, who's going to be surprised when she turns on him?"

The suggestion either confused or stunned the others back into silence.

All except Gonzalez.

"Brilliant," he declared.

His eyes traveled from one person in the group to the next, trying to assess each one's reaction.

"Whatever we do, it can't look like foul play." He shook his head. "We capture her, then move her back inside the park."

"Back into the park?" Conway replied. "I don't get it."

"We can't do it anywhere near here. Not after my call to Shewmaker. We hold McCarroll until we capture the grizzly, then we get her back in the park. It happens there. That distances me...er, *us*...and this place—the call I made to Shewmaker—from it. And it's believable. Shewmaker knows that Will's been tracking that sow day and night. He just got done telling me so."

Clay appeared interested, but not convinced.

"I can see trying to capture the bear, but just how do you arrange for it to take care of McCarroll?"

Gonzalez almost looked surprised that anyone would be dumb enough to have to ask. It was Conway who answered.

"I know someone who can make it happen."

Gonzalez didn't miss a beat.

"Stucky?"

"Yes, Stucky."

"Holy shit," Simms said quietly.

"Afterward," Gonzalez continued, his mind clearly racing, "we release her back on the Thunderer."

Everyone in the room could practically see the wheels turning as the words spilled out of the park superintendent's mouth.

"Under my direct supervision, the park conducts an intensive hunt for the killer bear. When she's found, the analysis of the sow's gut reveals she's the bear that killed McCarroll."

Clay's expression of apprehension had transitioned into a grin.

Simms did not share the enthusiasm.

"So what do you propose if we don't manage to capture her and pin the blame on her—and off of us? That's obviously a possibility. More likely, a probability."

"The wounded sow would be best," Gonzalez answered, unfazed, "but there are plenty of bears that can be lured into a trap, especially this time of year, when they're trying to fatten up before they go into hibernation. If we can't get McCarroll's bear, we'll have no trouble capturing another." He appeared to be loving this idea more and more as it took shape in his mind. "McCarroll's been living in dangerous bear country. Any bear could've gotten him well before now. It's just more believable if it's the wounded grizzly. Like Liz said, everyone knows he's been tracking her."

This didn't come close to appeasing Simms.

"I'm not on board with what equates to murder. Something goes wrong and any connection I might have with this would end my political career; that is, if we don't all end up in prison."

"None of us can afford that to happen, you idiot," Clay replied.

"Think of it this way," Gonzalez offered. "It's practically what McCarroll's been asking for. You've heard about suicide by cop? We play it off as a form of suicide—and with McCarroll's history, which is well known, the public will not only buy it; hell, they'll think it's beautiful. He'll become a legend. I think it's what McCarroll's wanted all along."

"I love it," Conway said, noticeably proud to have been the idea's origin.

She turned to Simms defiantly.

"With all due respect, Senator, can you come up with anything else that could solve this problem?"

Simms seemed to be rattled, and not wholly on board.

"I want to know what McCarroll knows. Maybe he didn't hear anything. Maybe none of this talk is necessary."

"That's naïve," Gonzalez offered. "Still, you're right. We need to get the guard to find out what McCarroll heard. Meanwhile, I'll arrange to get traps set up along the Emigrant Creek trail, and other nearby trails. If that grizzly's out there, we'll get her."

He turned to Conway.

"I obviously can't ask my bear biologists for traps. How do we get ahold of Stucky?"

"He's here," she answered. "I didn't see him at the meeting this morning, but he came up to me at the bar last night."

Even before she was done speaking, she had lifted her phone and begun double-digit texting.

"He's our man," she said excitedly. "He'll have all the traps we need."

• • •

Will had finally fallen into a restless half-sleep. Now he startled awake.

The bathroom door stood open, its frame filled with a hulk of a figure.

"Bet you gotta pee."

Flipping the bathroom light on, the guard's gaze went to the crotch of Will's jeans.

"Or maybe you already did."

"Fuck off," Will replied, instinctively turning his head away from the sudden rising sun that now streamed through a window high above the house's entryway.

Scanning the bathroom for a perch, the guard crossed the small room, shoved the shower curtain aside, and settled onto the edge of the cast iron tub.

Seemingly practiced in interrogation, he waited a full minute or two, surveying Will, before speaking.

"So," he said, his tone casual, "just what did you hear last night when you were eavesdropping under the window?"

"Fuck off," Will repeated.

The guard shook his head in mock frustration.

"That's too bad," he said. "I mean, give me a little something and maybe I can leave you alone. But give me nothing…"

His large paw of a hand reached behind his back, into the back pocket of his cargo-style pants. When it appeared again, it held what might look to some like a heavy metal necklace for a Kid Rock concert.

But Will recognized it for what it was. Brass knuckles.

"Okay," he said calmly. "I'll give you something."

The guard leaned forward eagerly, his boot-clad feet tapping the cement flooring.

Will met his gaze dead on.

"Here's what you can tell them. Tell them I saw you standing under the window, eavesdropping, until all the others left."

Will did not miss or mistake the spark in the guard's blue eyes.

"Cut the bullshit. I was hired to guard the perimeter during that meeting, and that's what I was doing."

"Guarding the perimeter?" Will echoed. "Or recording the meeting?"

It was a gamble, born mainly of instinct—something about how the guard had been standing, face squarely to the cabin wall. Something about how he had adjusted his clothing multiple times.

Now Will could see the gamble paying off.

"You're fucking crazy," the guard snapped.

"Am I?" Will paused. "Problem is, no matter how much you deny it, all it'll take is me suggesting you were wired for them to want to get rid of you. Like they're no doubt wanting to get rid of me."

Will sensed he'd rattled the guard.

"Where the hell were you that you think you saw so fucking much?"

"In the teepee," Will answered calmly, before breaking into a smile. "They might not like that either—that I managed to get up there and hide in a teepee on your watch."

Eyes dropping to the floor, the guard shook his head slowly before looking back up at Will, studying him for several seconds.

"They were right about you," he said, rising to his full six foot five. "You're good."

Then, as quickly as he had appeared, he disappeared through the door, brass knuckles still clasped tightly in one hand.

26

AS HE WALKED PURPOSEFULLY THROUGH the lobby and down the resort's first-floor hallway, each door of which posted a notice of a meeting taking place inside, Gonzalez glanced down at the second page of his program.

Schedule of Saturday forums and committee meetings

His eyes scanned the page.

1 p.m. Enough Is Enough: our states are burning because of Forest Service mismanagement, Room 2B

He cringed as the entry below it caught his eye.

2 p.m. National Parks (mis)Management—Yellowstone in Crisis, Main Conference Room

3 p.m. How to write op/eds and letters to legislators that will get attention, Room 2D

Entering the stairwell, he took two steps at a time to the second floor.

As he opened the door to the hallway, a flood of animated conference-goers began emerging from 2B and heading down the hallway, most of them away from the door Gonzalez walked through, apparently late to another session.

As one couple in their early forties, clearly agitated, passed him, Gonzalez heard the woman say, "All those poor people who've lost their homes from wildfires. It's criminal."

"We're going to put an end to it," her companion said confidently as they marched toward the stairwell door that had just shut behind Gonzalez. "That's what this is all about. The Alliance will change everything."

Ahead, in the sea of pale skin and fair hair flowing down the hallway, Javari stood out. Seeing Clay emerge from the meeting directly behind him, Gonzalez picked up his pace and called out.

"*Robert.*"

Clay, who had been following the flow, turned Gonzalez's way. Nodding, he tapped Javari on the back and cupped his hand around his ear.

Both men turned and headed toward Gonzalez, who stayed at the end of the hallway, which otherwise now stood empty.

"Who moderated that session?" Gonzalez asked as they approached.

"Liz," Clay replied. "Why?"

"Let's go inside. We need to include her."

The three walked back to 2B and stepped inside.

Liz Conway stood at the podium, gathering papers, her laptop, a remote for the projector that stood on a table at the front of the room, and her phone, all of which she was hurriedly shoving into a calfskin briefcase.

She looked up, surprised, when she heard Gonzalez close the door behind them.

"What's up?" she said, straightening to her full five foot nine.

"Good news," Gonzalez started. "I met with Stucky an hour ago. He's on board. As we speak, he's picking up traps to place along the Emigrant Creek trail and the two other trails that bear's been sighted close to."

While Conway beamed and lifted her hand to high-five Gonzalez, Clay's brow creased.

"Who is this guy? And how do we know we can trust him?"

Hand still raised, but to empty air, Conway responded with a chortle.

"Oh, we can trust him," she said, letting her hand drop good-naturedly. "Stucky's solid. And he's good. He's been a Wildlife Services agent for twenty years. He fucking loves killing wolves, bison, you name it."

"He liked our plan," Gonzalez added, "but I told him no killing. This grizzly has to be unscathed. No mistakes. And no signs left behind that it had been trapped."

Clay still was not convinced.

"Isn't Wildlife Services run by the feds?" he asked.

"Yep," Conway replied. "APHIS. That's why he hates the feds so much. He's worked for them all this time. He knows how incompetent they are." She hesitated briefly, then added, "I also think he's hoping for a role when the state takes over Montana's Forest Service lands. I haven't actually promised him anything, but…"

"He thinks he's been promised," Gonzalez said, his voice containing a hint of reprimand. "And if that's what it takes, we try to make it happen. But my sense is we can trust him. Besides, if he's got something on us now, just think of what we have on him."

"What do you mean?" Clay asked.

Gonzalez looked to Conway to respond.

"Stucky's been behind all our efforts to make the Park Service look inept," she explained. "The bison shootings, the bighorn sheep die-off from pneumonia they contracted from the domestic sheep. That was him bringing the sheep in."

"You mean the ones that got stolen?" Clay pressed.

"Yep. But they'd already done a pretty good job before they were taken. The pneumonia from that herd killed off most of the bighorn in the Gardiner Basin. And it's sure to travel to the other park herds. And you know, don't you, who stole Stucky's sheep?"

Clay shook his head.

"None other than our favorite backcountry ranger. Who just happens to be locked in your bathroom."

"You're kidding?" Clay replied.

"Nope. About the only thing Stucky can't claim any credit for were the maulings."

She looked startled when Gonzalez replied, "You never know." Almost as an afterthought, but with a side glance at Gonzalez, she continued, "And maybe the investigation into sexual harassment that's making headlines across the country."

Gonzalez took on a defensive look.

"That stuff was going on long before I got there, and the investigators know it. It's the rest of the stuff that makes me look bad."

"That was the plan," Clay was quick to remind him. "You signed on to it. And you're the one who stands to end up in D.C. running the fucking DOI. And out of this godforsaken state. I swear, these people all look like they've never seen the inside of a commercial plane."

Conway's smile disappeared in an instant.

"These *people*," she responded testily, "are leading the goddamn movement to transfer federal lands to the state so that companies like yours can trash the hell out of the land and make a fortune."

"And provide jobs," Clay reminded her, then added, "Mea culpa. But I just want to make sure some rogue asshole who makes a living shooting wildlife from a helicopter doesn't turn on us."

"You have my word," Conway replied.

No one paid note to Javari's half-smile at the tension building in the room.

"Okay, you two," Gonzalez declared. "That's enough. Let's just let this guy do his job. He said he'll have traps in place before nightfall."

"This better work," Clay said. "Simms took me aside first thing this morning. He has his panties in a knot over McCarroll. Hell, he was even starting to worry about that guard, and if we could trust him."

"You know, I had the same thought last night," Gonzalez said. "So I called my sources and they assured me he's top of the line." He took in a deep breath and let it out, shaking his head. "Top of the line with a major screwup on our hands."

"No shit," Clay replied.

Conway glanced at the clock on the wall above the screen at the front of the room, which still held her last slide:

WILDLAND FIRE CRISIS, 2018
Homes burned: 4,599

Lives lost: 34

...THANKS TO MISMANAGEMENT OF PUBLIC LANDS THE ALLIANCE CAN DO BETTER!

"Damn, I'm late," she said. Grabbing her bulging briefcase, she beelined for the door.

"Don't forget. Tonight's the wrap-up cocktail party. It's important to have a good show of influential figures. That means both of you."

27

"SO WHY ARE YOU REALLY HERE? What were you doing outside that cabin last night?"

Will had heard Clay leave the house, then, minutes later, footsteps climbing the stairs.

It had become a pattern. He wasn't surprised when the bathroom door opened and the guard entered, then took his seat on the edge of the tub.

"I told you," Will replied sharply. "I was headed up this way and saw the vehicles pulling into Pray. I recognized one of them. It belongs to someone I'm not exactly fond of. When I got inside the lobby, I saw Gonzalez. I'd never expect those two to be within a mile of each other, much less at the same function. I knew something was up."

"Okay," the guard replied, "let's say I buy that. For now."

"I don't give a shit if you buy it. Now or ever."

The guard broke into a toothy grin, patting the back pocket that still held his brass knuckles.

"It might be a good idea to start giving a shit."

He paused, watching for a reaction from Will. None came.

"Where were you headed when you got sidetracked?"

Will gave him an icy stare.

Why would the guard be hammering him with questions?

He'd no doubt been charged with finding out just what Will knew, which would help the group Will had eavesdropped on the night before determine Will's fate.

That was real—and the most obvious—possibility. But Will had another suspicion as well.

Still leaning against the toilet, he nodded toward the wall behind him. Toward the east. "I was headed up above the resort. To the Emigrant Creek trail. To camp."

The guard looked pleased.

"Okay," he said, nodding. "I buy that. I found your Jeep, saw all the gear in it. Looks like you planned to be gone for a while."

"Maybe."

"So why would seeing Gonzalez here mean anything to you?"

"Why?" Will replied, his scowl making clear his disbelief at having to be asked. "These nut jobs—the Alliance members—are all about the states taking over public lands. Why would the superintendent of Yellowstone National Park, the most iconic public land in the nation, have any business attending a meeting of a group like that?"

"Maybe he's just curious. Or here to argue his case."

It had become a game of cat and mouse. A dangerous game. One in which Will could either prove to have value to the thug seated in front of him, or prove to be a threat.

How to respond was a gamble.

"Or maybe he's working with them," he replied.

While the guard's expression did not change, his posture shifted, almost imperceptibly. Will picked up on it.

"Nothing about Gonzalez tells me he'd betray his own agency," the guard replied.

His agency.

"How about the fact that earlier this fall, he just happened to be in D.C. at the same time this movement had its first national meeting?" he asked. "One that Liz Conway attended?"

Will's captor snorted.

"That's all you've got on him? D.C. has people like Conway and Gonzalez coming and going twenty-four seven."

Will held back his smile.

So this guy knows D.C.

Calculating that he'd pushed the envelope as far as he dared, Will let it drop.

His lower back ached from the night and day without support, but not as much as his neck. He toyed with the idea of asking the guard to unwrap the chain around his waist and let him stand.

But he didn't dare interrupt their conversation. Not now.

The guard hadn't taken his eyes off Will. Leaning toward Will, hands gripping the curvature of the claw foot tub's rim, as if reading his prisoner's mind, he said, "You're a Yellowstone ranger. All that backcountry that you know like the back of your hand right on your doorstep. What made you want to go camping up here—which ended up with you chained to a fucking toilet?"

Will had begun to recognize the guard's strategy, but he had one of his own.

"You mean Gonzalez hasn't figured that one out yet?"

"If he has, no one's told me."

Being locked alone in a dark bathroom had given Will plenty of time to map out, in his mind, what had gone on over the past twenty-four hours.

After the guard broke into the meeting with Will in tow, Gonzalez would have called Shewmaker. Shewmaker would have turned immediately to Emma Day, and Emma would have shared the conversation she'd had with Will just two days earlier. All of which meant that Gonzalez and the others had to know what had driven Will to be in the vicinity.

Ironically, they might now even believe Will's story—that his presence at Pray wasn't planned.

Not that it would garner him any favor after he'd ended up outside their window. But that didn't mean they had shared what Gonzalez learned from Peter Shewmaker with the guard.

Will sensed he hadn't been kept in the loop.

Will's theory was beginning to seem all the more plausible.

"I was following a grizzly sow who'd been shot in the park," he answered. "She'd been sighted up here—or at least a wounded grizzly had been sighted. It might not have been the sow I'd been tracking. I came to find out."

"Why the fuck would you follow a wounded bear?" the guard asked. Then, like a light bulb going on, it hit him. "Oh, yeah. That's what you guys do to keep park visitors safe. You kill bears that are injured. I saw the firearms in your car. Hell, man, you could hold off an army with that cache."

"I wasn't going to shoot her," Will said, making no attempt to hide his disdain. "I was trying to protect her."

The guard drew back in surprise. "From what?"

"From the park killing her."

"Why the fuck would you do that?"

Will did not answer.

Maybe he'd said enough. Maybe this bozo was as dumb as he looked and Will had given him too much credit.

The guard was clearly assessing Will at the same time.

"You gotta be hurting," he said. "Sitting there that long."

Will looked him in the eye. Tried to read him. "I'm okay."

"Want me to unlock you, let you stand for a couple minutes?"

Knowing it was risky, Will replied, "That'd be good."

"Then answer my fucking questions."

Will shook his head, smiling. The kind of smile that said he wasn't amused.

"Were you hired to guard the meeting, or ask questions?"

"I like knowing who my clients are," came the guard's answer. "Besides, I get bored. Outside of when I went looking for your car, I've been sitting in this cabin almost twenty-four hours now. And they want me in here for another night while they have another fucking cocktail party.

"So entertain me," he continued. "Tell me more and I'll let you stretch your legs. Why would you want to save the bear from being killed? I'm curious."

Will looked him straight in the eye.

"Because that's what I do. That's why I'm here. Why I'm still alive."

"What does that mean, why you're still alive? Did that fucking bear save your life?"

"Yes. She did. And so have all the others. And the bison who were shot from the air. And the wolves who've made the park healthy again but are hunted and trapped as soon as they step outside its boundaries."

The guard laughed.

"You some kind of nutcase? A crusader?"

"Yeah. That's what I am. A nutcase."

"I don't get it. I'm serious now. Maybe I can actually learn something on this job. How did all of those animals save your life?"

Will looked at him hard, took his measure.

What the hell did he have to lose?

"When I first started in Yellowstone, as backcountry law enforcement, my wife and baby were out on a hike. An illegal hunter's bullet killed them both. Just one bullet. The only thing that kept me from going insane was making sure no one ever carried a fucking gun into the park again." He paused. "And the animals. Protecting them, like I hadn't protected Rachel and Carter. The animals helped me heal. They kept me sane."

"I thought guns are legal in the park now?"

Bitterness ripe in his voice, Will replied, "They are."

"That's heavy shit."

The room fell silent.

"What about the bison that got shot? What was that about?"

"Three bison were shot and killed in the Lamar. Bullet entry indicated they were shot from above. The guy I told you about, the one I saw turning into the resort last night—Stucky—did it. He works for Wildlife Services. Stucky hates bison. Hates wolves. Hates wildlife in general. And he loves his job."

"Which is?"

"Killing. Whatever APHIS decides to label nuisance wildlife, Stucky kills."

266

"I thought bison only got killed when they left the park." "Not this time."

"So how'd you know this Stucky guy did it?"

"Because I saw the report. Gonzalez pulled me off that investigation, knowing full well I was the best person for it. I broke into the Lamar Station, where the ranger he assigned to the investigation worked. I saw his files. Those bison were shot from above. Had to be from the air. Stucky flies a helicopter. That's how Wildlife Services work. They shoot whole packs of wolves, coyotes—you name it, and by the thousands—from the air."

"Why would Gonzalez want to pull you off if you were the best man for the investigation?"

"You tell me," Will replied. "He's your client."

The guard had nodded along as Will talked, taking it all in. When Will stopped, the room once again fell silent.

"One more question," the guard said. "How the hell were you going to save that bear?"

Will eyed him for several seconds.

"I was going to talk to her."

Will was surprised when the guard didn't laugh.

"What the fuck were you going to tell her?"

"That she's going the right way. Back to Glacier, where she was born. That she can make it before winter if she keeps going. And that if she returns to Yellowstone, she'll be killed. Eventually they'll find her and kill her."

The guard took several seconds to respond.

"And you're gonna tell her all that."

Silent, Will nodded.

"I suppose you've named her."

"She's Two Coyote."

Suddenly the guard reached for the firearm in his holster. Bending over, Glock in one hand and key in another, he crossed to Will, opened the lock, then straightened.

Stepping back, he lifted the gun, aimed it at Will.

"Get up. Stretch your legs."

They had struck some sort of a bargain. And they both knew it.

• • •

Superintendent Al Gonzalez stepped out of his cabin on the second tier of hills above the resort to a light morning drizzle, hurried across the gravel driveway and down the steps, and entered the back door of the main building. His pace gave away his sense of urgency.

In the lobby, conference attendees were already milling around the front desk to check out. Gonzalez eyed the line.

Seeing Conway standing at the door, thanking departing attendees, he hurried past the line and grabbed her, mid-sentence, by the elbow.

Conway looked annoyed, until he whispered in her ear.

"We've got a griz."

Releasing the hand she'd been shaking, with a dismissive nod of the head, she turned to Gonzalez.

"Already? You're kidding."

"No," Gonzalez answered, "I'm not. Gather everyone together."

"Simms is in the restaurant, eating breakfast. I just saw Clay and his Brazilian shadow."

"Get them all. Tell them ten minutes. Outside, by the pool."

28

TRUE TO GONZALEZ'S EXPECTATION, the chairs surrounding the outdoor pool fed by a natural hot spring sat empty as attendees—energized by their weekend of meetings and eager to return home and put their newfound knowledge and skills to use— packed bags and checked out, and the rain increased in intensity.

Gonzalez, Conway, Simms, Clay, Javari, and the guard sat gathered under the roof that sheltered the hot tub adjacent to the pool.

A new face had joined the group. Conway nodded in the newcomer's direction in acknowledgment while the group pulled their chairs into a tight circle.

Gonzalez made the introduction.

"Everyone, this is Bill Stucky, the Wildlife Services agent we've been talking about. Bill has some news to share."

Short, stout, with wild gray hair and a beard that brushed the top of his belly, Stucky cleared his throat.

"I set four traps last night. First thing this morning I checked them, and sure enough, we got ourselves a grizzly. Just off the Emigrant Creek trail."

Clay was the first to respond.

"Is it her? Is it the one McCarroll's been trying to protect?"

His expression giving away how idiotic he considered the question, Stucky replied, "Once a bear steps inside a culvert trap and sees a human on the other side, you better fucking believe they don't turn their back. I can't see whether or not it's taken a bullet on its ass."

"What does it matter?" Gonzalez added. "It's a grizzly."

"Yes," Conway, as the originator of the idea, said proudly, "all that matters is it's a grizzly. That's all we need to fit the narrative. McCarroll was obsessed with the wounded grizzly, and he was taking daily risks up on the Thunderer to protect her. Which means he was exposed to the other grizzlies, too."

"Exactly," Gonzalez replied.

"So what's next?" Simms asked. He turned to the guard. "What have you learned from McCarroll? How much did he hear? And why is he really here?"

The guard leaned in, lowering his voice.

"He's not talking about what he heard, but my gut tells me he got an earful. For what it's worth, I buy his story, that he came here trying to find out if the bear was the same one that got shot in the park." He paused. "I believe him. I think he's fucking nuts, the way he feels about that bear, but I believe him."

Stucky muttered, "Fucking nuts is right."

"Good," Gonzalez proclaimed. "That's just what we want. Everyone who knows him will believe it."

As if in a classroom, Simms raised his hand.

"One of us needs to talk to McCarroll," he said. Then, nodding toward the guard, he added, "Not just *him*."

This clearly made the guard uncomfortable.

Looking at the mining executive, he said, "You don't want to draw attention to Mr. Clay's cabin. We need to keep everything as quiet as possible up there. I've already turned housekeeping away twice now. I'm an experienced interrogator and I believe McCarroll. He stumbled into this by accident. And now he knows too much."

"I agree," Clay and Gonzalez said, practically in unison.

Clay followed with, "Last thing I want is to draw attention to a cabin in my name that has McCarroll locked in it. By the way," he turned to Gonzalez, "how the hell do we get him out of there without someone seeing he's in handcuffs?"

"I can handle that," the guard answered.

Gonzalez nodded his confirmation.

"That's what he was hired for. So here's the plan. Bill and I have already worked it out."

"Bill's going to haul the bear up close to the Thunderer Cutoff Trail right after this meeting. You," he looked at the guard, "you're taking McCarroll up. No one is to see the two of you—you and Bill—together at any time. That's critical. Bill will text you GPS coordinates for you to be able to find the bear. You wait until you get his text to head out."

The guard leaned in closer.

"And then what?"

The question seemed to startle everyone, including Clay.

Stucky answered for Gonzalez.

"I'll have left the trap with the bear inside, but I'll be waiting nearby. You text me when you get there with McCarroll."

"And...?" the guard said, brow furrowed in confusion.

"Then you and Bill make sure McCarroll and his beloved bear get reunited," Gonzalez replied testily.

Looking directly at the guard, Stucky said, "Let's you and me talk for a minute after this."

The guard nodded his consent.

The group fell into a stunned silence at the reality of what they were planning.

Simms seemed especially shaken.

"This is crazy," he said, staring at the waters of the jacuzzi. "Fucking crazy."

Under his breath, Javari, seated next to the guard, said, "No crazier than Brazil."

The guard immediately perked up. He leaned toward the Brazilian.

"Brazil?" he asked. "What happened in Brazil?"

Clay shot Javari an angry look, but once again, Javari was all too happy to answer.

"The Brazilian government has a program called the Lost Tribes Project. Because of that program, we wouldn't have gotten a mining permit if anyone thought Indians were living on the land the company bought." Issuing a short laugh, he added, "So we made sure none were."

This was too much for Clay.

"Believe me," he said, "no one in the government, much less the whole country, was worrying about those fucking Indians. Suddenly the press gets religion, talking about what a great tragedy it was. What's tragic is all that gold sitting beneath the land they were squatting on illegally. Losing all the jobs that mine's going to provide for a poverty-ridden country. That would have been the tragedy."

Shaking his head, eyes closed, Simms uttered, "Oh my god."

Gonzalez's expression grew increasingly concerned.

"Senator," he said to Simms, "listen to me. None of us could have dreamed we'd end up in this position. But don't forget what McCarroll may have heard outside your window the other night. Talk about a bombing." He paused to let his words sink in. "And even if he didn't hear that part, the fact is right now, chained to a toilet in Bob's cabin. McCarroll has enough on all of us for *all* of us to be screwed. All of us to end up indicted for kidnapping, if nothing else." He paused again. "Do you actually want to take that chance— when this grizzly bear idea stands to take care of all of it, and look like it was all McCarroll's own doing?"

Simms simply nodded, while Clay, unfazed, said, "It may be crazy, but McCarroll has to be taken care of. No one planned for the fool to stick his nose in our business. He's left us with no choice."

Conway had remained mostly silent, but now she echoed Simms' disbelief.

"Oh my god. What have we gotten ourselves into?"

"Now *you* suddenly got religion?" Clay said, looking at her accusingly. "When this whole thing was your idea?"

Javari cleared his throat.

"I think it was my idea, Boss," he said proudly.

The guard had fallen silent, clearly thinking about the plan, before he turned to Gonzalez, then Clay.

"You're sure that's the decision?"

"I'm sure," Clay, resolute, replied.

The guard's demeanor subtly changed with Clay's answer.

He leaned back in his chair, agitatedly tapping his foot on the concrete patio.

"This is far more dangerous than what I signed on for. It's going to cost you more. Considerably more."

All eyes turned to Clay, who apparently controlled the finances of the endeavor.

He let out a sigh.

"What say we double what we told you?"

The guard's laugh startled everyone in the group.

"A hundred grand for accessory to murder? Or murder itself?" He paused, clearly pleased with his newfound leverage. "I'd say $250k is more like it."

Shaking his head in resignation, Clay replied, "At this point, what choice do we have?"

"Up front," the guard added.

"You already got paid up front to come here."

"Not the new number."

Clay's eyes suddenly shifted to a waitress, who had just stepped out of the coffee shop and looked to be headed their way to take orders.

Waving her away, Gonzalez called out, "We're good, thank you."

With a smile and nod of acknowledgement, the heavyset brunette pivoted and disappeared back into the café.

The guard had not taken his eyes off Clay.

After several more seconds, the mining executive finally broke the standoff.

"Okay. Two-fifty. But you don't get the rest until you show back up here," he declared. "With proof you did your job."

"In the form of…?" the guard said, leaning in closer.

Clay had reached the limit of his patience. Raising his voice, he said, "What the hell do you think? You get paid the full two-fifty when you bring me a fucking picture of McCarroll." Then he added, "After the bear's done."

While the rest of the group shifted uncomfortably in their chairs as they glanced around to make sure no one was within earshot, the guard smiled and nodded his agreement.

"Okay," Gonzalez said with finality, rising to his feet

"Let's make this happen."

29

AS HIS PICKUP PASSED THROUGH the iconic Yellowstone Arch and approached the two lines of vehicles entering the park at the North Gate, Stucky shifted into the right lane.

The smaller station, which had been erected three summers earlier for park employees and contractors who displayed the appropriate window sticker, usually allowed faster entry and, if manned at all, tended to house a novice seasonal employee.

Rolling forward, Stucky eyed the culvert trap through both the truck's side mirrors and the back window, grateful for the lack of wind. He'd taken extra pains to ensure the canvas tarp covering it stayed in place. Now he just hoped the bear inside sat still, which bears in transport tended to do. If not, he could deal with it. No one was quicker on his feet than Bill Stucky.

Still, when his truck pulled within one vehicle in the line at the smaller station, he cringed at seeing the familiar face at the main gate.

Jackie, who had manned the booth for over two decades, leaned out the window and waved, calling, "Whatcha got today?"

Rolling his window down as he inched past the young, ranger-uniformed brunette standing in front of the new station, Stucky called back.

"Empty for now. But there's a trouble bear down at Lake and they're short on traps."

Just then a honk from back of her line redirected Jackie's attention to her current vehicle, and Stucky cruised on through the gate, into Yellowstone National Park.

• • •

They had been sitting at the crest of Papesh Road, waiting, for over two hours.

From the truck's front seat, the guard scanned the landscape—the frothy waters of the mighty Yellowstone River to the Gallatin mountains rising like monarchs on the opposite side of the Gardiner Basin.

His eyes came to rest on Devil's Slide.

"What the hell? How was that made?"

Will had been giving him a geology lesson.

From the floor of the truck's back seat.

"It's made of beds of limestone, sandstone, and quartzites that eroded at different rates. Wind and water did that over time."

"What the fuck made that red streak?"

"That's Triassic rock. It's how Cinnabar mountain got its name."

The guard studied the formation and colors for another couple minutes.

"I have to admit," he said, "it's pretty amazing country."

"Then why don't you flip sides? Come live in it. I could make that happen."

The guard just chuckled. And then grew serious.

"You screw things up when we go through the entry gate, neither of us will be living here. Hell, I guess neither of us will anyway, but no one within fifty feet of us will either."

While the inference was clear—a bomb—Will suspected the guard was bluffing. But before he had been forced to the floor of the back seat, he had seen the guard lock a suitcase in the metal toolbox built into the truck's bed.

He had also seen the small leather case—just the right size to hold a detonator—the guard kept close to him.

He had not yet decided whether he dared risk calling the guard's bluff.

Instead, he tried another tactic.

"So who do you really work for?"

"Whaddaya mean, who do I work for?" the guard shot back. "I'm with a company that provides security. Gonzalez and Clay hired me for that conference. So I guess right now I work for that wacky Alliance group." He paused, eyes on Devil's Slide. "I never see the actual contract. I just get sent out on a job, mind my own business."

"Yeah, right," Will replied.

He could feel the guard shifting in his seat.

"So what makes you think I'm anything but that?"

"Seeing you outside the window that night. You were wired," Will replied, then added, "Plus my gut. My gut tells me."

"And what does your gut tell you? Who the fuck do I work for then?"

"I haven't figured that out, but I'm pretty sure of one thing. You're as dangerous to Gonzalez and Clay…and the Alliance…as they seem to think I am. Maybe even more so."

The guard did not respond.

Will kept at it.

"You're not government, I'm pretty sure of that."

"Okay, genius, why am I not government?"

"What I should say is you're not from one of our agencies. I've worked with American interagency task forces. You don't have the same discipline."

"What the fuck do you mean by that?"

"You wouldn't be trying to cozy up with me, for one. Anyone in an American agency would know all about me within a few hours of my getting caught outside that cabin."

"So who do I work for?"

"Maybe Canada. Or Europe."

The guard did not respond, and the truck fell silent until Will heard a beep from the guard's phone.

He knew what it was.

A text.

Within seconds, the guard started the truck back up.

"Here we go."

Conversation was the only tool, the only hope, Will had left. He didn't want it to end.

"Or you could be an industrial spy."

The guard laughed as they rolled down Papesh and pulled onto Highway 89, heading south, toward Yellowstone.

"You got some imagination."

"You," Will said from directly behind the guard, "maybe your company, if there even is one, could be double dipping…getting paid by both Clay and a competitor. That's industrial espionage."

"And just what am I supposed to do for this industrial competitor?"

"Get Clay indicted."

"For?"

"For starters, some of the stuff I heard outside the window," Will said, then, almost as an afterthought, added, "And now there's kidnapping, if anyone ever even finds out."

Reaching up, the guard adjusted his rearview mirror, as if to make sure Will hadn't popped up in the seat behind him.

"So you *did* hear what was said?"

Will would not appease him with an answer.

"Okay," the guard continued, "so let's say you're right. What would my industrial espionage accomplish?"

"Eliminate the competition. They just approved fracking in Yellowstone Country, just north of here, along the Yellowstone River. Clay's already got the Antelope Mines contract. He'd love to sew the fracking contract up too, especially since he's already got his team and equipment here. Hell, if he had his way, he'd love to tear the whole fucking Yellowstone ecosystem up. But he's gonna have plenty of competition for that fracking deal. Millions—maybe billions—will be at stake."

"Yeah, well, interesting theory."

Sensing he wasn't getting anywhere, Will decided to try another approach.

"You sleep okay at night?" he asked. "Or do you actually get off on this stuff?"

Something about the guard's silence made Will feel he'd touched a nerve. The truck suddenly picked up speed as it approached the town of Gardiner.

"I got a family I need to feed. And I'm good at what I do. I get paid good. So why don't you just shut the fuck up and let me go about my business?"

Several seconds later, almost as an afterthought, the guard added, "Sad thing is you're not a bad guy. I wouldn't have minded learning more about bears and wolves and shit like that."

Will already knew precisely where they were when the truck pulled over and his captor hung his thick head over the seat. He reached down, saw that Will had managed to shake the tarp off his face. A large duffel bag—the kind military used when taking off on missions with an undetermined end date—filled the front seat next to him. Swinging it over the back of the seat, he tossed it on top of Will, ensuring he was hidden. It landed on Will's chest.

"We're about to go through the gate. You move an inch, you say a fucking word…," the guard said, negotiating around foot traffic on the bridge over the Yellowstone River, "and we all blow sky high."

The wait at the gate only took a few minutes. Will knew it was late enough in the afternoon that most traffic was exiting, not entering, the park.

As the truck pulled even with the entry building, he recognized the voice. His friend Jackie.

"Good afternoon. Day pass?"

Nodding, the guard handed her a twenty and a ten-dollar bill in silence, making it clear he did not want to engage in conversation.

A seasoned park ranger, Jackie knew his kind and simply handed him a receipt, along with a folded map.

"All the park's rules and regulations are on the back of the map," she said cheerfully, as the truck had already started rolling away.

Once they cleared the gate and the guard closed his window, he turned his head sideways and spoke to Will.

"Good decision."

As the truck climbed the five miles between the entry gate and park headquarters, Will managed to shake the tarp off his face again. Passing through Mammoth, the only thing he could see from his position on the floor was rooftops. He recognized every one of them.

The post office and medical clinic on the left, the new Justice Center on the right. The corner of the newly remodeled hotel. And the Albright Visitor Center.

As the truck started into a left turn, toward Tower and Roosevelt, Will knew it would be his last chance. Perhaps ever.

Using all his abdominal strength, straining against the expertly wound restraints on his wrists, which were tied behind his back, and the duffel bag weighting down his torso, he lifted his shoulders and head enough to be able to see Liberty Cap and Minerva's steaming springs cascading down its terraces.

He had just enough strength, and time, to glance to their right and see the Stone House. Annie's home.

Falling back to the floor, Will gave up on the dialogue he had hoped might lead somewhere.

He could both hear and feel the truck crossing the bridge where, two summers earlier, he'd helped recover the body of a female tourist—a mother of four—who had fallen over its railing while taking a selfie.

Where, during the winter, bison crossed on their way to lower ground, less snow, slowing traffic to a crawl, or stopping it altogether.

Where he had stopped countless times to watch the sun rise or set as he returned to or from park headquarters in Mammoth.

"I don't know where you're taking me," Will said quietly from where he now lay still, "but I suspect I'm not coming back."

He paused, closing his eyes—as if to do so would hold on to all the memories.

"But if I'm going to die, I ask just one thing."

The guard did not respond.

"Let it be here," Will McCarroll said. "Let it be in Yellowstone."

30

GONZALEZ NEGOTIATED AROUND THE CARS stopped in the middle of the road without even glancing up in the direction the dozen or so tourists had pointed their phones, cameras, and binoculars. He'd traveled the road between Gardiner and Mammoth enough times to know that the Rescue Creek bighorn sheep herd must be standing atop the precipitous ledges and hills overlooking the Gardner River as it descended into the Gardiner Basin.

Right now, he just wanted to get home, to his wife and their house, adjacent to the Albright Visitor Center. It had been a long and exhausting—emotionally and physically—weekend, and he needed a vodka and tonic on the balcony before the big Xanterra dinner.

When his cell phone rang, he felt so certain it would be Angela, eagerly checking on his progress, that he didn't even look at the screen before answering.

"Almost home," he said cheerfully.

The voice that met his was the antithesis of Angela's.

"Al, it's me, Clay. That fucking guard still isn't back, and I'm going to go out of my skin if I have to spend another night in this cabin."

Scowling, Gonzalez looked at the dashboard clock on his Land Rover.

5:49 p.m.

"There's no way he shouldn't be back by now. Maybe he stopped for dinner at Tower. Or the hotel."

"I told the fucker I had a nine-twenty-five flight out of Bozeman, that if he wanted to get paid, he had to be here no later than five."

Nodding at a law enforcement ranger managing the bighorn jam, Gonzalez's mood plummeted.

"Something's not right. I'll call Stucky."

"Get back to me."

With a sigh of exasperation, Gonzalez pulled over. He didn't have Stucky's number memorized, nor was it in his contact list. He'd have to search through the texts he'd sent and received while at the Alliance conference in Pray.

When he found a group text from Conway, he chose the only 406 number he didn't recognize and hit "Send."

Stucky picked up immediately.

"I've been waiting," he said. "What the hell's taken you so long?"

"Bill," Gonzalez said, "it's me. Not the guard."

"What? Why?"

"You haven't heard from him yet either?"

"No, and he was supposed to text me as soon as he got to the trap so I could go in there and we'd get the job done."

Waving off a law enforcement ranger approaching his vehicle, no doubt trying to get in good with the park's highest man, Gonzalez ordered, "Get back over there. *Now*. Call me the minute you get there."

• • •

"There," Will said, pointing toward the mound of rock and earth rising like a phoenix next to the river's rushing water. Smoke poured out of its top. "That's Soda Butte. I can walk from here."

Glancing in the rearview mirror first, then eyeing the road ahead, the guard pulled off the road as Will opened the door to the back seat of the truck and climbed out.

He started off, but then turned back and walked to the open window on the passenger side of the truck.

"I don't understand, don't know who you really are," Will said, "but thank you."

Keeping his eyes on the road before and behind him, the guard nodded.

"You may not have much time," he said. "Go save your bear."

31

GONZALEZ HAD JUST FILLED A sixteen-ounce glass with ice, poured vodka and tonic to its rim, and stepped out on the balcony, where his wife was waiting, when the cell phone in his shirt pocket vibrated.

Fumbling for it with his free hand, this time he recognized the number.

He pivoted, and stepping back inside their house, slid the glass door shut behind him.

"What took you so long?" he said, clearly exasperated.

"There wasn't service there," Stucky replied. "I had to drive back down to Pebble Creek to make a call."

Impatient, Gonzalez cut to the chase.

"What'd you find?"

"Nothing. I found fucking nothing."

Gonzalez watched as his wife turned his way, an inquisitive look on her face.

"What do you mean nothing?"

"The trap's there but that's it. No bear. No guard. And no

McCarroll."

"How can that be?"

"How the fuck am I supposed to know?" Stucky replied.

"*No* sign of the bear or McCarroll?" Gonzalez said, incredulous. "No blood? What about signs of an attack—a scuffle?"

"Nothing."

Seeing his wife stand, Gonzalez held his forefinger up, urging her to wait outside for him.

"Could the bear have carried him away?"

"Not without some sign…" Stucky replied. "A foot dragging, branches broken where he was hanging on…something. I've done this long enough, been called in after enough maulings, to know that bear never got ahold of McCarroll."

As he watched his wife pick up her wine glass and head toward him, Gonzalez lowered his voice.

"For Chrissake," he said, just as she reached for the handle on the glass door, "get back out there and get the trap out of there. Ditch it somewhere."

"I don't wanna bring it back through the park," Stucky replied. "I'll hitch it up, then pull off the road and wait till the Northeast gate closes and it's dark."

Gonzalez remained silent as his wife slid the glass door open and stepped inside.

"Then I'll ditch it in the hills above Silvergate."

• • •

Stucky glanced in his rearview mirror to make certain there was no traffic coming from either direction, then turned his brown Wildlife Services truck off the road, following the tracks he had made earlier—twice now—that day.

While no one would bat an eye at seeing him, or his tracks—Wildlife Services vehicles were commonplace, especially at the north end of the park and just outside its borders—he had a bad feeling about this one.

He chastised himself for telling that too-talkative ranger at the North entrance that he was heading down to Lake for a problem bear. Originally, that's what he figured he'd do once he pulled the trap out—take it down to Yellowstone Lake and put it in storage in the garage Wildlife Services had there.

But with Will McCarroll on the loose, he needed to get that fucking trap out of there as fast as he could, ditch it where no one would find it, and make sure he had an alibi if anyone came knocking on his door.

That meant going east, through Silver Gate and up into the hills north of town.

Two hundred yards off the road, he retraced his earlier tracks, crossed a small offshoot of the Soda Butte, drove through a stand of cottonwoods, into the clearing.

The trap sat just as he'd left it—its door wide open and facing the creek and clearing. He'd backed it in, bear inside, perfectly.

Something had gone wrong.

Stucky never failed on the job. He was renowned for his creativity and instincts. What a time to fuck up.

And where the hell was the guard?

Stucky was all-consumed by such thoughts as he jockeyed his truck into position, lining the ball on his back bumper up with the tongue at the front of the trailer.

Climbing out of the truck, eyes searching the ground for more hints of what had gone on earlier in the day—when the guard arrived with McCarroll, which had obviously taken place, since the trap now stood empty—he marched to the back of the pickup.

Leaning over, he saw he'd miscalculated, but only slightly. The ball was still a bit off to the side of the trailer's tongue, but they were perfectly aligned vertically. He wouldn't have to pull the trailer forward or back, just lift and shift it to the right.

No reason to get back in the truck and do more jockeying. After all, he prided himself in having the strength of an ox.

Placing his right leg over the frame of the trailer to straddle it, Stucky leaned forward and grasped the trailer's coupler with both hands, took in a deep breath, and, with a grunt, lifted.

As the trailer's front end came off the ground, he felt the hair on the back of his neck stand straight up.

Turning, he looked over his shoulder, and dropped the trailer—just as he heard the "woof" of her charge.

As he fumbled for the .44-caliber handgun at his waist, the last Bill Stucky—Wildlife Services agent extraordinaire—saw of the grizzly bear, the last he saw of anything, was how close set her eyes were.

The last thing he heard was the sound of teeth raking across his skull.

The last thought that passed through his racing mind, before it ceased to convey anything but pain, intense pain, was disbelief.

32

CLAY PICKED UP ON THE first ring.

"What's happening?"

Gonzalez had excused himself to go to the bathroom. He could hear his wife in the kitchen, talking to the neighbor that had just dropped by unannounced.

"Stucky checked the trap out. It was empty. And no sign of the guard or McCarroll."

"Holy shit, you're fucking with me, aren't you?"

"I wish I were. Right now Stucky's headed back there to pull the trap out."

The line went quiet as both men took the chain of events in, trying to make sense of them.

Clay spoke first.

"Either the guard let McCarroll go, or McCarroll overtook the guard, then went up and let that fucking bear out."

"That's how I see it. It's pretty clear the guard's not coming back. He's got our numbers, and I don't see him passing up the payoff that was waiting for him there. Somehow McCarroll managed to overpower him."

"In which case, the guard could now be captive."

"Either that, or dead."

"Holy shit," Clay repeated.

"Right now we have to focus on McCarroll."

"Any ideas where he would go?"

"Maybe," Gonzalez replied. "He and Judge Peacock have been off and on for years now. We need to get someone over to her place. I obviously can't call LE. Do you have anybody close by who can get on it?"

"Hell yes. I've got a security team at the Antelope Mines twenty-four seven. The off-duty guys stay in Gardiner. I'll call them now. Where does the judge live?"

Gonzalez heard a fingernail tap on the bathroom door.

Holding the phone close to his mouth, he whispered, "The Stone House. Right next to Minerva."

• • •

Annie couldn't shake the feeling.

As soon as she'd started packing to meet with Johnny, she began questioning herself.

Of course, that was after her mother had questioned her, before slowly climbing the stairs to her bedroom.

"I guess this means it's really true," Eleanor Malone had said.

Knowing better, Annie had looked up from her opened, half-full suitcase on the living room couch.

"What's true, Mother?"

"You've moved on from Will."

Moved on.

What an innocuous term for the hell she'd been through.

She had wished her mother a good night's sleep, then continued to pack.

It would just be a couple nights' trip, a chance to get away. Still, even without her mother's words, Annie understood what her mother meant.

It *was* a big deal. Maybe even monumental.

She reached for the toiletry bag she'd brought downstairs so she wouldn't bother her mother as she packed, by going in and out of their shared bathroom, and tucked it neatly into the corner of her suitcase.

When Archie began whimpering, wagging his tail, even before she'd heard the tapping on her window, she had almost known what—who—she would see when she opened the curtain.

Will McCarroll.

Eyes tearing as she raced Archie through the kitchen, Annie found Will standing on its other side when she unlocked the back door.

"Will."

He stepped inside, took in a deep breath, then bent to pet his friend, the friend whose life he had saved years earlier when Annie's mother was kidnapped.

Old now, the golden retriever twisted and whimpered like a puppy upon seeing his beloved pal.

"I can only be here a few minutes," Will said when he straightened to face Annie.

Annie studied him. He looked terrible, weak, ungroomed.

She reached for his hand.

"Where have you been? I've been sick with worry. No one has known where you are."

At first Will pulled his hand away, but when she grabbed it again, when she held on to it with a steel will that was also reflected in her eyes—that would not let his eyes go—Will relented.

He locked eyes with her, and in that moment, Annie could see into his soul. His heart. She could see his pain.

"I can't tell you," he replied. "You can't know. I came to warn you."

His next words shook Annie to her core.

"And to warn Johnny. They're talking about bombing the Safe Crossings Project."

Annie let out a gasp.

"Who?"

"A secret group that I discovered meeting at the Alliance conference in Pray."

Startled, Annie said, "Why would you attend that conference? They're all about turning all our public lands over to the states." She let out a gasp. "Oh my god. I just read a case involving the Alliance back East. A bombing."

Will took in a deep breath.

"I *didn't* attend. I forgot it was even going on, then I saw something that made me curious. I can't tell you more than that. The more you know, the more danger you could be in. But I overheard the leaders talking about bombing Johnny's project. The grand opening."

"Why?" Annie cried. "Why would they?"

"They see it as a threat, especially with Canada's involvement now. A step toward more federal lands, not less. A step toward Canada's socialism. Pro environment, not pro extraction. Bombing it would be their statement that they won't tolerate that."

Annie stood speechless, studying Will, trying to digest what he was telling her; thinking about Johnny.

As if reading her mind, Will said, "You have to warn him. You have to warn Johnny."

"He's up there now. At the first bridge, where the grand opening takes place day after tomorrow."

Will raised both hands to Annie's face, cupped it in his cold, calloused hands.

"I think they could move it up, Annie. Call the feds. But whatever you do, don't call LE."

Annie's mind raced with panic and confusion.

"Why wouldn't I call LE? I just saw Keith drive by. I can radio and have him come talk to you."

"No," Will said forcefully. "You *have* to go right to the feds. Keith would go to Peter Shewmaker. And Peter would go to Gonzalez."

"Will, you're not making sense. The feds would listen to LE before they'll listen to me. And LE would be the closest agency, the fastest to get there."

Will's expression—its determination, its fury—scared Annie. In that moment, she wondered if the rumors—that living in the wild, Will had "lost it"—held some truth.

But she knew better.

She knew Will better. And when he spoke again, she did not doubt him.

"Gonzalez is involved."

"Oh my god."

Suddenly Annie saw Will's eyes drift to the couch behind her. He'd caught sight of her half-packed bag.

"You're going," he said. "You're planning to be there."

A tear gathered in Annie's eye.

She nodded and reached for the hands Will had dropped from her face.

"You can't go," Will said, displaying no emotion. "And you have to let Johnny know."

"I can't reach him," she said, panic rising. "He told me there's no cell coverage up there."

"Call the feds. Now. Just trust me. Don't go up there, and make sure Johnny knows."

"Please, Will, stay. Let's do this together. Don't go."

"I have to. There's one more thing I have to do."

"What is it?" Annie replied. "What's so important that you have to leave?" And then she saw it, saw it in his eyes. "It's that grizzly sow, isn't it? The one who killed Stucky."

Will turned to go, but Annie grabbed him by the arm.

"Annie, I'm putting you in danger just being here."

"Look at me," she demanded.

Will pivoted.

He looked at her, locked eyes with her, and in that moment, Annie knew everything she needed to know. In that moment, Annie's heart broke.

"I love you, Will," she said. "I will always love you."

Will took in a deep breath.

"I love you, too, Annie. I have never stopped. But I'm no good for you. Johnny deserves you. Johnny can give you what you need. What I can't give you. Especially now."

A huge sense of foreboding overcame Annie with those words. *Especially now.*

"Please don't go. Please don't leave me again."

For a moment—something in his eyes—she thought he might stay. That he was considering her plea.

And then he turned, and as quickly as he had appeared, Will McCarroll vanished out Annie Peacock's back door.

33

"*THAT'S IT.*"

The hulk of a man seated in the Jeep Cherokee's passenger seat pointed through the windshield as the car passed the Mammoth Hotel, headed toward the Lower Terraces of Mammoth Hot Springs.

"Wouldn't you know?" the car's driver, a scrawny version of John Travolta's *Pulp Fiction* character, replied. "There are two stone buildings."

"It's that one," his partner replied, "the one closest to the boardwalk. I know. I've seen her come and go. Pull into that boardwalk parking area just past the house. I'm gonna have to walk up the boardwalk, then cut over and approach the house from behind."

"Damn," the driver said as he honked at a Suburban pulling too slowly out of a parking space. "I wish we had the van. We could sit right here and pick up both sides of any calls."

"No shit. But Clay said we need to get there STAT, and the van's up at the mine." The big man leaned forward and grasped a leather bag on the floor of the Jeep. "This contraption should at least work through a wall."

"Even if it's stone?"

"Let's hope so. If I can get up under that back window, I can hear for sure."

As they pulled into a spot just vacated by an RV bearing Utah plates, the two men focused their attention on the Stone House. Lights shone behind closed curtains on both floors.

"I only see one car," the driver observed, "and it looks like what Clay texted us—what the judge drives."

His passenger removed his ball cap, revealing a clean-shaven head, as he studied the situation.

"This guy is probably on foot. Plus, even if he's got a vehicle, he's not gonna pull up to her house."

"Yeah, you're right."

Both men scanned the activity surrounding them as they sat in the parked Jeep. Tourists still dripped down from the Upper Terraces, climbing into cars in the strip of parking spaces at the foot of the boardwalks or heading on foot toward the hotel or dining room.

"Look," the driver said, "that guy in front of the shit house."

Picking up the binoculars lying between them on the car's front seat, his partner zoomed in on the figure on the sidewalk passing a building marked *Public Restrooms*, as he walked toward the Park Store and Mammoth Hotel.

"I've seen Will McCarroll before," he said. "Snuck into an employee lecture he was at. He was grilling the idiot who was presenting. McCarroll's a good-looking guy. That guy's a scrub."

"He doesn't look any different from any of these assholes,"

Travolta's lookalike declared. "None of them ever look like they take a shower."

Grabbing the bag that had been sitting at his feet, his partner threw it over his shoulder as he reached for the door handle.

"So here's the plan. You stay here, in the car, and watch the house. I'll go see what I can hear."

Before climbing out, he slapped his ball cap back on.

"We text each other the moment one of us sees or hears something. Got it?"

"Got it."

"And whatever you do, don't take your eyes off that house."

"Whaddaya think I am, an idiot?"

34

JOHNNY YELLOW KIDNEY STOOD ON top of the barren foothill above the Yellowstone River, watching the activity below. The commercial floodlights they had rented to allow work to continue through the night had not yet gone on, but enough daylight remained for Johnny to see the machinery and figures below, moving about on the section of land they had been excavating for days.

When he saw the trail of dust headed up the hill toward where he stood, Johnny scrambled down the incline to the dirt road below, where he had parked his yellow pickup truck half an hour earlier.

Removing his ball cap, he stood grinning as the truck driven by David Easton slowed to a halt. Inside, in the passenger seat, a man smiled back at Johnny.

Johnny strode to the passenger door. As the door opened and the passenger stepped out, Johnny's grin grew even wider.

"Mr. Heyka," he said, grasping the other man's extended hand. "How was your flight?"

Wearing a smile almost as big as Johnny's, Bob Heyka answered, "Couldn't have been smoother. I left Seattle in the rain and a fog that almost grounded the plane, so this"—he gestured toward the valley splaying out below them and a sky displaying gorgeous ribbons of pinks and yellows—"is a real treat."

Johnny beamed with the pride he had always felt about his homeland upon someone seeing it for the first time.

"Seattle's nice," he said. "But nothing beats this."

"You went to school there, didn't you?" Heyka replied. "I remember Tracy Blessings telling me you were a track star for the Huskies. It's a pleasure to finally meet. And now that we have, please, call me Bob."

David Easton had climbed out of the truck and now joined them.

"Thanks for picking Bob up from the airport, David," Johnny said with a nod of acknowledgement. "I didn't want to take the chance of missing the flatbed."

"Flatbed?" Heyka asked.

"We're expecting a flatbed trailer that the Canadians are sending down. It's carrying the habitat modules for the crossing."

"That glass of wine on the plane must have made me a little foggy," Heyka replied. "I don't remember any discussion of modules, or seeing them on the plans you sent."

"That because the plans you saw were drawn before Canada stepped in," Johnny replied. "Canadian engineers have developed the newest, most innovative design for wildlife crossings." He nodded toward Easton. "DuWayne and David were already working similar designs for the second crossing when we got our funding cut."

Eager to step in, Easton pointed downhill, to the activity below where they stood.

"The Canadians are way ahead of us. In fact, DuWayne and I were basically designing a less expensive variation of their system—the system that's going in right there below us—when DuWayne had his accident. It's a modular system—kind of like a kit of parts. It can all be assembled locally. What you see down there is the crossing itself. It was actually about to be put in place in British Columbia, but the Canadians gave it to us instead. Those two huge pieces you see lying on their sides are double-curved inverted arcs. They're basically ramps whose surfaces, once the modules get here, will mimic the landscape. Not only do they look like they belong, the animals literally can't tell them apart from the ground and other natural surfaces they're used to."

Easton's enthusiasm and appreciation for the state-of-the-art design could be heard in his every word.

"Those arcs are overlaid with a micro-grid lattice that gets filled with plastic habitat modules. The habitat modules can be planted off-site, then transported and inserted here."

"The beauty of this," Johnny added, "is that the habitat modules the Canadians had planted for their newest crossing in British Columbia are ideal here, too, since our landscape and vegetation are so similar. Those arcs will be upright and ready for us to insert the vegetated habitat modules arriving tonight." He paused. "We should have the modules inserted by morning."

Heyka shook his head in wonder.

"Amazing," he said quietly, "just amazing."

"It's incredibly lucky for us," Johnny went on, "in that there's such a close fit in terms of environment and dimensions. And incredibly generous of the prime minister."

"Of course," Heyka replied, "it's also a political move. The prime minster wanted to expedite the completion of the project in part to put it in our president's face, and to let the American people know that regardless of his relationship with the president, Canada values its neighbor. Oh, and by the way, I heard from the prime minister's office just as I boarded the plane. Michael Kornberg, the prime minister's right-hand man, is due in on a private jet tonight, just after midnight."

"Fantastic," Johnny said. "I'd like to pick him up, if the modules have arrived by then."

In addition to being anxious to meet the man who played such a pivotal role in the Canadian stepping forward to help the project, Johnny liked the idea of picking him up for another reason.

That's when I can call Annie.

"Great," replied Heyka. "I just wish the rest of the Safe Crossings Project could see this. I'm the only one who could come on such short notice. The rest of the board would love to be here."

"They will definitely be missed," Johnny replied. "I got a call today from one of my colleagues who worked on the People's Way Partnership." As the reality of the next hours, the next days, and what they meant suddenly hit, Johnny had to fight back a wave of emotion. "A carload of our old team is on the road tonight to see this crossing get put upright."

Heyka picked up on the emotion in the biologist's voice. His eyes had been focused on the activity below, but now he turned them to Johnny.

"What an honor to have them here. Yours was the first name Tracy Blessings brought up at our initial meeting. She was so impressed with that project. All the different tribes and agencies working together to create—how many was it?—safe crossings for the wildlife on the Flathead reservation."

"Forty underpasses and one overpass," Johnny replied proudly, "the Animals' Bridge. The native people believe that roads are visitors and that they should respect the land and the Spirit of the Place. The People's Way Partnership crossings have now been used over 100,000 times. Vehicle and wildlife collisions near the crossings have been reduced by at least fifty percent. I suspect after seeing the design and beauty of this crossing, my colleagues will go back and build a second overpass."

He paused briefly, letting the significance of it all sink it. "Many of the same animals that will have safe passage due to this project— the project your Tracy Blessings began—will end up using the People's Way Crossings on the Flathead, including grizzly bears on their way to the Northern Continental Divide Ecosystem. Those two populations connecting could ensure the species survives."

"It's a beautiful thing," Heyka added quietly.

"A beautiful thing, indeed," Johnny echoed.

Looking to the now blackened sky—to its stars—softly, just loud enough for his own ears, Johnny Yellow Kidney uttered, "Aho Creator."

• • •

Clay's security specialist strode purposefully up the boardwalk. Stopping midway, as most visitors do to view the waters cascading down Minerva's steps, he glanced around.

With the sun having set, the boardwalk had emptied. No sign of tourists, or law enforcement.

When his phone vibrated, he raised it, pretending to take a selfie, Minerva's steam rising in the background.

Coast is clear.

Hurriedly, he stepped off the boardwalk and headed toward the judge's house, working his way through the thinly forested land behind it at a fast pace.

Time was of the essence.

Approaching the house, now engulfed in darkness, he stepped up to its back door and, dropping his bag to the ground, retrieved a flat, box-shaped piece of equipment from inside.

Inserting ear buds in each ear, he held the box up to the wood door, then began adjusting the sensitivity knob on the front of the device.

At first the voice he heard was muffled. The only thing he could tell was that it belonged to a female, but as he turned the knob, it became clear.

"This is not a prank call," he heard it say, followed by a silence.

Damn I wish we had the van.

If they had the van, he could be sitting inside and listening to both sides of the conversation. Instead, he was standing out in the cold, dark night, where a fucking bear or wolf could sneak up behind and get him. But at least the device was working.

He turned the volume up another notch.

"Yes, I know there are penalties for prank calls," the voice said. "I repeat. My name is Annie Peacock. I'm the magistrate judge at Yellowstone National Park. This is *not* a prank call."

While she spoke firmly, as he imagined a real judge would, her voice was growing increasingly impatient. And he could hear a note of panic in it.

Standing there listening, he halfway felt sorry for her, while, at the same time, he found himself becoming aroused being within mere feet of her, listening to her plead for help.

"That's what I'm trying to tell you," he heard Annie Peacock cry. "A bombin*g*."

He thought he heard her stifle a sob.

"They're planning a bombing."

35

"LOOK," DAVID EASTON EXCLAIMED, POINTING down, to just west of where he stood with Johnny Yellow Kidney and Bob Heyka.

A stream of racing headlights dotted the east-bound interstate below, but one vehicle—a long flatbed truck—had moved into the right lane, as cars and semis raced past it.

They watched as the flatbed slowed to a crawl to take the precarious turn off Interstate 90 and on to the exit ramp.

"That must be them," Johnny declared. Already beginning the scramble down the hill, he added, "We'd better get down to the site."

As he waited inside his pickup for Easton to do a three-point turn on the narrow dirt road, another set of headlights below caught Johnny's attention.

These lights came from the east and traveled west, at a slower pace than the interstate traffic. Johnny concluded the vehicle had to be moving along the frontage road. It was dark enough now, especially on the unlit road, and far enough away, that he couldn't tell whether it was a truck or car.

As he sat there observing it, the vehicle's lights suddenly swept south, off the frontage road, and started up the foothills.

I didn't think there were any side roads down there.

Johnny watched the lights continue climbing for almost a full minute, until the undulating hills swallowed them.

Guess I was wrong.

Turning the key in the ignition, Johnny Yellow Kidney executed his own tight three-point maneuver, and with a growing excitement, followed Heyka and Easton down the hill.

36

AS HE STOOD OUTSIDE THE BACK of Annie Peacock's house, Clay's security chief's anxiety grew by the minute.

"I don't *have* the precise location," he heard Annie say from the other side of the wooden door. "It's somewhere east of Livingston. Please, take this seriously."

He had hoped he might be able to pick up a word or two of the voice on the other end, but so far, he'd had no luck. Of course, he was focused on other sounds as well.

What the fuck was that?

Eyes wide, free hand frantically reaching for the butt of his gun in its holster, he looked back over his shoulder.

It sounded like a branch breaking. Or, worse yet, maybe several branches.

The thick stand of trees behind the judge's house stood pitch black. Anyone—*anything*—could be in there, watching him. Waiting.

He had become desperate to get out of there, but he still hadn't determined who was on the other end of the judge's phone call. Clay would want that information.

Then, almost as if she could read his mind, he heard Annie Peacock eliminate one possibility.

"No," she answered forcefully. "I haven't called park law enforcement. I was specifically advised not to."

So it wasn't Yellowstone law enforcement. That left local police. Or the feds.

He turned the dial to its highest setting and tried to ignore the woods behind him.

"Please. My name is Judge Annie Peacock. Look me up. My informant is a long-time law enforcement ranger with Yellowstone. The bombing is planned for the grand opening of the Safe Crossings Project."

Silence followed. The security guy knew she was being interrogated.

"It's a wildlife crossing. To keep animals off the highways."

Another silence, then, "The day after tomorrow." A pause. "Yes, I told you, I don't know the precise location. The manager of the project is there now. He's not reachable because there's no cell coverage at the site, but I'll be hearing from him tomorrow."

Suddenly, as if the idea had just come to her, Annie Peacock added, "Call the Canadian embassy. The prime minister is sending representatives to the grand opening. He may even attend. Someone there will know. Maybe they can give you the location."

For the first time, the security specialist was able to hear the voice on the other end. A male.

All he could make out were two words: "park" and "superintendent."

"No, no, no," Annie cried. "Do not call Superintendent Gonzalez. He cannot know of this call. Please assure me that no one will call him."

Her voice bordered on absolute terror. Despair.

Clay's security chief almost felt sorry for her. He'd seen her before. She was hot.

Maybe he should stick around and find some way to go to her rescue. Just think about how she might repay him.

If it weren't for those damn sounds in the trees behind him....

• • •

Guest of honor and closing speaker at the annual gathering of Xanterra executives, Yellowstone National Park Superintendent Al Gonzalez sat at the head of the table in the elegant dining room of the Mammoth Hotel. Gonzalez had put his cell phone on silent after Robert Clay's call earlier in the evening, which had prompted him to step outside. That didn't keep his wife, seated next to him, from hearing it vibrate in his pocket.

"Al, not now," she whispered in his ear. "This thing's gotta wrap up soon, and you're the next speaker."

"Be right back," Gonzalez said as he pushed back from the table.

Stepping into the hallway that led to a back door, Gonzalez glanced at the caller ID before raising the phone to his ear. Robert Clay again.

"What now?" he said, clearly irritated.

"I just got off the phone with my security guys," Clay replied. "They heard your judge call in a warning about the opening ceremonies being bombed. We need to move. Now."

"Now?" Gonzalez echoed, his voice loud and surprised enough to turn the head of a housekeeper standing just outside the door, smoking a cigarette. "You mean tonight?"

"Yeah, tonight."

"How's that even possible?"

"I can make it possible," replied Clay, without offering the fact that he'd already set the wheels in motion.

"We have to consult the others," Gonzalez said. "The ceremony's a couple nights away. Maybe we move it up, if that's what the consensus is, but first we need to get everyone on board."

At the silence that followed, Gonzalez looked at the phone screen to see if he'd lost the signal.

"Bob?"

"Yeah, I hear you," Clay said, his displeasure audible. "I think it should happen now."

"After your guys heard Annie Peacock call it in? And with McCarroll maybe out there, knowing what he knows? That's crazy. I'll arrange a call in the morning to figure out what's next. What time are you available?"

Clay fell silent again.

"As far as I'm concerned, the group's already spoken."

The door to the dining room suddenly swung open and Gonzalez saw his wife stand up—no doubt to come look for him.

"Bob," Gonzalez said hurriedly. "Do you hear me? We're not doing anything without everyone on board. I'll set up the call. What time works for you in the morning?"

• • •

Robert Clay pressed the red icon on the bottom of his phone's screen, dropped the hand holding it to his side, and then, determinedly, jerked it right back up.

The familiar voice answered on the first ring.

"We're moving," Clay announced. "Tonight."

"But Boss, we're not ready."

"How close are you?"

"After you called last night, my guys got in there. They planted a couple ANFOs, mostly on the perimeter of the site, but they got one dead center."

"What about a blasting machine?"

"That's just about ready. It's set up, on a hill above. The bridge crew started showing up so they got out of there fast."

"Damn," Clay said softly, shaking his head in disgust. "You mean they're working nights now?"

"That's what it looks like," his explosives expert replied. "I need to check it all out, make sure everything complies." When Clay didn't respond right away, he continued. "My team is actually on their way back there now. They'll let me know if everybody clears out, so I can go in and inspect what they did last night."

Clay fell silent as he tried to calculate the group's reaction to moving the bombing up on the call Gonzalez planned to convene in the morning.

Gung-ho Conway would be on board. She was up for re-election and wanted to please her base, which had become increasingly debased, especially after the recent barrage of commercials for her opponent, which had a civil-war, violent undercurrent to them. His numbers had risen from obscurity to heading the field. Hell, Conway no doubt wanted some of that.

Simms, on the other hand, had grown increasingly cowardly the past few days, even though he wasn't up for reelection for another two years.

Javari and Stucky would be totally up for it, but neither had any say.

And then there was Gonzalez.

No one—not one of them—had as much at stake as Clay.

Not only would this wildlife bridge be just the first in a chain of dozens, perhaps hundreds, of such crossings—the majority of which were planned for prime mining country—he could practically predict the governor and Democratic U.S. senator using the publicity and celebration reverberating from the grand opening to justify pulling the plug on the Antelope Mines.

And something about Gonzalez, including his reaction on the phone just minutes earlier, was gnawing at Clay.

He had stepped outside the door of the saloon at Pray when his security chief called, and remained standing there in the empty parking lot to make the call to Gonzalez. Now a clearly inebriated couple emerged from the bar and headed his direction. When the loud-mouthed millennial lifted his remote key and pointed it in Clay's direction, the lights on a Dodge Ram, two vehicles down from where Clay stood, flashed in response.

Turning his back to the couple, Clay took several steps away and pressed his mouth to the phone.

"Blow it," Robert Clay, mining executive, ordered.

"Blow it sky high."

• • •

It was after midnight in Washington, D.C., but the night operator's voice came across crisp and clear.

"Interagency Task Force, please identify yourself and the nature of your call."

The voice on the other end sounded calm, but deadly serious.

"Al Gonzalez," it replied. "We have an emergency on our hands."

37

THE GROUND WAS HARD AND cold, but Will did not even try to sleep. From his perch on top of the foothill behind the Chittenden House, he could monitor most of Mammoth, including Annie's house. It had taken him over two hours to travel from the Stone House to the Chittenden House, then climb the hill—a process that usually took no more than fifteen minutes. As he crossed the parking lot behind the Mammoth Hotel, the back door had opened and several employees, including a pianist friend of his, stepped outside for a break. He'd had no choice but to drop and roll under the nearest vehicle.

He'd wanted to get right up the hill so he could monitor anything going on at Annie's, but from his hiding spot under the hotel van, he could hear and see the road leading from the Albright Visitor Center to her house—the road any EMT vehicles or LE would have taken—and had seen nothing to indicate Annie had called law enforcement.

By the time he got up on the hill, only one room in her house had a light on, and that was the living room. He imagined Annie sitting in it, worrying—about him, and about Johnny.

He knew she would have done the right thing, called the feds.

At least Annie should be safe now.

• • •

Inside the Stone House, Annie picked up her phone again. It would be her twelfth attempt. She was becoming frantic.

When he answered with a cheerful "I was just about to try you," Annie's eyes teared with relief.

"Johnny, where are you?"

"On my way to the airport to pick up Michael Kornberg, from Canada," Johnny replied. "And listen to this. I just got a call saying the prime minister may be with him."

"Oh thank god," Annie sighed.

"What do you mean?"

"I'm so relieved you're not at the crossing."

Johnny's voice instantly turned sober.

"What's going on?"

"They're planning to bomb the grand opening," Annie blurted out. "But Will thinks it could even happen before that."

"*Who?*" Johnny cried. "*When?*"

"The Alliance, rogue members," Annie replied.

She willed herself to stay calm. After all, she'd been able to get ahold of Johnny.

"A couple hours ago, Will came to my house to tell me not to go to the grand opening. He said I needed to warn you. He overheard a meeting of Alliance members talking about bombing the safe crossing, maybe even the grand opening. But Will thinks they might move it up."

At first, when Johnny didn't reply, Annie assumed their call had been cut off—until she heard what sounded like his truck braking, and then wildly lurching.

"Johnny, what's going on?"

"I'm doing a U-turn," Johnny yelled.

"Where? Why?"

"On the pass."

"Johnny, no!" Annie cried, visions of the rocky terrain that separated the west- and eastbound traffic on Bozeman Pass racing through her mind.

"Are you okay?" she yelled, with no response. And then, "Do I hear sirens?"

Something had gone wrong. Something had gone horribly wrong.

She heaved a sigh of relief when Johnny answered.

"The cops. They saw my U-turn."

"I don't understand. Why would you do a U-turn? Don't you have to pick up the Canadians?"

As the fast-approaching sirens began to drown out his voice, Johnny had to shout to be heard.

"*Annie, there are workers at the site.*"

Annie gasped.

"And I have friends from the People's Way who should be arriving any minute."

Annie was barely able to make out Johnny's last words before her phone went silent.

"*That must have been the lights I saw.*"

"What lights?" she cried, refusing to let go her grip on the phone, as if by doing so she could bring him back.

"Johnny," Annie yelled into the phone. *"What lights did you see?"*

• • •

When the second police SUV raced onto the highway at Quinn Creek and joined in the pursuit, it sped past both Johnny and the Livingston sheriff's department vehicle that had been tailing Johnny ever since his U-turn, lights flashing and siren blaring, and literally cut his truck off.

Boxed in by both vehicles at eighty-five miles per hour and left with no other option but to veer off the freeway, which would result in plunging one hundred feet, Johnny pulled onto the shoulder and braked to a jarring stop.

As four officers surrounded his truck, guns drawn, he lifted his hands off the steering wheel and into the air. The driver of the Gallatin County sheriff's SUV threw open the truck's door.

Johnny's thoughts immediately turned to a friend he grew up with on the reservation.

Billy Madplume had never made it out of a situation like this.

38

PASSING THE MAKESHIFT PARKING LOT, Johnny sped toward the glaring floodlights.

Despite the hour, the construction site looked like a camp of worker bees. When Johnny left for the airport, workers had been maneuvering two thirty-foot-tall cranes to either side of the front half of the bridge the Canadians had delivered the day before. Now it stood upright, facing south, half a piece of a giant puzzle, with the cranes still securing it, until its mirror image could be set in place.

Heads turned as the police and sheriff's vehicles came over the hill behind Johnny's truck, sirens blasting, lights flashing.

Racing over a ditch dug earlier that evening for an electric cable, Johnny's truck flew into the air momentarily, his head hitting its roof.

Workers had stopped their various jobs and, confused, headed his way, some at a run.

As Johnny threw open the truck's door and jumped out, a new sound—that of fire engine sirens—joined the clamor.

Johnny began running toward the workers, hands in the air.

"Bomb," he yelled as several of the police and sheriff's deputies caught up with him, yelling alongside him, "there may be a bomb. Evacuate."

"Evacuate. Everyone head for the hill," he kept yelling, motioning to the overlook on which he had stood just ninety minutes earlier with Bob Heyka and David Easton.

As he ran, he scanned the crowd for Easton and Heyka but realized immediately it would be impossible to identify either in the mass of workers fleeing in the direction Johnny and the officers shepherded them.

When a dozen or so men reached the dirt road that wound its way to the top, Johnny turned to a foreman.

"Miguel," he ordered, "keep them moving up the hill. Get everyone as high as you can."

"But Boss, where are you going?"

"*Just go!*"

The fire engines had arrived but could not traverse the earth that had been chewed up and turned over by the heavy machinery. Forced to stay on the perimeter, five firemen unraveled hoses while a booming voice from a loudspeaker urged everyone to clear the area.

"*Don't stop moving away from the lighted area,*" it instructed, and then, over and over, "*In the event of an explosion, drop to the ground, face first. Cover your face and head.*"

Johnny turned and began to run back down the hill, toward the site.

Where were Easton and Heyka? And could his friends from the Flathead Reservation have arrived—or be about to arrive? He suddenly veered toward the bridge itself, sprinting up its new southern slope at a pace that rivaled his college track days.

He would be able to see the entire site from up there.

He was almost to the top when he remembered. And abruptly froze.

With a sense of dread that bordered on premonition, Johnny turned toward the hillside to the east, where he had seen the vehicle lights earlier in the evening.

High on the hill, along its ridgeline, with the moon rising behind, he could see movement—figured he could not clearly make out. But he could tell one thing.

They were not antelope, or wolves, or deer.

They were men. Three of them. And they, too, were running. In the opposite direction.

Pivoting back to the scene of chaos now mostly playing out on the hill across from him, Johnny placed a finger in each corner of his mouth and let out a whistle that pierced the night, drawing the attention of all those racing to safety.

"*It's gonna blow!*" he yelled.

At that second, as if triggered by his voice, a deafening explosion catapulted Johnny into the air.

When he came back down, Johnny Yellow Kidney lay motionless.

39

THE FALL WINDS WOKE HIM. That plus the running water.

He had had no actual contact with humans for days now. He had seen hikers, and more importantly, law enforcement and biologists—the Thunderer was crawling with them as they searched for her, the bear that killed Stucky. But by now he was so adept at hiding, at avoiding contact, that he hadn't come across a single human being since the mauling, since he'd resumed looking for her, too. He had become used to quiet—the quiet of wilderness. The solitude.

Sleeping alongside the creek felt soothing.

He had decided to move off the Thunderer, go north, after just three days and nights looking for her. For signs of her. But all he saw were others searching for her, too—including Emma Day. The fact that they were still searching was a good sign. It meant they hadn't found her yet. That was the only good thing about Will's privacy—his world—being invaded.

He believed that Emma sensed his presence. From his outlook on the rock, he could see her glancing around, at one point even looking directly toward him with her binoculars. But she had a ranger with her—if Will had his binoculars he would no doubt have been able to identify him—and it was clear to Will, even from that distance, that Emma was trying not to alert her search partner to the fact that she was on a mission to find not just one, but two that day: one four-legged and the other two.

For Will knew they were searching for him as well, that Gonzalez would not rest until he knew where Will was.

Will was curious about the stories Gonzalez would have come up with, preparing for the chance Will would be found and tell *his* story. Had Emma Day believed those stories?

He feared Annie would lose her judgeship. She wouldn't allow Gonzalez to deny his involvement. But the world Will thought he knew had been turned upside down and Will could no longer predict, no longer had confidence in, someone good, like Annie, being believed over someone powerful, like Gonzalez.

One thing Will did know is that the relentless presence of dozens of park rangers and biologists on the Thunderer would have driven Two Coyote away, to one of two places—either back up the Absarokas, or back down to the Thorofare. But fall traffic going south, toward the lake, fall hikers, was also dense right now. And the reality was that Will knew in his heart where she was headed, that she would again move north. And the path she was most likely to take from where he had last seen her, when he opened the culvert door and released her, would be to cross to the north side of the road transecting the Lamar Valley and start climbing.

She would likely follow one of three creeks—Pebble, Slough, or Hellroaring—to continue her path in the safety provided by the wilds of the sky-scraping Absarokas. If Will's instincts were accurate, she would continue along the east side of the Paradise Valley and, once she'd crossed the Yellowstone River, on into the Shields Valley.

Deciding which creek she would follow from where he'd last seen her was a crap shoot. Something in Will's gut told him it would be Slough.

So he had moved north, crossing into Montana after midnight, following trails made by wildlife, not hikers; guided by a full moon. Now, with dawn breaking, he lay along the waters of Slough Creek, its soothing sounds lulling him back to sleep, urging him to stay inside the sleeping bag he had stolen—just a few minutes more— and masking the sound of his company.

He should have known better.

Maybe he did.

"You're still here," he said quietly as his eyes squinted open. They had been partially glued shut with crust, but he dared not wipe them. Dared not move.

"You're still in the park."

Two Coyote did not move. She simply stood, ten feet away, staring at him, with piercing, empty eyes.

"You have to leave, Coyote. You were going home when they trapped you above Pray, weren't you? Back to Glacier, where you were born?"

She shifted weight on her front legs. Right to left. Left to right.

With no gun, no bear spray, Will knew he had but one option. She was listening to him, he could tell. He could not change the tone of his voice. He had to keep talking.

"Do you know I was on the team that collared you when you and your brother first came here?" he said calmly, as he lifted his head and rose to one elbow.

She didn't startle, but she stopped shifting weight.

"Is that why? Why we have this connection?"

Now he was on his knees, and out of the bag.

"It's time to go back to Glacier, where you were born. You've healed now."

Avoiding her eyes, ever so slowly, voice calm as he continued to engage her interest, he stood.

"You can make it, but you must leave, Two Coyote, you must leave the park. They are looking for you and they'll eventually find you. The two-legged you killed was a bad man. He has killed many four-leggeds, many of your kin. But it means you can't stay.

"If you go now, you can still make it by winter. If you go now, you'll be safe."

Heart racing, Will looked straight at her, stood his ground as her hackles rose like a row of soldiers on her hump. As a low, guttural sound issued from her open mouth.

"This is my home, Coyote," he said, looking directly into her dark eyes, as he had told countless visitors never to do. "This is where I belong. I think you've been trying to get back to your home ever since they took you from it. Ever since you lost your mother, and your brother. I'm sorry my kind ever took you from there. Go home now, Coyote. Go home.

"That's what the Creator wants for you. Just as he wants for me to stay here. Forever. This is where I belong. This is where I choose to die."

EPILOGUE

"WE ARE HERE TONIGHT TO celebrate a remarkable achievement."

Bob Heyka leaned into the microphone on the podium that was framed with balloons and banners. As he stared down at the mass of people below, his voice cracked with emotion.

"It's been just eighteen months since seventeen-year-old Kylie Blessings died tragically on her way home from a youth trip to Yellowstone. The van she and eleven other young people were in collided with an elk.

"Kylie's mother, Tracy Blessings, whom many of you know either personally or through her work at KOMO TV in Seattle, vowed to do something to make sure no other mother has to suffer the same tragic loss.

"It was Tracy who came up with the idea to create the Safe Crossings Project. A project that would build safe crossings for wildlife, saving both human lives and the lives of countless wild animals that Kylie, her mother, and every person in attendance tonight," he looked around, waved his hand across the crowd before him, "every person in attendance cherishes.

"As you know, more tragedy followed, and while Tracy couldn't be here in person, she is most assuredly here in spirit. And we are so grateful to have the original SCP bridge engineer, DuWayne Masters, here with us tonight."

The crowd's response was overwhelming. His wheel chair situated in the middle of the row of seats behind the podium, tears streamed down DuWayne's face, as well as that of his wife, and many in the audience, all of whom at the same moment lit a candle and held it high in the air.

"Tonight," Heyka went on, "tonight we are here to celebrate. And we celebrate not only this first crossing and those that will follow, tonight we celebrate the friendships and partnerships born during this project, the dedication, integrity, and pure intentions of all involved in making this become a reality. We celebrate the lives that will be saved. The grizzly bear who now has a better chance for long-term survival thanks to the connectivity between diverse populations this project will bring. The wolves that can travel more safely across vast territories."

Heyka turned to face the row of dignitaries seated behind him on the stage that had been set up in front of a bridge that, for just this one day, hosted visitors of the two-legged kind.

"We celebrate," he said, staring directly at Canada's prime minister, "the beautiful, long-standing friendship between two countries, two neighbors, who have stood together to make this world a better, safer, and healthier place for decades."

With that, wild applause broke out in the crowd standing or seated on blankets in front of the stage, and the row after row of chairs set up beyond.

Several Canadian flags waved below him, raised by members of the audience.

Heyka beamed, raising both arms high in a thumbs up, as the cheering continued.

"There are some in this country who believe projects like this, that protect wildlife, and more importantly, our citizens, are of less importance than projects that extract, that tear up, destroy, and exploit our lands for the short-term financial profit of a privileged few."

The cheering turned to jeers and shouts of protest.

"Today repudiates that way of thinking. Today sends a different message," Heyka cried, his voice rising in response. "The message that we will *not* give in. We will never, ever give up fighting to protect the Earth and *all* of its inhabitants."

The crowd's response drowned out Heyka's attempt at a few more words. When it died down, smiling widely, he again turned to those seated on the stage behind him.

Representatives from Canada, France, and Germany sat alongside tribal chiefs and elders from Canada and each of Montana's seven reservations.

"And now, I'd like to introduce the man who made this message, made this *night* a reality. From Blackfeet country, Glacier National Park biologist Johnny Yellow Kidney."

When Johnny stepped forward to another wave of applause and cheers, the two men embraced.

Once at the podium, before speaking a word, Johnny's eyes searched the crowd below.

When they found Annie, seated several rows back, she met his gaze and nodded.

Yes.

Johnny took a deep breath and looked toward the sky. "*Aho Creator.*"

"*Aho Creator*" echoed through the crowd.

Johnny clasped his hands together in front of his chest and bowed his head in gratitude. Then, his expression solemn, he began. "The grizzly bear plays a critical role in my culture. She is not only sacred, she is our family, to many, our god. Our rituals and legends, our dances, our religion, celebrate and honor the grizzly bear and her spiritual power."

He paused to let his words linger, to make sure they were heard.

"The recent delisting of Yellowstone's grizzly bears and hunts planned in Wyoming and Idaho are, to my people, nothing short of cultural genocide. Delisting amounts to the government saying, 'Forget how sacred the grizzly bear is. Forget your sacred ways.'"

Johnny looked to his friends and colleagues from the Flathead Reservation, seated in the front row, several of whom nodded their agreement, while others appeared to have bowed their heads in prayer.

"But this project," Johnny declared, twisting nimbly at the waist to enable him to see the structure that many in the crowd before him had not taken their eyes off, "this beautiful bridge standing tall behind me, amounts to another voice. A collective voice that says we will not only *honor* the grizzly bears, we will work to protect them.

"Unlike the states of Wyoming and Idaho, who want to allow them to become trophies for hunters, we will *fight* to protect them. To ensure they continue to survive, and roam free in the great state of Montana, as they do in our neighbor to the north, Canada. The same holds true for wolves, the buffalo, wolverine—for the many species of wildlife the Creator has blessed us with, that all too often we have seen lying lifeless on the side of a highway."

As if part of a tightly coordinated plan, signs began rising into the night air from within the crowd.

338

Some featured crude drawings of buffalo, some passionate words scrawled across a piece of cardboard. Some pictured wolves, in the eyes and hand of a child.

Johnny fell silent as his speech was interrupted by cheers and shouts of "Yes!" and a deep male voice from the back of the crowd yelling repeatedly, "Save them all."

Within seconds, "Save them all" became a chant, echoing through the starlit night. It was soon accompanied by two or three drums at the back of the crowd.

Johnny took a deep breath and willed himself to ignore the lump forming in his throat.

"The Safe Crossings Project..." he tried. When he suddenly—and visibly—lost his battle, it only served to further incite the crowd.

Stepping back from the microphone to allow all the voices to be heard, all signs to be seen, Johnny scanned the faces before him.

What he saw was a diverse mix—young and old, male and female, dark skinned and light, well-groomed and just in from a week at backcountry campsites—all with one common denominator: a passion and conviction made visible by a handmade sign, an expression of determination or joy, a fist held high, arms joined in solidarity.

He had attended a lifetime of powwows, sacred ceremonies, sweats. At that moment, for the first time Johnny felt the same sacred connection with those standing before him that he had known his entire life with his own people.

Strengthened, emboldened, he stepped back to the podium, cleared his throat, and raised his hand high. Eager to hear more, the crowd fell silent.

"The Safe Crossings Project," Johnny continued, "will not only provide safe passage for wildlife and us two-leggeds who travel our highways, it can help ensure survival of species like the grizzly bear." Once again, he looked for Annie. She sat, hands crossed on her lap; but when Johnny's eyes stopped on her, she lifter her right hand and softly tapped the left side of her chest.

"Even as we celebrate tonight," he continued, "just a few miles north of here, at the mouth of the Shields Valley, workers are clearing a site for the second crossing—across the mighty Yellowstone River. From there, a series of crossings both under and over highways will be constructed that will allow grizzlies to travel up the valley and over to the Big Belts, and from there north and west to the Swan or Mission Mountains, the Scapegoat Wilderness, and on into the Bob Marshall. And you know the next step...."

Johnny's eyes scanned the crowd for an answer, until he heard several shouts.

"*Glacier National Park.*"

Laughing, Johnny nodded.

"Yes, Glacier National Park. Along the way these bears may cross any number of highways: 89, 12, 287, Interstates 90 and 15, and finally, Highway 2. When this project is complete, each of these high-speed roadways will have multiple possibilities for dozens of species of wildlife to cross safely, avoiding wildlife vehicle collisions that can turn deadly.

"At long last grizzly bears from Yellowstone—a once isolated population—will have a chance to connect with their brothers and sisters in the Northern Continental Divide Ecosystem." He nodded toward the Canadians on the stage behind him. "And, if they so choose, continue on into Canada.

"This project has been fraught with tragedy and loss, with controversy and opposition, even with violence…but tonight we all stand together, united by a common vision, common values, a common love for one another and for the four-legged, winged, and finned inhabitants of this Earth we have been blessed with."

Tears visibly rolling down his face, under a spectacular blanket of stars, Johnny brought his speech to a conclusion.

"Tonight we celebrate. Tonight," he finished, "we give thanks."

• • •

Emotion washed over Annie as she watched the crowd's reaction to Johnny—his soft-spoken, heartfelt words; his humility; his pride in and commitment to his native heritage, the wildlife he cherished, and this project.

Two decades ago she had let him go. When he re-entered her life, it had been easy to love him again. But Annie's pride in him tonight was overshadowed by an almost unbearable pain. One that she knew would be visible to Johnny.

After Bob Heyka stood again to thank the crowd for its support and bring the ceremony to a close, Annie was relieved to see Johnny's Salish Kootenai colleagues surround him at the base of the stage.

It gave her the chance to slip away quietly.

She did not want to diminish Johnny's hard-earned cause for celebration. Not after he had left his beloved Blackfeet Reservation and taken a leave of absence from the wolverine study he'd spent over a decade working on to ensure Tracy Blessings' vision would not die.

Not since he'd put his life on the line, literally, to see the Safe Crossings Project through.

Johnny would understand.

Weaving her way through the crowd heading for their vehicles, Annie had just reached the makeshift parking lot when a firm grasp on her elbow caused her to stop and pivot.

She found herself face to face with Yellowstone National Park Superintendent Al Gonzalez.

"Still no word from him?"

Unable to voice the answer, Annie simply shook her head.

"If anyone can survive out there," Gonzalez said, his voice tinged with a kindness that took Annie off guard, "it's Will."

"Thank you, Al."

Eager to escape further conversation, she quickly turned away, only to be drawn back again by that voice.

"Annie?"

"Yes?"

"If you do hear from him, I know it wouldn't be a priority, but I would be grateful if you'd explain what I was doing. It haunts me to think Will might be out there believing I would actually take part in what he heard at Pray, and what he experienced after that."

Turning to face him squarely, Annie replied, "Will *does* believe it."

She paused and could see Gonzalez understood her refusal to accept any suggestion that Will was *not* out there somewhere. That he was gone.

"How do I explain it to him," she went on, "when I can't even understand?"

As if to confirm her reaction, Gonzalez nodded as she spoke.

Then he began his story.

"When I was called back to Washington earlier in the year, after the bison shootings, the bighorn dying, and with the press on fire about Yellowstone being mismanaged, I assumed it was to let me go. Instead, I learned a covert investigation that I wasn't even aware of had already concluded that the Alliance was behind both the bison shootings and the bighorn, and more—and that Robert Clay was involved. Clay's company was being investigated by an international intelligence agency task forced for its role in wiping out a small Brazilian tribe that no one knew existed. Had anyone known of them, the Brazilian government would not have approved World Resource Extraction's mining permits. During that investigation, Clay's ties to the Alliance, here in this country, were discovered. Based on what the investigation indicated about his role in the killings in Brazil, investigators became convinced he might be willing to do whatever it took to get his mining applications approved in Yellowstone Country, too. Especially when they learned he'd brought his right-hand man, Raul Javari, into the country.

"I was already being trashed in the news, with calls for me to be let go. The task force decided it could be believable for me to approach the Alliance and offer to make a deal—that, since I was about to be fired, I would help them in their efforts to discredit the park." He zeroed in on Annie, locked eyes with her, "by doing things like firing its most famous and beloved backcountry ranger, as part of their campaign to transfer public land to the states. In exchange, I told them I expected Clay and Simms to use their influence to land me another job.

"Well, the task force was right. Those key members of the Alliance jumped on my offer. In reality, I had already become part of the interagency task force.

"There I was, investigating Clay and the Alliance and their mission to have Yellowstone shut down altogether or cut in half—so the states could take over—when the best damn investigator I've ever known shows up outside our window at the conference." He shook his head in a disbelief that clearly still lingered. "Will McCarroll."

Now, as Gonzalez's explanation sunk in, Annie found herself nodding her acknowledgement.

"And that mission, to privatize public lands," she offered, "was the antithesis of the Safe Crossings Project—another federally funded wildlife protective program."

"Exactly," Gonzalez replied. "Led by Clay and with the help of his highly skilled employees, a few select members of the Alliance tried to stop the crossings project before it ever got started by attempting to kill Tracy Blessings, and then, when that didn't work, arranging for DuWayne Masters to have an accident. He had just bought a high-tech car that Clay's security experts were actually able to take out of his control and drive remotely. They had him going so fast he could never have made that turn at Yankee Jim."

When Gonzalez paused, Annie couldn't tell whether it was to let her digest what he was sharing or a result of his still trying to come to terms with it all.

"And when all of that failed to stop the project, Simms used his influence to get the federal funding cut."

Gonzalez shook his head in dismay.

"Who would have thought? At first, I figured I had nothing to lose. My name was mud after all the stuff that had gone on in Yellowstone, all the media talk about mismanagement. When they called me back to D.C. and made their proposal, I thought it would be my key to keeping my job, trying to turn things around, but once I got involved, I realized just how important the mission was. Far more important than my future with the Park Service." Another pause. "I entered a dark world, Annie. And I couldn't even confide in my wife.

"Ironically, Clay bought my turning on Yellowstone hook, line, and sinker. In fact, he's the one who promised me the Interior job."

"You had Will convinced, too," Annie replied. "He told me not to call park law enforcement the night he warned me."

Gonzalez shook his head.

"I've obviously had time to think about all of this a lot. From what I learned when I was undercover, Tracy Blessings getting shot and DuWayne Masters' accident were Clay and Javari's doing, not the rest of the group's. Conway and Simms were instrumental in the chaos taking place inside Yellowstone, but they may not even have known ahead of time about Blessings and Masters, and if they *had* been consulted, I don't think it would have gone anywhere. But everything took a turn at the Pray conference. Once Will showed up and overheard talk of bombing the Safe Crossings bridge, they got in over their heads. There became no choice, in their minds, but to get rid of Will."

Annie found his last words so chilling she could not bring herself to respond.

Picking up on her reaction, Gonzalez grimaced.

"I'm sorry. I can be so oblivious." He locked eyes with her. "They will pay, Annie. They will all pay."

Eager to put an end to the conversation so that she could retreat to the solitude of her car, Annie replied, "I'll do everything in my power to make sure they do."

"I hear you've already recused yourself from Stucky's trial."

"Yes, I had to. As you know, I have no jurisdiction over the other alleged crimes—Tracy Blessings, or DuWayne Masters, or anything else that took place outside of the park. And I had no choice in the kidnapping and attempted murder case since Will was the intended victim. They're bringing a well-known Cheyenne judge in to hear that. But I'm not about to recuse myself from the bison shooting—or any other charges they bring for violations that took place inside the park." She couldn't stop the tears that sprang to her eyes. "That's the least I can do for Will."

Gonzalez reached out, placed his hand under her chin, forcing her to meet his gaze.

"I want you to know," he said, his voice holding a note of pleading, "there was no way I would have let anything happen to Will. No way. I wasn't the only one undercover in that conference in Pray. The guard I arranged to be hired for the Alliance was part of the task force, too. He and I made a pact after Will showed up at the conference—to make sure Will was not harmed."

His sudden grin took Annie aback.

"Leave it to Will," he went on. "The last time I spoke to the guard, he told me that right from the start, Will suspected he was some kind of undercover agent. Will just wasn't sure who he was working for."

Gonzalez quickly fell serious again. He'd said all he needed to say.

Placing a hand gently on Annie's shoulder, he leaned in to kiss her forehead, then turned and started to walk back toward the rows of emptying chairs, where Annie had seen his wife sitting earlier in the evening.

Now it was Annie who called out after him.

"The guard saved Will's life. I'd like to thank him, but I don't know his name."

Gonzalez pivoted to face her again, and for a moment Annie could see it all washing over him—the reality, maybe even disbelief, at what he'd experienced.

Al Gonzalez's life may have returned to normal, but Annie could tell he was not the same man she had known all these years.

"Neither do I," Gonzalez replied somberly. "I've never known his name."

• • •

Annie had been sitting outside in her car, which she'd deliberately parked around the corner from Johnny's office, for almost half an hour.

It had been a month since the grand opening for the first Safe Crossings bridge. Between Johnny's determination to get one more crossing constructed before the snow started flying, Annie's full court docket, and her determination to work herself to exhaustion, they had only seen each other twice.

When Johnny called that morning and invited her to his office in Livingston, just hearing his voice had shaken her.

"I have something I want to show you."

Not lunch, not a drive, which is how they often spent time together, and not "something I want to tell you," which Annie had been waiting for—Johnny's announcement that he'd soon be leaving, returning to Glacier. To his wolverine study.

Annie knew she could trust Johnny and his intentions—after all, he sounded cheerful—but still, as she sat in the car, she debated about starting it back up and heading back down to Mammoth.

Taking a deep breath, she finally opened her car door to crisp fall air, and Livingston's famously gusty weather, the katabatic winds that the Gallatin and Absaroka mountain ranges to the south funneled into town with a vengeance.

As she climbed the stairs to Johnny's second-floor office, Annie saw that the door stood open several inches. When she reached it, she could see Johnny inside, his back to her as he focused on his computer's monitor. For a fleeting moment, she considered turning away.

Then, as if he sensed her presence, Johnny looked over his shoulder.

His smile upon seeing her—that beautiful smile she'd fallen in love with as a co-ed, the one that transformed his face—erased any trepidation she'd felt. She stepped inside, met him halfway across the room, and wrapped her arms around his waist as he stuffed his cell phone in his jeans pocket and engulfed her, saying, "Thank you."

"For what?" she teased. "A hug?"

"No, for coming up to Livingston right away. I didn't know if I had it in me to wait."

Frowning, bracing herself for his answer, Annie echoed, "Wait for what?"

Dropping his arms to grab her hand, Johnny pulled her toward his desk.

"Over here, come see."

Pulling the chair out from the other desk in the room—DuWayne Masters' desk—Johnny slid it up beside his, motioning for Annie to sit down.

He lowered himself into his chair, the two of them facing the large monitor on his desk. Its screen had gone black. When Johnny pressed a key on the keyboard, it came alive.

At first, Annie had no idea what she was looking at.

She could tell it was a video, but it was obviously taken at night, and the quality was grainy. She turned to Johnny, whose eyes bounced from Annie to the screen and back.

"There," he exclaimed suddenly.

Annie finally made it out. What she was looking at. The movement caught her eye.

"The crossing!" she cried, leaning forward to get a closer look. "Here, let me zoom in a little," Johnny replied.

Hearing the excitement in his voice, Annie suddenly felt an enormous joy and sense of pride. She reached for Johnny's left hand as his right hand worked the mouse.

"Yesterday we collected the videos taken by the cameras we set up last week, at both ends of the bridge, and at the top." He paused, eyes glued to the screen. "This big guy was our first recorded crossing."

Annie's smile might just have outdone Johnny's.

"A moose!"

The two fell silent as they watched the tall, gangly animal stop and graze at the base of the bridge. While not visible, the video soundtrack picked up cars and trucks whizzing by one the interstate.

Twice, the moose started to turn back; then, after looking again toward the south, from where he'd come, he took a tentative step up, onto the bridge, still stopping to graze from time to time.

Johnny let the first video play out, then switched screens to the footage taken by the camera on top of the bridge, which caught the moose moving with more purpose, as if he now knew he was safe. As if he knew the bridge was built for him.

"Oh, Johnny," Annie said. "You must be so proud."

"Wait, there's more," Johnny replied.

For the next half hour, the two sat side by side, eyes glued to the sight of one animal after another cautiously approaching the new structure. A coyote, the camera's lights reflected in its eyes, who, after sniffing and lifting her head high into the night sky, decided to turn back. To try another night.

Two young elk, all legs, one in velvet.

A white-tailed deer and, so close behind that some frames of the video caught them together, a bobcat.

They had watched all the videos, some two or three times, when Johnny said, "Just one more."

Immediately, Annie detected a new note in his voice.

When Johnny clicked on the next video to open it, she caught her breath.

As she leaned into the screen, with Johnny silent beside her, watching her—she could feel his eyes—Annie's tears began to fall.

What looked like nothing more than a mass of dark fur lumbered slowly, purposefully up the south side of the bridge. Her gait was strong, but she walked with just the slightest limp.

"It's her, isn't it?" Annie whispered.

Clearly having already done so—already having studied the video over and over—Johnny zoomed all the way in, revealing a scar on the grizzly's rear end.

"She's healed, Annie," he said softly.

He fell silent again, allowing Annie to process the sight.

Finally, after several minutes of Annie staring at the screen, Johnny spoke.

"Should I report it?" he asked. "If it's her…" he let his voice trail off, not willing to speak the unspeakable.

Annie turned to him.

"No," she replied softly. "Let her go. Let her finally go home."

Johnny wrapped his arms around Annie, held her as she sobbed into his chest.

"It's what Will wanted," he whispered into her hair. "For her to go home."

In that moment, eyes back on the screen, Johnny returned to who he'd been, long after he and Annie broke up, long before they reconnected—a biologist; a wildlife expert—and smiled.

"And as good as she looks," Johnny Yellow Kidney declared, "she just might make it before winter."

ACKNOWLEDGMENTS

This morning, the morning I send off my final manuscript, is a glorious morning. Less than twenty-four hours ago, on September 24, 2018, a federal judge in Missoula, Montana, restored Endangered Species Act protection to Yellowstone-area grizzly bears. There would be no 2018 trophy hunts in Wyoming and Idaho. While the battle is not over, as the U.S. Fish and Wildlife Service is determined to delist the Northern Continental Divide Ecosystem grizzly bears by the end of 2018, today is a very good day.

I am always deeply impressed by the generosity of those who share their knowledge, expertise and passion during my research and writing. That was especially true with this book. My heartfelt gratitude to the following for their contributions:

For the inspiration born of their passion for *Ursus arctos horribilis*: former Yellowstone bear education ranger and author of *Grizzlies On My Mind*, Michael Leach; my friend and tireless wildlife activist, Ramona Coyote; Yellowstone pianist extraordinaire, Randy Ingersoll, who attributes his spiritual rebirth to his encounter with a grizzly on the Thunderer twenty-four years ago, and my brother, Wayne, who instilled in me at a young age his reverence for the great bear.

Many experts have theorized the route grizzly bears might take between Yellowstone and the Northern Continental Divide Ecosystem. I turned to my friend Mike Dailey, one of the founders of the Bob Marshall Wilderness Foundation, to map a route for this book.

Thank you, Mike, for your decades of dedication to Montana wilderness and its four-legged, finned and winged inhabitants.

Ashley and Ryan Sherburne once again provided thoughtful insight and knowledge regarding the landscape and culture of their beloved Glacier country. I am deeply proud of Ashley for her work as a teacher on the reservation and grateful for the opportunity it has given me to know her beautiful, spirited students.

To Steve Johnson, ultimate warrior for grizzly bears and the wolves he has dedicated much of his life to protecting. Thank you, Steve. Yes, let's save them all. And yes, science just won.

T.J. Carroll and Dale McCormick shared not only their expertise on legal and law enforcement matters, but also a contagious passion for and commitment to protecting the Northern Rockies ecosystem.

I am immensely grateful to Ken Atchity, producer and Story Merchant publisher. No one I know has a greater love of story; no one has nurtured more writers yearning to be heard. Thank you, Ken, for believing in me as a storyteller.

To Jennifer Williams: you have graced this book not only with your impeccable talent, but also with the reverence we share for the world you inhabit so lovingly and respectfully. And to Lisa Cerasoli and her design team: you made this book visually stunning. I am forever grateful.

To my beloved four-legged family, who keep me company as I write and hopeful in a world I sometimes barely recognize; especially to those I lost during the writing of this book.

To Steve, whose daily fight to save the lives of the animals in his charge fills me with pride and love.

To Amanda for her grace and gentle spirit, and for always being there.

And to Kamiah and Mira, both of whom have known the thrill of living on the very ground the grizzly bear walks today, and both of whom inherited the love and passion required to save not only grizzlies, but also the wolves, buffalo, wolverine and other wild creatures we are blessed with in this big, wild country we've chosen to call home. One day the fate of these iconic species will be in *your* hands. That gives me immense peace.

GRIZZLY
JUSTICE